The Cunning Man
by
Elizabeth Andrews

A World of Magic Myth and Legend
First published September 2016

Find out more about the author and her other books at:
http://www.magic-myth-legend.co.uk

The Cunning Man

*Cunning folk: practitioners of folk magic used for healing
and expelling evil spirits, prophecy etc.
The term 'Cunning Man' was most widely used
in southern England.*

Chapter One

The wide sweeping cove of Widbarrow Bay spread out before them, with the popular holiday resorts of Weymouth to the west and Swanage to the east. This part of the Jurassic coastline with its gentle sloping beaches of sand and shingle and benign winds offered a safe haven for the countless pleasure crafts found in the English Channel and the local fishermen. Sheltered from the land by green rolling hills, the tiny fishing village of Bindon crouched along the narrow strip of land between the wooded hillside and the sea. The collection of whitewashed houses looked sturdy enough to withstand the battering from winter storms with the closest dwellings sheltering just feet behind the sea wall, the detritus from countless storms piled against the weathered stones.

It was a typical summer day with the sun just warm enough for an outing. A few light clouds scudded across the sky while down in the bay sunshine glinted on the white horses breaking onto the beach. The large coach squeezed down the narrow lane, brushing past the overhanging cow parsley and nettles, the gentle thwacking sound on the side of the bus rousing Queenie from her doze. She sighed and yawned, 'Are we there yet?'

Sybil glanced round from staring out the window. 'Nearly, had a nice sleep?'

'I wasn't asleep, merely resting my eyes.'

Sybil snorted slightly. 'You were snoring dear. I am sorry you are finding the trip so boring' she added, with a slightly sarcastic edge to her voice.

Her sister straightened up on the hard coach seat and pushed a lock of bright pink hair out of her eyes.

'Outings with the jolly ladies of the WI aren't my thing, you know that Sybil.'

'Then why did you come?'

'You sounded so put out on the phone that your friend had let you down at the last minute that I felt duty bound as your loving sister to come.'

'Merrill is always unreliable so I shouldn't have been surprised, and anyway I haven't seen much of you recently, so this will give us a good chance for a natter, if you can stay awake that is,' she added.

The two elderly sisters hadn't seen each other since Queenie's last visit to Sybil's home in the small remote village of Medbury when she had rushed over in response to her sister's urgent phone call. The arrival of some new residents had brought to light the strange death of a previous resident of the village. The subsequent haunting of Sybil's new friend Kitty had caused her enough concern to call her older sister Queenie for advice. The resulting events weren't quite what the elderly duo had envisaged but using their unusual expertise in the occult they had managed, with Kitty and her husband Gordon's help, to unravel the old mystery surrounding the woman's death and lay the ghost of her murderer.

Picking up Sybil's thoughts Queenie suddenly asked, 'How is Kitty these days, no more ghostly apparitions in the house I hope?'

'Nothing that she can't handle, Hannah appears occasionally. Kitty says it is a bit of a shock when she does but she is getting used to it. Nobody else, thank goodness.'

'Well, that's good,' said Queenie pleased. 'I think we have solved that little problem.'

'I don't think you could call Robert Beamish's ghost a little problem.'

'Whatever. He's gone now, that's the main thing.'

'And good riddance to him.'

'And how is....?'

'Fine,' replied Sybil quickly, blushing slightly.

Queenie grinned wickedly. 'Still bringing you flowers?'

'Oh shush! William is just being nice; there is nothing in it at all.'

'Just as well, you're far too old for that sort of thing Sybil.'

Sybil sat up indignantly, a flush mounting over her cheeks. 'We're not too old; we can go out together if we wish.'

'Ah hah,' chortled Queenie.

'Oh shut up, you old bat.'

The level of chatter in the bus suddenly intensified as the coach rounded the last corner and presented them with a clear view of the beach and the handful of small fishing boats pulled up on the shingle. An elderly woman from across the aisle nudged Queenie's elbow. 'Isn't this lovely? Aren't you pleased you came? It must be so nice for you to have a day out.'

Queenie smiled sweetly at her. 'Oh yes! I am so lucky that they let me out today, I just hope I don't get too excited and have one of my 'violent turns'.' She looked at Sybil out of the corner of her eye, who was desperately trying to keep a straight face. 'Isn't that right, Sybil?

Sybil closed her eyes briefly and tried to avoid looking at her friend Maud.

'Just you wait till we get off this bus, Queenie, I am going to push you into the sea,' she muttered, contenting herself with a jab in her sister's ribs.

Queenie smiled brightly at both of the women and settled back into her seat, chuckling silently to herself. The startled Maud quickly busied herself with her bags and engaged her friend seated next to her in a whispered conversation. Sybil tried her best to ignore the pitying looks from her and pretended not to hear the muttered comments of 'poor Sybil' and 'probably dementia'.

'They will be gossiping about this for months now,' Sybil glared at her sister and whispered, 'Of course, you do realise that I am going to tell them you are as mad as a bag of frogs?'

'I don't care; you can tell them what you like. In fact you can tell them all about us. See what they make of that!'

'They would never believe me; they would just assume I was going potty as well.'

Sybil looked out of the window momentarily distracted as the coach slowed for the last bend at the foot of the hill, and navigated the tricky turn into the small car park on the edge of the village. It was still only half full which gave the driver ample room to manoeuvre it as close to the main street as possible.

The aisle was suddenly frantic with activity as the WI members grabbed their coats, bags and umbrellas from the overhead lockers and clambered off the bus. Getting impatient, Queenie elbowed and pushed her way down the crowded aisle, ignoring the disapproving looks from the other women until she got to the door. Breathing a sigh of relief she clambered down the steep steps and waited for Sybil to join her. She breathed in deeply enjoying the fresh sea air and muttered to herself,

'At last I am off that blasted bus!' Smoothing her tweed skirt she started fumbling in the pockets of her favourite purple fleece for her cigarettes.

'Queenie! I thought you had given up?'

Queenie jumped guiltily before lighting up. 'I'm trying to, Sybil, honestly.' She inhaled deeply, blew a smoke ring, and ignoring the disapproving looks she offered the packet to the surrounding women.

'Anyone?'

A few muttered refusals came her way as the women, laden down with bags and coats gathered around the front of the coach waiting for Mrs Marshall, the trip organiser, to hand out the itineraries and detailed instructions on where to find the open gardens in the village participating in the NGS scheme.

The sound of seagulls filled the air as they all waited for her to distribute the pile of leaflets she had produced from her handbag.

'Does that mean there is a storm at sea?' wondered Queenie.

'What?'

'The seagulls, I thought they were supposed to come inland when there is a storm at sea.'

Sybil looked towards the clear horizon. 'It's a beautiful day Queenie, what are you talking about?'

Her sister shrugged. 'Nothing, it is just the sound of the birds, it made me think of storms.'

'No storms predicted, the weather forecast is fine for today,' called across Mrs Marshall, who was handing out maps to anybody who was paying attention.

Mrs Marshall, aptly named thought Queenie gloomily, waved an all encompassing arm.

'Everybody, everybody,' she repeated, raising her voice above the chatter. 'Right, now I have your attention, there are three open gardens in the village today. They are scattered along the length of the main street so should be easy to find,' she consulted her notes, 'the last is right at the end of the village, near the church. All the information is on the sheets, has everybody got one? Good. So,' she looked around, beaming, 'have a lovely time and we will meet back at the tea shop at three 'o' clock. Don't be late, ladies.' She nodded to her cronies who fell in behind and set off for the village, carefully consulting her map on the way.

There was a small gift shop in the cottage nearest to the car park and Queenie busied herself examining the postcards on display outside, hopefully she thought, giving the other women time to get far enough in front.

'Queenie! Stop hiding behind the postcards and come on.'

'I was just looking,' she protested innocently, holding up a card. 'Look at this one, isn't it nice?'

Sybil lifted an eyebrow and said, 'Very nice dear, now put it back. If you're a good girl I will buy it for you later, and I will get you a nice stick of rock as well.'

'Thank you dear, but I don't think my teeth can cope with rock these days. She slotted the post card back into the stand and muttered to the woman behind the counter, 'I'll be back.'

She joined her sister at the front of the shop, sighing dramatically, 'If I must!'

Sybil slipped an arm through hers, 'Yes you must, now come on, we are getting left behind. And wipe that look off your face!'

Tubs of colourful bedding plants marked the entrance to the village and the narrow cobbled street. On the sea ward side the cottages, having no gardens, had to content themselves with colourful hanging baskets while farther down as the village widened, more tubs of bedding plants edged the road. The gardens of these cottages were much more substantial front and rear, and packed with a riot of flowering plants. No spent blooms or dropped leaves spoiled the immaculate displays. Halfway down on the right was the local public house, The Anchor, a small building painted a brilliant white and its front festooned with the obligatory hanging baskets.

As the two sisters strolled through the village towards the church, Queenie chuckled as she gazed at the larger cottages, 'Ah, this must be the posh end of the village.'

'Bindon has won loads of competitions. 'Best Kept' village for the last two years, and runner up for five before that.'

'How do you know that?' enquired Queenie.

Sybil smiled and waved a piece of paper at her sister. 'Because I have been reading Mrs Marshalls leaflet.'

'Well, it's all very pretty and the cottages are immaculate; no flaking paint anywhere. Considering all the salty sea air, that's quite surprising. Do you know,' she carried on, 'I haven't seen a stick out of place anywhere, or a litter bin or anything.'

Sybil looked up and down the street, 'Well there must be litter bins somewhere, Queenie. There is probably one by the car park.'

'I wonder what would happen if I littered? Do you think I would be made to walk the plank?

'You are getting muddled dear, that's pirates.'

Just in front of them some of their fellow travellers had reached the first open garden and were clustered around the gate consulting their information sheets. One of her friends looked up and saw Sybil and Queenie walking towards them and signalled that they were about to turn in to the garden.

'How many of these gardens do we have to do?'

'All of them,' Sybil said firmly.

Queenie slowed to a halt and watching the women crowd through the first gate, said quietly to her sister, 'Right! Those old dears are all disappearing in there so we will head for the farthest one.' She pulled her protesting sister quickly along the street, almost breaking into a trot.

'Slow down, for goodness sake.'

'After two hours on a bus with that lot I need to escape. It's either them or me Sybil.'

'Oh, stop being such a drama queen, my friends are not that bad. I shan't invite you again.'

Queenie grinned wickedly. 'Is that a promise?'

They scuttled all the way to the end of the village, coming to a stop at the last cottage. Beyond that was just the church. The yellow NGS sign was tied to a small wrought iron gate set into a low stone wall. Queenie lifted the latch and pushed, the hinges shrieking loudly as she opened it wide enough for them both to walk through.

'Now this sounds like my kind of place!'

The gravel crunched underfoot and the flowers growing on either side of the path brushed against their legs as they slowly walked up to the cottage which was covered in pink rambling roses and honeysuckle.

The front door stood open invitingly hinting of a cool retreat from the sun. On either side of the door the building stretched out long and low, the gravel path that had led them to the front door carried on to the left leading to the rear of the cottage, and through another small wrought iron gate was a tantalising glimpse of a cool arbour.

Sybil breathed in the heady scents from the roses and sighed, 'This is delightful, isn't it?' she asked, turning to her sister.

Queenie was moodily staring at the front door. 'Hmmm,' she answered vaguely.

'Stop sulking dear,' Sybil said briskly, bending down to examine a delicately coloured rose.

'Hmm, yes dear.'

Sybil gave her a suspicious look 'What's wrong with you?'

'Nothing, I suppose it's only natural, Queenie muttered. 'Fishing families are always superstitious I suppose. It's just...,' she stopped when a figure appeared in the doorway.

'Good morning, welcome to the garden.'

An elderly woman stepped shakily over the door step and walked carefully towards them, leaning heavily on a walking stick.

'This is beautiful,' said Sybil, gesturing at the garden.

'Thank you,' the old lady beamed, 'I wish I could take credit but my granddaughter looks after it for me. I gave up gardening several years ago after my hip operation so Serena took over. She has such green fingers I swear she can make anything grow. She is tickled pink that we have won 'Best Kept Village' for the second year running.'

'Your granddaughter is involved in that as well?'

'Oh yes, she took over the running of the committee when she returned home, Serena has put so much hard work into the village, organising everybody. Of course there are always a few who moan about her pushing in and taking over, but she is a perfectionist and everything has to be done right.'

'How old is the house?' Queenie suddenly asked, interrupting the two women.

'I believe it was built in the late 1600's, my husband's family bought it about 1750.'

'So his family have been here a very long time,' exclaimed Sybil.

'Were they fishermen?' asked Queenie, staring at the old woman curiously.

The old woman hesitated briefly before answering, 'Something like that.' She turned slowly back to the house. 'Now you carry on and wander where you like, I will be in the house if you need me.' She cast a quick glance at Queenie. 'I hope you enjoy the garden,' she said before disappearing.

Leaving her sister to admire the roses, Queenie slowly followed the path that led to the back of the property. Conscious of the dark windows to the side of her and disliking the feeling of being overlooked she quickened her pace until she was out of sight of the cottage. The path wandered on past more flower beds then into an immaculate vegetable garden before joining up with a narrow lane that ran up the hillside between the church and the cottage. The lane became even narrower as it led upwards into the trees and became rougher the higher Queenie climbed. The end of the women's property was marked by a small wooden gate set into a dry stone wall, on the other side the path led on finally disappearing through a cut in the cliffs. She resisted the urge to open it and follow on, reasoning that Sybil would be rather put out if she disappeared so soon after arriving in the village. Built into the wall next to the gate was a crude stone seat, worn smooth from years of use; she turned away from the path and sat down on it with relief. It had been quite a climb and although she would not admit it to anybody, least of all Sybil, she was starting to have a twinge of rheumatism in her knees. Queenie stared out across the roof tops of the village to the sea, from here she could see the entire bay and beyond. Quite a vantage point, she suddenly thought to herself.

Behind her the wood was silent and dark, no bird sound came from the trees and even the seagull's plaintive cries were oddly muted. A dark cloud crossed the sun bringing a feeling of chill to the wind. Queenie shivered, the hair on the back of her neck prickling. Behind her, the failing light made the shadows under the canopy even darker and a sudden breeze stirred the leaves. A few stones clattered down from above, Queenie jumped and stared up the path straining her eyes to see what had dislodged them. She relaxed when over the rustling canopy she could just make out muffled hoof beats.

What a steep path for a horse, she thought in surprise. She waited expecting at any minute for a horse and rider to appear, but nothing came into view and although the hoof beats slowly faded away, Queenie still felt that there was somebody up on the hillside with her, somebody waiting in the dark of the trees. Her skin prickled again and she strained her eyes to see farther up the path.

'Queenie!'

Down below in the garden Sybil had rounded the corner of the house in search of her and was waving to get her attention. A slight feeling of relief swept over her at the sight of her sister. Queenie waved in response before starting slowly back down the steep path to the garden.

'What were you doing up there?' called up Sybil, shading her eyes against the sun. 'That's a steep climb for your old legs.' Knowing her sister she expected a quick retort, but Queenie remained quiet and thoughtful, casting a backward glance up the hill to the trees.

'I followed the path. There is quite a view from up there. You know, I think this is quite an odd place.'

'Odd? It's just a little fishing village.' Sybil patted her arm affectionately. 'I don't think there is anything strange about it.'

'Honestly Sybil,' said Queenie in exasperation. 'I believe you must have been walking about with your eyes shut, you of all people. Didn't you pick up anything at all, especially talking to the old biddy down there? You must be getting rusty,' Queenie suddenly grinned, 'or is your mind on other things?'

Sybil carefully repositioned her handbag on her shoulder, ignoring her sister's last comment and slipped her arm through Queenie's. 'Why can't you just relax and have a nice day? There is nothing strange about this village, it's perfect.'

'Perfect little chocolate box village,' mused Queenie. 'The trouble with perfect, it just makes me want to rip the lid off to see what is festering underneath.'

'Queenie, you can be so weird sometimes.'
They walked slowly back along the path to the front of the cottage.
'So you didn't notice the marks by the front door?'
'What marks?'
'Witch marks. Carved into the door jamb.'
'Is that all? Lots of old buildings have those marks. We have seen enough of those in our time Queenie, why so bothered about them now?'
Queenie took a firm grip on her sister's arm and impatiently pulled her closer to the front door and pointed dramatically at the door jamb.
'There! See? They are fresh!'
'Oh... Well, as much as I hate to admit it but you're right.'
Sybil peered at the strange daisy shaped marks freshly carved into the wood. These strange markings had been used in more superstitious times, and were even now still clearly visible on many ancient buildings. They were believed to deter witches and protect the inhabitants against evil spirits. She reached out and carefully traced one with her finger before turning and grinning at her sister.
'Not working though, are they?'
Queenie stared at her silently for a second before starting to laugh. 'Not at all,' she spluttered.
'You sound as though you're having fun,' a quavery voice spoke from inside the darkened hallway.
Queenie peered inside, trying to adjust her eyes to the dim light inside the house. 'We were just admiring your witch marks.'
The old lady tottered closer to the entrance; she looked surprised at Queenie's comment.
'You know what they are?'
'Of course,' replied Queenie, keeping her face expressionless 'Doesn't everyone?'
Sybil put in, 'Although it is unusual to see fresh marks. I thought this tradition had died out years ago.'
The old lady shrugged dismissively. 'It's nothing to do with me; my granddaughter is keen on that sort of thing. Serena insists on carving them everywhere. It's a tradition in the village and she likes everybody to keep to the old ways'
Queenie folded her arms and asked flatly, 'And what are the old ways?'
'I wouldn't know,' she snapped, the old woman's eyes narrowed and she looked frostily at Queenie. 'It's all nonsense anyway, now if you will excuse me I have things to attend to.'

'Perhaps we will get the chance to meet your granddaughter later, what was her name again?'

'Serena, Serena Moon.'

'Moon, that's quite unusual. Is that your family name?'

The old woman glared at her before slamming the front door shut

'Oh dear, we have upset her. I hope she doesn't close the garden, my friends will be so disappointed.'

Queenie stared at the closed door for a minute, cocking her head on one side convinced that the elderly woman was listening on the other side.

'I'm sure she won't, Sybil. It is such a pretty garden she will want to show it off.'

She turned slowly away and walked back along the front path to the street. Pausing at the gate she waited for her sister.

'There is something strange here though, an atmosphere. Here and in the village. It's oppressive. I wonder what this Serena Moon is like?' Queenie mused.

'Why do you ask?' a voice asked from behind them.

Queenie jumped, before turning slowly to face the young woman. Bright curls framed a pale face that would have been pretty but for the cold blue eyes. Dressed casually in jeans and a t-shirt she eyed the two sisters thoughtfully. She glanced towards the house where her grandmother had reappeared in the doorway.

'Has granny been giving you a tour of the garden?'

Sybil smiled calmly at her, 'Yes indeed, it's beautiful and apparently all down to you. You have very green fingers. Your grandmother has been telling us that you are the guiding light behind the entry for the 'Best Kept' village.

Serena smiled briefly. 'Yes, I was very proud of the result last year. It takes a lot of work of course and there are always a few of the residents who will oppose any change to the committee. People can be so difficult to motivate. But it was all worth it in the end.'

'And the rest of the village, were they as pleased?' asked Queenie, eyeing her thoughtfully.

Serena glanced at her briefly, a slight expression of annoyance flitted across her face before replying, 'Of course, why wouldn't they be?' She pushed open the gate. 'Are you leaving?' she asked politely, standing to one side.

Sybil nudged her sister in the back, 'Yes, we were just going. Thank you very much; we really enjoyed looking around the garden.'

'And the folk art on the door frame,' added Queenie slyly. 'It's so nice to see the old superstitions kept alive.' She laughed inwardly at the surprised expression on the young woman's face.

'I'm sorry?' she enquired, assuming a blank expression.

Queenie walked slowly through the gate and stopped just in front of her. 'The witch marks on the door frame. I was just pointing out to my sister how unusual it is to see freshly carved marks.'

Serena's face remained impassive. 'Just a tradition of the village.' She eyed the two elderly women, taking in Queenies pink hair and her favourite purple fleece that mixed oddly with the sensible tweed skirt. Next to her sister, Sybil seemed very normal.

'Of course I suppose you are of the generation that would remember that sort of thing.'

'Yes, you are right, we do remember all about that quaint custom, and so much more,' murmured Queenie before moving slowly away. Over her shoulder she said sweetly, 'Well goodbye for now, I'm sure we will be meeting again.'

Serena's cold gaze followed the old women, replying briskly, 'I look forward to it.'

Sybil followed her sister out into the street and smiled. 'Goodbye Serena, it's been delightful. Oh, by the way I meant to ask your grandmother if Moon was a local name. I haven't heard of any other families of that name around here.'

'We're a local family,' the women replied shortly, before turning into the garden and pulling the squealing gate shut behind her. She walked briskly towards the house without a backward glance and disappeared into the darkened hallway where her grandmother was waiting for her.

'Hmm... Do I detect a slight atmosphere?' Sybil muttered. 'All is not perfect in paradise after all.'

'She is probably just a control freak and has made herself unpopular. You know what these small villages are like, they don't like newbies coming in and 'taking over' as they put it,' said Sybil.

'Villages need an injection of fresh blood every now and then, and anyway what are we saying.... She isn't a newbie as you put it if she is that women's granddaughter.'

'Well, then she is just unpopular.'

They paused in front of the small white washed church, perched precariously between the boulders at the far end of the beach and the towering wooded cliffs. Behind it, hugging the walls as if for comfort was the small graveyard; the leaning haphazard stones worn smooth by the weather and sea air. Beyond the church set into a rocky outcrop on the beach and silhouetted against the bright blue sky stood a large worn and rusty metal cross, years of waves pounding up around the base of the monument had undermined its fixings and it was now leaning drunkenly to one side. With the salt water adding to the corrosion of the metal it was quite a sorry sight.

'I wonder what that memorial is for? Lost fishermen perhaps,' said Sybil, shading her eyes against the sun to see it clearly. 'Strange spot to put it though.'

'It looks a bit worse for wear, it's probably years old and I bet they have even forgotten what it's for,' Queenie said dismissively, being more interested in exploring the church.

Sybil pushed open the small gate set in the stone wall. 'Let's see if it is open, I do like these small churches. Who knows what little hidden gems are inside? And we can see how many Moons are buried here.'

Queenie followed her curiously, 'What's bothering you about her surname?'

'I don't know, it just rings a bell somewhere. I can't put my finger on it.' She turned to her sister and smiled. 'So let's do some poking about!' She trod briskly up the path to the iron studded door and pushed it open. Inside it was dim and surprisingly chill, the scent of fresh lilies filling the air. Rows of worn pews stood firmly to attention facing the plain altar which was lit by a small stained glass window. The walls, rough and whitewashed, were decorated with a modest memorial plaque commemorating the dead of the village killed during the First World War. The name of Moon did not appear anywhere in the church. Queenie followed her sister's gaze.

'Perhaps the Moon family were all heathens,' she joked.

'Maybe. It's a charming little church though, quite peaceful in here.' Queenie frowned slightly. 'But if the family have been here for so long you would have thought their name would have appeared somewhere. After all there wouldn't have been a large population here.' She carefully read the ancient plaque listing, in flaking gold paint, the previous rectors of the church. 'No rectors called Moon either.'

'Let's have a look outside at the gravestones; hopefully they won't be too worn to read.'

'The church records would give us more information, if we could get at them,' Queenie mused. 'I wonder who we could ask about them.' She grinned slightly maliciously. 'Unless Serena is in charge of that as well.'

'Now that would annoy her! Of course we may be making a fuss about nothing but I have got the strangest feeling about her.' Sybil raised her eyes to the vaulted ceiling and sighed, 'I wish I could remember, my memory is getting worse every day.'

'Yes, it's called old age, dear. It happens to everybody. Except me of course, I have perfect recall,' Queenie smirked.

'I shall remember that the next time you lose your keys, which if you recall happens quite regularly.'

'I thought we were going to look outside?' said Queenie, ignoring the comment.

'We are going to look completely mad, scrabbling around the gravestones. I hope my friends are busy elsewhere in the gardens, otherwise I will never live this down.'

'Just blame me.'

'I intend to.'

'And anyway it's better than trailing around after Mrs Marshall and praising the petunias.'

Sybil tightened the collar of her coat against the chill of the church and shrugged slightly.

'Maybe.'

'Oh go on, admit it Sybil; this is more our style. Strange mysteries, weird goings on,' she added gleefully, 'this is fun!' She followed her sister out into the warmer air and pulled the door shut firmly behind her. 'Wait for me.'

Sybil was already walking off down the path to the nearest headstone. 'Well come on then, let's get started. Although,' she peered at the weathered stones,' I don't think we will be able to decipher anything, they are so worn.'

They walked arm in arm along the path to the side of the church where the majority of the graves lay, huddled between the wall and the wooded hillside. The grass verges, neatly trimmed, edged the gravel pathway that circumnavigated the church. Their footsteps disturbed a lone rook in a nearby tree, it flew up cawing dismally.

'It's very well kept; Serena's influence has reached here as well.'

'Hmm,' agreed Queenie absently.

Her attention had been caught by the sound of running footsteps on the gravel path. They turned expecting to see a fellow tour member hurrying to catch them, but paused in surprise as a ghostly figure of a child rushed past them with a frightened sob, leaving a trail of terror so strong that they could almost taste it. They watched in silence as he disappeared amongst the farthest gravestones.

'Well!' said Sybil. 'I wasn't expecting that. Shall we follow and see where it leads us?'

She set off in pursuit across the cropped grass, avoiding the sunken and broken kerb stones to the far corner of the cemetery where a worn headstone lay in the grass. Apart from the fact that the headstone had toppled over it was well tended, and placed on top was a small bunch of honeysuckle, horse daisies and red campion neatly tied up with a twist of grass. Sybil bent closer to read the inscription, wincing slightly at the sharp twinge in her back. 'It's very difficult to read.' Running her fingers lightly over the worn letters she said, 'It's sometimes easier like this, like reading Braille. I believe that is a T,' she carried on, rubbing the grey lichen from the stone.

'Thomas,' Queenie whispered.

'The lettering is worn away completely. What a shame,' said Sybil regretfully. 'I wonder if this was the grave of the young boy. Of course it might just have been a coincidence that he disappeared here.'

'It might be,' replied Queenie briskly, looking around the quiet graveyard, 'but not likely.' Nothing moved amongst the stones and she sighed. 'I need a cup of tea,' she stated, 'and time to think.'

'A cup of tea sounds like a good idea; let's wander back to the cafe. We will be a bit early but that will give us time before the others turn up.' Sybil straightened slowly from her examination of the stone, ruefully massaging her lower back. 'We're getting too old for this.'

'Speak for yourself, you old crock.' But Queenie took pity on her younger sister and took her arm to help her back to the path. 'Perhaps we could find a resident to ask, see if anybody knows about the boy. He may have appeared to others as well.'

'He died a long time ago, nobody will remember him now.'

'But somebody does and leaves flowers for him.'

'Well we can ask, but don't get your hopes up.' Sybil shook her head sadly. 'I hate to hear a child cry like that, it's going to haunt me now until I find out who he was.'

Queenie patted her gently on the arm before pulling it through hers. 'We'll do our best as always so don't worry. Now... tea!'

Jenny's Tea Room was still very quiet considering the time of day, most of the visitors to the village were still exploring while enjoying the fine weather.

Queenie scraped the chair back from the table and sat down with a relieved sigh. 'First here Sybil and we have the place to ourselves.'

Her sister consulted her watch and frowned. 'Hmm, plenty of time.' She plumped her handbag down on the stained table cloth and sat opposite her sister.

A middle aged woman arrived with a tea cloth draped over her shoulder to take their order. Gazing askance at Queenie's bright pink candyfloss hair she politely handed her the menu.

'What would you like ladies?' she asked briskly, whipping a notebook and pencil out of her apron pocket.

'A pot of tea for two please,' ordered Queenie, not giving the menu a glance, 'and have you any cake? Preferably something chocolate and fattening.'

The waitress smiled slightly. 'How about double chocolate fudge cake?'

'That will do nicely, two slices please.'

She nodded briskly and disappeared into the small kitchen at the back of the cafe.

Sybil looked around curiously at the interior of the dimly lit room. 'This isn't very clean, is it?'

Her sister followed her gaze to the cobwebs festooned over the clutter of plates and various knickknacks displayed on the picture rail.

'I wonder what Serena thinks about this, it's a bit of a blot on the pristine village.'

'Perhaps her influence doesn't reach this far.'

'I don't know, I got the feeling she would want to control everything in the village.' Queenie put her arms on the table and leaned forward. 'There is a guest house over the road, why don't we stay for the night and see what mischief we can get up to?'

The interior of the cafe was quite warm and stuffy so Sybil unbuttoned her coat, she sighed and said firmly, as she loosened her scarf, 'I would rather sleep in my own bed tonight, thank you and if we don't go back on the bus with all the other women we will be stranded here.'

'Could be worse.'

'No Queenie,' she said firmly, 'we can come back another day.'

'Tomorrow?'

'We'll see. And besides it will give us a chance to find out more about the village. We can ask Kitty to research it on that computer of hers.'

'She did well last time.'

The chink of cups announced the arrival of their tea and cake.

'That looks yummy,' said Queenie, eyeing up the generous slices of cake the waitress placed on the table.

'Thank you,' she replied, putting the teapot and cups carefully before the two women. 'I make all the cakes myself.'

'Then you must be Jenny, have you had the tea shop long?'

The waitress carefully placed the napkins and cutlery on the table before answering, 'Over thirty years now.'

'So you know the village really well?' Queenie added mischievously, 'and the residents?'

'Well enough,' she replied cautiously.

Queenie decided not to beat about the bush and plunged straight in, ignoring Sybil's sigh.

'We met Serena Moon earlier.'

'Oh yes?'

'Her grandmother informed us of her success in the 'Best Village' Competition. It seems she is the leading light of the village.'

'Well that's not how I would have put it, but still one mustn't be uncharitable,' said the woman with a slight flush to her cheeks.

'Has she been getting up peoples noses?' asked Queenie bluntly.

'Queenie!'

'Best to be honest, call a spade a spade I say. She got up my nose earlier.'

The woman smiled slightly and visibly relaxed. 'I have to be careful what I say as it always gets back somehow.' She glanced around at the nearly empty cafe. 'But she is such a pain, always interfering. Suggestions, she calls it. I told her this cafe has nothing to do with the competition. I put the flower tubs outside and keep it tidy but the inside is my business,' she bridled. 'She didn't like it, didn't like it at all! She even inferred I was letting the village down.' She sniffed in disgust, 'we managed well enough before you came back I said.' The woman absentmindedly rearranged the cutlery and carried on slowly, 'She is a strange one though, always has a funny look in her eye. And it's not just me that gets spooked by her; old Albert won't even answer the door to her now.' She folded her arms and pursed her thin lips, nodding at the seated women. 'We're running scared of that woman. It's ridiculous!'

Sybil stirred her tea thoughtfully, 'Is Moon a local name? I have heard it before somewhere.'

'Moon was her married name; her husband was from up north somewhere.'

'Where is he now?'
'Oh, he died suddenly and a few months later she turned up here unannounced and moved back in with her grandmother. And now we are stuck with her.... still, no use complaining. We just have to get on with it.' She gave the table a last wipe with her tea cloth and nodded at the duo. 'Enjoy your tea and call if you would like a refill.'
'We will; thank you.'
Queenie looked across the table at her sister who was staring blindly into the cup while she continued to slowly stir the tea.
'You are going to wear a hole in the bottom of the cup. Sybil!'
'What?' she answered, with a start.
'Stop stirring and talk to me!'
'Moon and sudden deaths... the bells are clanging in my head.'
'Then we must get hold of Kitty and put her to work.'

Chapter Two

The sisters sat in front of the unlit fire in Sybil's home in the tiny
Devon village of Medbury. Priddy Cottage was situated in a row of
small stone cottages, behind which was the cemetery and the church of
St John the Baptist
Sybil had already kicked off her shoes and inserted her aching feet into
a pair of comfortable slippers.
'What a long day,' she sighed. 'I must say I am glad to be home.'
Queenie yawned and nodded in agreement. 'Travelling in buses always
tires me out, I would rather drive myself.' She stretched out her legs
and carefully prised off her shoes. 'Ah, that's better, now I can relax.'
She peered up at the mantel clock 'I suppose it's too late to call on
Kitty?'
'I am not moving from this house tonight,' stated Sybil. 'My poor feet
have done enough walking.' She raised a finger and wagged it at her
sister. 'And don't suggest driving up there either, it can wait until the
morning.'
'I hope Gordon won't mind us asking for Kitty's help.'
'I don't see why he should; after all we only want her expertise on the
computer. We certainly won't be dragging her into anything.'
'Not after last time.'
'But she did cope very well, better than Gordon.'

An early morning mist hung in the valley as they walked up through the
village to Orchard Cottage. Sybil's little dog Nigel was pulling at the
lead desperate to investigate all the lovely smells coming from the
damp hedgerows. He whined in excitement as they reached the entrance
to Castle Farm and tried to pull his mistress into the farmyard. Sybil
paused and looked across to the front door. It was closed and the
kitchen curtains were still pulled. Queenie cast a sideways glance at her
sister and smirked slightly.
'You can wipe that look off of your face,' Sybil said firmly. 'I was
seeing if he was up and about, that's all.'
'I never said a word,' protested Queenie innocently.
'No, but you were thinking it.'

Queenie grinned and pulled her sisters arm through hers. 'Stop being so touchy dear.'

Inside the farmhouse William's collie hearing their voices started to bark.

'Now we have disturbed the dog, let's get on round to Kitty's before William comes out to see what the disturbance is. And before you say anything,' Queenie added, interrupting her sister. 'William will want to know what we are doing out so early and if he hears what we are getting into... well you know how upset he gets.'

'Yes I know,' agreed Sybil reluctantly. 'He wouldn't approve.'

'Not at all, so let's go.'

The house, built inside the old walls of the orchard, had already mellowed over the few months since it had been built. A vigorous early flowering Montana had been planted near the front door and was already scrambling over the house while in the back garden the six new apple trees were flourishing. A few little green apples had already appeared on the branches while underneath Kitty's new additions, a trio of bantams, scratched contentedly in the grass.

'Kitty, Kitty!' Queenie rapped loudly on the front door of Orchard Cottage and peered impatiently through the hall window. 'Ah, there she is.'

The door opened and Kitty smiled at the two women in surprise.

'Good morning Queenie, Sybil.' She looked from one to the other. 'Is everything okay?'

'Fine, fine. Are you going to invite us in?'

Kitty grinned. 'Of course, come in. I was just making some coffee.' She stood to one side and ushered the two elderly women through to the kitchen where Gordon was eating some toast.

'Good morning you two, isn't it a bit early for house calls?'

'Early? It's the middle of the morning,' Queenie answered tartly.

Gordon looked at the kitchen clock; its hands were set at 8.15.

'We have been up for hours.'

'And why?' he asked calmly. He looked from one to the other. 'And what are you up to now?' he asked, recognising the mischievous gleam in their eyes.

'Well, you are not going to believe this...'

'Oh, just try me,' he said drily.

'We have stumbled across an intriguing puzzle and we would like Kitty's help to find out a little background information for us.'

'Is that all? You're not going to involve her in any more séances, ghost laying, etc, etc?'

'No, no, don't worry!' Queenie pulled out one of the kitchen chairs and sat down opposite Gordon. 'Are you going to finish that toast?' she asked, eyeing the remaining slice on his plate. He wordlessly pushed the plate in front of her and then as an afterthought passed her the marmalade.

'Would you like some more Queenie?' asked Kitty.

'Don't make any especially for her, Kitty, she's already had breakfast.' Sybil watched her sister slap a thick layer of marmalade on the toast and raised her eyebrows as Queenie mumbled around a mouthful, 'That would be nice, white if you have any. Wholemeal gives me indigestion.'

Gordon snorted and tried to stop himself laughing.

'Well if you didn't eat so much you wouldn't get indigestion, I keep telling you,' Sybil said irritably. She sat down next to her at the table and watched as Queenie started spreading marmalade on the toast Kitty had just handed her. 'And now I will have to listen to you moaning about your indigestion all the way home.'

Kitty placed two mugs of coffee in front of them and sat down next to Gordon. 'Now what information did you need?' she asked, interrupting their bickering.

'Well... yesterday we visited a small village on the coast called Bindon; it's just past Lulworth Cove.'

'It was a WI outing,' muttered Queenie, raising her eyebrows.

'The WI? I'm surprised they let you in as a member,' grinned Gordon.

'I'm not a member!' she said in disgust, glaring at him. 'I went to keep Sybil company and that's the only reason.'

'But while we were there,' continued Sybil calmly, 'we encountered; let's say a few strange things, and a name. Serena Moon. It rang a bell for some reason.' She sipped her coffee and looked across at Kitty. 'We were wondering if you could perhaps check it out, type it in on your computer and see what comes up. Can you do that?'

Kitty shrugged and looked at her husband, 'Well, Gordon is better with that sort of thing than I am. What do you think?' she asked him.

'I don't see why not. When did she die?'

'Oh no, she's alive, very much alive.' Sybil looked at her sister questioningly 'What age do you think she is? Late twenties, early thirties. Something like that?'

Queenie shrugged, 'Maybe.'

'You might get lucky,' he paused and raised an eyebrow, 'and I suppose you want me to do it right now?'

'Well,' put in Sybil before her sister could answer. 'That would be helpful.'

He sighed and pushed back his chair, 'I'll get my laptop.'

'Wonderful' said Queenie serenely, finishing the last piece of toast.

Sybil helped Kitty clear the table, whisking Queenies plate away before she could ask for more and stacking it in the sink with the rest of the breakfast things.

'More coffee?' Kitty asked. 'Gordon?'

He shook his head as he came back in with the laptop tucked under his arm. 'No, I'm fine.' He opened the top and turned it on. 'Now what was the name again?'

'Serena Moon.'

'Anything else to go on? Anything at all?'

'Well now, let's see. Moon was her husband's surname. He was from up north somewhere and so I assume died up there.'

'When?'

'It must have been about two or three years ago.'

'Now how did you come to that Sybil?' Queenie queried.

'Well..... If this was the second year of The Best Kept Village competition and I imagine Serena started working her way into the committee shortly after arriving.'

'But that is just a guess, dear.'

'Yes, yes I know,' said Sybil irritably, 'but let's just go with that for now.'

'Well I will start within that time frame and I can go back farther if need be.' He tapped briskly on the keyboard for a few minutes and then sat back and waited.

'Well?' asked Queenie, trying to peer over the top of the laptop.

'Patience,' he answered calmly.

'I'm afraid my sister hasn't got any,' said Sybil, nudging her arm.

'Ah, here we are, this might be helpful,' he adjusted his glasses and started to read. 'This is The Poppleford News. *Tragic accident of local man* blah... blah....' he muttered quickly, scanning the text.

'Don't do blah, blah Gordon,' Queenie tapped him on the arm. 'Read it properly!'

'Okay! *Tragic Accident* is the headline; it goes on *well respected local builder Terence Moon, 45, dies tragically at his home. He was believed to have been electrocuted while working on new wiring in his home. His wife of one year Serena, 34, discovered his body Sunday on returning home from a business trip. Terence, a benefactor of the local hospice and church warden of St Peters Catholic Church, Poppleford will be sadly missed in the community. His funeral...'* Gordon looked up. 'You don't want me to read all the funeral arrangements as well, do you?' Kitty interrupted, looking puzzled, 'But what is unusual about that?' It was just an accident.' She looked at the two women. 'Wasn't it?'

Queenie shrugged. 'Sybil has heard the name before, that's all. She said it was ringing a bell for some reason.' She looked across the table at her sister who was staring blindly out of the window. 'Sybil... Sybil! Well? What do you think?' she questioned.

'Poppleford,' she replied slowly.

'What?'

'Poppleford. Emily Forbes, remember Emily? She lives there, at Poppleford.' Sybil turned from staring thoughtfully out of the window. 'Emily runs a circle in Poppleford. That's where I have heard the name Serena Moon from.'

'A circle of what?' asked Gordon, looking confused.

'They have sessions once a week for mediumship and psychic healing.' Gordon groaned. 'I knew it was going to involve that sort of thing again.' He looked slowly from one to the other. 'Let me make myself clear on this, you are not going to get Kitty involved in any of this.'

'Now Gordon, we said we wouldn't,' Sybil patted him reassuringly on the arm.

'It's not you I'm worried about, Sybil. It's your sister,' he said bitterly, staring at Queenie.

She studied him calmly, a slight smile playing on her lips. 'I'm sure we will be able to manage, we usually do. After all,' she glanced across at Kitty, 'It's not Kitty's thing, she has little experience in such matters.' She raised an eyebrow and continued coolly, 'So she's safe enough,' and smiled slightly at his expression of relief. 'For now.'

Kitty pushed back her chair impatiently and walked over to the sink where she stared in exasperation at all three of them.

'I wish you would all ask me what I think instead of treating me as though I wasn't here!'

Her husband looked startled at her outburst while Queenie just smiled to herself.

A concerned frown wrinkled Sybil's forehead as she asked, 'Well my dear, do you mind getting involved?'

Kitty's chin lifted in defiance. 'I would be very happy to help, in fact I will start now. I can get in touch with the Poppleford newspaper and see if they can add anything to the report.'

Queenie smiled faintly at the annoyance on Gordon's face before she turned to Kitty.

'Well that sounds safe enough. Making a simple phone call isn't going to put Kitty in harm's way.

Gordon ran his hand through his hair in frustration. 'I'm not happy about this but,' he looked at his wife's determined expression and said grudgingly, 'I suppose calling them won't hurt.'

'And I,' said Sybil suddenly standing up, 'am going to go and find Emily's phone number and call her. As far as I can remember Serena was part of her circle. I haven't spoken to Emily for months so it will be nice to catch up.'

Sybil and Queenie linked arms as they walked slowly back down the lane to the village. It was turning out to be a beautiful morning, the mist had been burnt off by the warm sun and the birds were singing in the hedgerows. The smell of coffee and bacon drifted out from one of the cottages as they walked past.

'I still think we should go back to Bindon,' said Queenie thoughtfully.

'Let's wait to see what Kitty can find out and I would like to speak to Emily first.' Sybil unbuttoned her coat 'I think it's going to be a lovely day.'

'Yes. Nice day for a drive?' prompted Queenie.

'No, we will wait,' she replied firmly. 'I wonder if Serena and the little boy we saw in the churchyard are connected in some way?'

'I think so,' Queenie paused, 'I can feel a link between them. And an overwhelming sense of fear.'

Sybil shrugged. 'Well, you are better than me at picking up things like that.'

They paused outside of Sybil's cottage while she fumbled in her pocket for the key. 'We will drive over tomorrow.' she said decisively. 'That's what we will do, otherwise you and I will be thinking of nothing else.'

'So you are ready for an adventure then?'

'Not an adventure Queenie, just a little bit of poking about.'

Queenie put her arm around her sister's shoulder. 'Here's to poking about then.'

'But we will be subtle.'

'I don't do subtle.'

'Well, it's time you started. I don't want to rock the boat so to speak. I just wish to ask a few questions and it's better not to set peoples backs up first.' She opened the front door. 'Now let's go and call Emily.'

The phone rang for a few minutes before it was finally picked up.

'Hello?'

'Emily, it's me, Sybil.'

'Sybil! How lovely to hear from you. How strange, I was thinking about you this morning. Haven't heard from you for ages, how are you?'

'Very well dear, and you?'

'Well as can be expected at my age,' Emily chuckled slightly.

'I know what you mean,' she said sympathetically, at the same time turning her back on Queenie who was mouthing and gesturing at her to hurry up. 'How is the circle going?'

'Oh, I stopped that a few months ago, I just haven't got the energy to cope with it at the moment.'

'Queenie and I met a member of your group yesterday.'

'Really?' Emily sounded surprised. 'Who was that?'

'Serena Moon.'

There was a deathly silence on the other end of the phone.

'Emily, are you still there?'

'Yes Sybil.'

'Do you remember her?'

Sybil heard Emily laugh slightly.

'Who could forget Serena!' she replied.

'She seemed quite a strange young woman.'

'What did she say about our circle?'

'Nothing dear, she didn't mention it at all. I just recognised the name.'

'Oh I see. Well, she was a nightmare! Never content with what we were doing,' Emily said indignantly. 'She always wanted to take control of the meetings, and her temper! Well I pitied her poor husband having to put up with it. When she realised we weren't going to allow her to take over she flew into such a rage, she was like a mad woman.'

'Her husband died, didn't he?' asked Sybil tentatively.

There was long pause and then a hesitant, 'Yes.'

The following silence from both of the women was too much for Queenie and she took the phone impatiently from her sister's hand.

'Let me speak to her. Emily dear...it's Queenie.'

'Queenie! I haven't spoken to you for years. How are you?'

'Oh I'm fine. Now about Serena. What did she want to do in the circle exactly? You said she wasn't happy with what you were doing so what did she want then?'

Queenie heard her laugh. 'You haven't changed have you? Always straight to the point. Is this the reason you rang?'

'Sorry but yes.'

'Well... she wanted to lead us more down the occult path, and summon and bind spirits to our will. She is a very strange woman! We refused of course, tried to explain how dangerous that could be but she wouldn't listen. That's when she exploded.'

'Really?'

'Not literally Queenie! I meant lost her temper, I have never seen anybody lose it like that before. She was practically foaming at the mouth. And after that she never came back to any of the meetings. And we weren't sorry about that either! She always seemed to think she had special powers which she inherited from her grandfather.'

Queenie looked intrigued and raised her eyebrows at her sister who was trying to follow the conversation.

'What powers? What was special about her grandfather?'

She heard her friend sigh. 'Well, she was always saying that he had immense power at his command; that he could protect his village against evil forces. Cunning Man,' Emily said suddenly, 'that's what she called him. A Cunning Man. I guess now that she meant more than being wily!'

'What village? Did she mention a name or where it was? This is really important Emily, try and remember.'

'Oh dear, you are putting me on the spot. I didn't recognise the name I'm sorry but I do remember it was on the coast. I'm sorry I just can't remember any more.'

Queenie sighed. 'Well you have been very helpful Emily, thank you. But tell me one thing before you go, did Serena have any psychic abilities?'

The sound of laughter came from the telephone and it was a few minutes before Emily had enough breath to answer Queenie's question. 'Abilities? Queenie, I have seen bricks with more psychic abilities than her!'

'I will tell her you said that!' chuckled Queenie.

'You can tell her with my compliments! But seriously, be careful if you run into her again, she really has got a screw loose. Several in fact.'

'So we're agreed then? We'll go in the morning,' asked Queenie.
Sybil nodded, looking up from her knitting. 'I will have to ask Kitty to look after Nigel for a few days but I'm sure she won't mind.'
Queenie watched her busily knit for a few minutes; Sybil's lips were pursed as she concentrated on the difficult pattern of the sleeve. Queenie's eyes began to gleam with mischief. 'Why don't you ask William? I'm sure he would love to help.'
Her sister gave her a withering look.
'Well?' prompted Queenie innocently.
'Because I would have to explain where we are going and why and I'm no good at lying. He would have the truth out of me in no time at all. So it's better if he doesn't know anything about it.'
'Very true, keep him in the dark,' she chuckled.
'As you have reminded me, I will ring Kitty now,' Sybil said, folding up her knitting and putting it into the sewing bag.
Queenie smiled and put her head on one side, lifting a finger she said thoughtfully, 'Don't bother, she's just walking up to the door.'
'I wish you wouldn't do that.'
'Do what? I am just saving you the cost of a phone call that is all. You should be grateful.'
A gentle knock sounded at the cottage door and Sybil sighed. 'Just for once can't you be wrong!'
'No,' Queenie said simply.
The door opened slowly and Kitty peeped in. 'Hello?'
'Hello Kitty. Come in.'
'Did you have any luck with our research?'
'Queenie, let the poor girl get in the house first,' Sybil interrupted before she replied.
'Come and sit down Kitty, would you like a cup of tea?'
'I would,' put in Queenie. 'I thought you were never going to stop knitting.'
Kitty grinned at the pair of them and took the armchair near the fire; she leant forward and gave the little cairn a pat.
'No thanks Sybil, I'm fine,' smiling at Queenie's disgusted look.
'Now she won't make any,' she complained.
'Ignore her Kitty; she knows where the kitchen is. I was going to ask if you would look after Nigel for a few days while we have a little trip to Bindon.'

Kitty gave the dog another pat. 'I would be very happy to look after him. So you are going?' she questioned, looking from one to the other, a slight expression of concern on her face.

'Oh yes. Definitely,' said Queenie. 'Did you find out any more information on Serena's husband?'

Kitty sighed. 'Not much, I'm afraid.' She pulled out a few notes from her jacket pocket.

'Now let me see; I checked with the newspaper. They couldn't add much to what we already know although I did get the impression it wasn't an open and shut case. There was no evidence so it didn't go any further.' She consulted her notes again. 'As for Bindon, there wasn't much I could find out about it either. Just a small fishing village. During the war most of the men answered the call to help with the Dunkirk evacuation and a lot of them didn't make it back. Apart from that nothing of interest I'm afraid.' She looked up frowning. 'Sorry, I haven't been much help at all.'

'Don't worry. It was a long shot anyway but it was worth checking. There might be nothing at all going on in the village and we will be wasting our time, but,' she went on smiling at Queenie, 'at least we'll get a few days away.'

'Paddling and ice creams?' teased Kitty.

'Something like that.'

'You will be careful though won't you? And please let us know how you are getting on and if you need any help.'

Queenie shook her head in disgust. 'Really Kitty, we can look after ourselves.'

Chapter Three

Sybil placed her overnight bag in the boot of Queenie's car and looked around as her sister slammed the front door of the cottage.
'Anything else to go in here?'
'No, that's it, dear.'
'Right,' she closed the boot and moved around to the passenger side of the car. 'And you're sure you are alright to drive that far?' She looked worried as Queenie fumbled in her fleece pocket for the keys.
'Of course, stop fussing. It's not that far.'
'It's just there is so much traffic on the road nowadays.'
'I'll be fine Sybil,' she replied impatiently. 'Now get in or I will leave you behind.' She settled herself behind the wheel pulling out a pair of thick glasses and perching them on the end of nose. 'Have you got any mints?'
'What are those? Sybil asked in surprise, looking across at her sister. 'Mints?'
'No, the glasses. Since when have you been wearing glasses to drive?'
'Oh, not long,' she replied airily. 'I don't really need them.' She looked at the expression on her sister's face. 'Don't worry, we'll be fine.'
She put the car into gear and pulled away slowly, down through the narrow lanes of the village and out onto the main road.
'Now,' said Sybil. 'Which way are we going?'
'Well, we are going straight along the A35 to Dorchester then follow the A352 and then turn onto the B3070 to the coast. We'll be there in no time at all.' She glanced across at Sybil's blank face and sighed, 'We're going to drive to Dorchester, turn off as though we are going to Aunt Gracie's then follow the road that flooded in 1963 then turn off at Hangman's Corner to the coast road. Okay?'
'Now why didn't you just say that?' Sybil sighed, then clutched at her seat as Queenie sped past a slow lorry grinding up Abbey Gate hill. 'And slow down!'

By the time the little car crested the hill overlooking Widbarrow Bay the sky had clouded over and a light rain started to fall.

'Oh, what a shame,' said Sybil peering through the misty window. She could just make out a few boats anchored below in the bay. 'I hope it won't rain too hard.'

'It will be a nuisance if it does, it might hamper our snooping.'

'Investigating,' she reminded Queenie.

A small river of rainwater was already flowing down the narrow lane leading to the cove. Queenie drove down very carefully avoiding the potholes and the larger puddles, mentally keeping her fingers crossed that no vehicle would be coming up from the village.

'Call it what you like Sybil; investigating or snooping, it's all the same.' She glanced in her rear view mirror in exasperation. 'I do wish this jackass would get off my bumper!'

Sybil looked surprised at her sudden outburst and peered over her shoulder at the large four by four that was following closely behind as Queenies little yellow car crawled down the narrow lane.

They rounded the last bend and pulled into the car park. Queenie drove through the few parked cars that were already there to the far side where it was allocated for the residents parking. As she pulled into a vacant space the following car roared into the adjacent space and stopped.

'Are you sure it's okay for us to park here?'

'Mrs Butler from the guest house said to park here, but I have to get a permit or something to put in the window. She will give it to us when we book in.'

Sybil peered through the misty window at the four by four that had pulled up so close to them. 'Oh bother,' she exclaimed.

'What?' asked Queenie, struggling to get her seat belt off.

'It's Serena and she doesn't look very pleased to see us.'

By then Serena had got out of her car and was walking around to Queenies door, she bent and peered in the window then opened the door.

'What are you doing here?'

'Hello, how delightful to see you again Serena,' gushed Queenie. 'Mrs Butler said it would be okay for us to park here,' she gave the young woman a bright smile.' So you needn't worry.'

'Are you staying here?'

'Oh yes! We enjoyed ourselves so much the other day that we thought a nice little break by the seaside would do two old ladies the world of good.'

Sybil watched amused from the passenger seat as a variety of emotions flickered over the young woman's face.

'Well, Mrs Butler must have made a mistake; she has no vacancies at the moment.'

Queenie raised an eyebrow. 'There's no mistake, we've booked, and paid for a room. However I will let Mrs Butler know that you are concerned about the way she is dealing with the bookings. She must be delighted that you take such an interest in her guest house.'

Queenie opened the car door pushing Serena out of the way and swung her legs out. 'Excuse me dear but I must get out and stretch my legs.' She ducked her head back into the car 'Come along Sybil, let's get booked in.' She straightened up and looked at Serena in mock surprise. 'Still here, dear? Queenie smiled brightly at the frustrated expression on her face and slammed the door shut. 'I am so looking forward to this.' Serena's mouth tightened for a minute.

'You will get bored, there's nothing for two old women to do here. We have no knit and natter groups for you to join,' she added maliciously.

'I can't knit,' replied Queenie calmly. 'And don't worry about us; we have plenty of things planned.' She smiled brightly at her and winked at her sister. 'Haven't we Sybil?'

'What's that dear?' Sybil was struggling to pull the cases from the car. She looked up and smiled sweetly. 'I say Serena you wouldn't be a dear and help us with our bags would you?'

The woman glared at them both and didn't bother answering, just swung her handbag onto her shoulder and stalked off across the car park followed by Queenie's cackle of laughter.

'Nice one Sybil!'

'No, actually I was serious; I need some help with these.' She hefted her sister's bag and raised her eyebrows. 'What have you got in here? It weighs a ton.'

'Just a few essentials. Put it down Sybil, it has wheels on it.'

She peered at the bottom of the case. 'Well so it has, how clever.'

Queenie locked the car and took the case from her sister. 'Come on.' They rattled their way across the car park following in Serena's footsteps, past the little gift shop and the tea shop which was just opening. Sybil waved cheerfully to the owner who after a surprised stare, waved cheerfully in return and opened the door.

'Hello, how lovely to see you again.' She looked at the cases inquiringly. 'Are you staying?'

'Just for a few days, we thought we could do with a little break and this seemed such a nice quiet little village,' Sybil replied, smiling calmly.

The woman looked from one innocent wrinkled face to Queenie's, who was grinning mischievously.

'Really?'

'No, my sister is trying to be subtle, we've come to snoop.'

Sybil sighed in resignation. 'That's it Queenie! You have just blown our cover!'

The women laughed. 'Now that explains why Serena has just stormed past here with a face like thunder,' she smiled, 'so I suppose we can expect fireworks now you are here?'

Queenie straightened her fleece and hefted her case. 'Well, I think we have just lit the touch paper, time to stand back and watch!'

Sybil took her sisters arm. 'Come along dear, now let's go and find our room,' she nodded to the woman. 'We will probably see you later for a cup of tea.'

'Good luck.' She retreated into the tea shop and watched through the window the two old sisters picking their way carefully over the wet cobbles to the guest house. 'They will need it,' she muttered.

Sea View Guest House was a delightful little white washed cottage overlooking the beach; its brightly coloured shutters framed the sparkling windows and hanging baskets hung from the front of the building. A narrow passageway ran down the side of the cottage to the beach which could be accessed by a set of narrow stone steps. The back door of Sea View opened on to these steps and placed on the beach below were some tables and chairs for the guests' convenience.

The front door of the guesthouse was firmly closed, the sound of raised voices could be heard coming from inside.

Queenie rattled the door handle and rapped loudly on the glass panel. The voices stopped and a small thin woman hurried into the hall and peered through the glass at them. Her mouth dropped open in dismay and she hurriedly opened the door.

'I'm so sorry to have kept you waiting.'

Queenie smiled at her calmly, 'That's alright Mrs Butler, how nice to meet you. I'm Mrs Beresford, we have booked.' She looked inquiringly at the women who remained fixed in the doorway.

'Oh yes, of course,' her lips worked nervously for a minute and drawing a shaky breath, 'I'm sorry but...' her voice trailed off and she glanced nervously behind to the darkened interior.

Queenie sighed, took her by the arm and pushed her gently into the hall. 'Come along,' she said reassuringly. 'Everything will be fine, just show us to our rooms.' She glanced down the hallway to a door marked private which was just slightly on the jar. 'Hello Serena,' she called out cheerily. She felt Mrs Butler start under her grasp and saw her gaze in dismay at the door.

'It's okay,' she hefted her bag and nodded towards the staircase. 'After you.'

A door slammed in the depths of the guest house.

'Oh dear,' Mrs Butler moaned, pressing her fingers to her mouth. 'She's going to be so angry with me.'

Sybil placed her arm around the woman and gave her a hug. 'Now, now, dear, there's nothing to worry about. After all this is your guest house isn't it and it's up to you who you have staying here.'

Mrs Butler nodded in agreement. 'I know, but she gets so worked up. I don't usually worry, my husband deals with the bookings and he doesn't take any nonsense from her.'

'Where is your husband?'

Her lip quivered. 'He's in hospital at the moment, he had a fall.'

'Oh no,' sympathised Sybil. 'Nothing serious I hope?'

'A fractured skull and concussion.'

'Goodness, how awful for you,' exclaimed Queenie, looking at her sympathetically. 'So you have to cope on your own.'

Mrs Butler nodded as she led the way up the narrow staircase.

'Well, we won't be any bother so you don't have to worry.'

She smiled at them and paused before a door. 'This is yours. I hope you will like it. It has a sea view,' and opened the door to a sun filled room; light curtains stirred in the breeze from the open window, the sea air mingling with the scent of polish. The room was spotless, the twin beds covered in white bedspreads and plump cushions.

'This is a lovely room,' exclaimed Queenie, moving to the window.

'And I can see the whole bay.' Her sister moved to stand beside her and admire the view.

She turned back to Mrs Butler who was hovering in the doorway. 'This is very nice, thank you.'

'Well, I'm glad you like it,' she smiled uncertainly. 'I'm sorry about the mix up just now.'

'That's alright, we met Serena in the car park and she didn't make us welcome then either.'

Queenie laughed. 'That's an understatement.' She hefted her bag and plumped it onto a small chair near the window. 'We're looking forward to a nice relaxing stay, aren't we Sybil?'

'Absolutely,' she agreed, trying to keep a straight face.

Mrs Butler's expression relaxed and she nodded happily. 'Well that's good, now I will go and make some tea for you. I'm sure you could do with some refreshment after your journey.'

'We never refuse tea, do we Queenie?'

Mrs Butler pulled the door closed behind her and they could hear her descend the creaking stairs on the way to the kitchen. Sybil waited until she was sure their host was out of earshot.

'Well, I didn't think Serena would go that far to keep us away.'

'Which makes it all the more interesting, doesn't it! I wonder what she is up to? Very strange,' Queenie mused as she busied herself throwing handfuls of clothes into the small set of drawers. She looked at her sister who was still staring out of the window.

'Which bed would you like?'

Sybil shrugged. 'Not bothered.'

'Right, I will have the one nearest the window. I can lie here tonight listening to the sea.'

Sybil unzipped her bag and began meticulously arranging her clothes in the wardrobe, pausing while hanging a blouse on a metal coat hanger she suddenly said, 'I must ring Kitty later just to let them know we have arrived safely.'

Queenie snorted. 'Honestly, they are treating us like children. Having to check in, really!'

Sybil smiled 'I know but I did promise. I think Gordon believes we are in our second childhood.'

'Huh, he's so bossy.'

'And you're not?'

'Who me? I'm not bossy,' replied Queenie, not meeting her sister's eye. In the short silence that followed a little tinkling bell could be heard coming from the hall, they paused in their unpacking and looked at each other.

'I wonder if she is ringing it for tea?' mused Sybil.

Queenie threw her wash bag down on the bed and opened the door. 'Let's go and find out, shall we?'

Down in the hall Mrs Butler was waiting with a loaded tea tray in her hands.

'Ah, you did hear me; I thought you might like to have tea in the sitting room. It's more comfortable in here.'

She led the way into the room overlooking the street. Although a light rain was still falling, inside it was warm and cheerful. The small cosy room was filled with comfortable armchairs and little tables arranged around the fireplace. She placed the tray carefully down on a little three legged table.

'I could light the fire if you are feeling chilly,' she looked in concern at the two elderly women. 'It's all laid, ready to go.'

'No we're fine, it's nice and warm in here.' Sybil looked at the tray with its plates of cucumber sandwiches and array of delicate pastries jostled with the delicately patterned china tea set. 'This looks wonderful, you are spoiling us.'

Queenie reached towards the tray and helped herself to a sandwich. 'This is splendid, just what we need.' She glanced at Mrs Butler whose cheeks were pink with pleasure at the compliment.

'It's no trouble at all,' she hesitated. 'It will be nice, having you here, having some company,' she confided, looking slightly embarrassed. Queenie paused in the act of helping herself to another sandwich, 'Aren't there any other guests?'

Their host looked uncomfortable for a minute. 'No,' she said slowly. 'With my husband in hospital Serena thought it best that I cancelled all the bookings.' She looked bewildered for a minute. 'Until I got your call Mrs Beresford, I don't know why... I just thought I would enjoy having you both here.'

'Queenie, please.'

'Well,' she looked pleased, 'I'm Beryl.'

'Well, Beryl,' Queenie threw an arm around her and gave her a hug, 'We are going to have a great time together.'

She nodded and smiled. 'I think you are right Queenie, and?' she looked inquiringly at Sybil who was calmly pouring tea.

'It's Sybil, dear,' she smiled at her, 'Would you join us for tea?'

'Oh, that would be nice; I'll just go and fetch another cup.' As Beryl disappeared to the kitchen Sybil warned her sister in a low voice, 'Now behave yourself Queenie and don't pump her for too much information, I don't want to upset her.'

'Okay,' she shrugged, before piling a handful of the sandwiches onto her plate. She settled down in one of the armchairs in front of the fireplace and taking a cup and saucer from Sybil sipped on it thoughtfully.

'She is taking an awfully long time to fetch one cup.' She placed her own back on the tray and stood up. 'I will go and investigate.' She picked up the teapot 'And I will get this topped up at the same time. She headed for the nether regions of the guest house with a purposeful air, tapping politely on the door marked 'private' before pushing it open.

Beryl was sitting at the kitchen table with her head sunk in her arms, shoulders shaking and muffled sobs coming from the folded arms.

'Oh goodness! What's wrong?' Queenie asked in amazement. A quick scan of the kitchen supplied the answer before Beryl could speak. Her days baking of the pastries and cakes that they had just been enjoying had been taken and dashed against the walls of the room in a vindictive act. The fruit and cream splattered the paintwork and as Queenie watched a raspberry tart that had clung onto the surface of the wall gave up and slid slowly down leaving a bright red smear and plopped onto the floor where it joined the crumbled remains of the rest.

Queenie banged open the door and shouted down the hall for her sister before turning back to Beryl.

'Now dear what happened?'

Beryl raised her tear stained face. 'I can't stand much more of this,' she moaned. 'If my husband were here it would be different. He always stands up to her.' She began to cry again as Sybil walked calmly into the room, cup and saucer in hand.

'What's going on?' she enquired, pausing in amazement at the sight of the kitchen. 'Oh.'

Queenie walked past Beryl to the back door which was wide open and swinging in the stiff breeze blowing off the beach.

'Did you leave this door unlocked after Serena left?'

Beryl nodded miserably. 'I didn't think. I was too busy getting you settled into your room. Why would she do this?' she said, blowing her nose.

Queenie and Sybil exchanged looks. Because she doesn't want us here, they both thought.

Sybil said soothingly, 'We'll get this cleaned up in no time at all. Such a shame, those cakes were delicious.'

She busied herself about the kitchen clearing away the broken cakes and squashed fruit and wiping down the walls. In no time at all the kitchen was clean and tidy again, the only evidence of the destruction was the broken plates and the red stain on the wall. Sybil looked at it ruefully, 'Sorry, I can't shift that at all.'

Beryl sniffed and blew her nose. 'Never mind' she said bravely. 'It's time the kitchen had a lick of fresh paint.' She looked around the room. 'Perhaps a yellow, what do you think?' she appealed to the sisters.

'A nice yellow would do the trick, bright and cheerful,' said Queenie, putting the kettle on to make some more tea. She paused, 'I will just go and get those cakes from the sitting room and we can continue our tea party in here.'

Queenie pottered out into the hall, checked the front door was securely locked before collecting the tea tray.

'Here we are,' she said cheerfully, laying it on the kitchen table. 'Good job Sybil hasn't eaten all the cakes.'

Her sister gazed at the seriously depleted stock of sandwiches.

'And it's a shame you didn't leave more of the sandwiches, Queenie.'

Beryl jumped up pleased to be able to do something, the comforting presence of the elderly women made her feel more positive and secure since her husband had been taken to hospital.

'I can make some more, it's no trouble,' she offered eagerly. 'As long as Serena hasn't thrown out the bread for the seagulls.'

'I hope not!' Queenie shook her head indignantly. 'Such a waste if she did.'

With Queenie making the tea and Beryl making a few more rounds of her delicious cucumber sandwiches they were soon installed back at the table with filled plates in front of them.

Sybil propped her elbow on the table and rested her chin in her hand. 'Now Beryl, what is going on here?'

Beryl gazed at the two women 'I don't know. I really don't understand her. She just doesn't like us having guests. She has even written a few bogus reviews on our website.'

'Bad ones?'

'Terrible. They were so... well, just nasty and spiteful. I can't understand how anybody can be like that. How she thinks we are going to make a living if we don't have paying guests I just don't know.'

Tears began to well up again and Sybil reached over to give her a soothing pat.

'It's okay, everything will be fine.' She smiled reassuringly. 'We'll deal with Serena.'

For the life of her Beryl couldn't understand why she suddenly felt so comforted but looking at their two calm wrinkled faces she did.

'When is your husband coming home?'

'I'm visiting the hospital tonight and if all is well then I can pick him up tomorrow.'

'Well, he will have to kept quiet and rest when he comes home. So it will be best if you don't say anything about this,' suggested Sybil.

Beryl's brow furrowed and she looked momentarily anxious. 'I hope we won't have any more trouble.'

'Don't worry,' Queenie said firmly, reaching for the last sandwich. 'We'll deal with Serena.'

Chapter Four

'As it has stopped raining a breath of fresh air will do us good,' suggested Sybil. 'Come on, stir yourself.' She looked impatiently at Queenie who was stretched out on the bed. 'You need to walk off those sandwiches.'

Queenie pushed a lock of pink hair out of her eyes and yawned. 'Okay,' she muttered. 'But I was just getting comfortable.'

'Well... if you are too tired... and after all you have had a very long day dear. Perhaps you should stay and rest. I'm sure Gordon would approve.'

Queenie swung her legs over the side of the bed and stood up. She straightened her skirt.

'Bother Gordon, I'm fine. Stop treating me like an old woman.'

Sybil's lips twitched as she handed her sister the purple fleece.

'Okay if you insist. Now would you like a nice warm scarf to wrap around your neck?'

'I'll wrap something around your neck,' she muttered, zipping up her fleece. She headed towards the door. 'Well come on then!'

It was late afternoon and although the rain had stopped and the sun was struggling to peep out from behind the clouds the village was deserted. The day's inclement weather had been enough to deter the most enthusiastic holiday maker.

Sybil pocketed the back door key and drew a deep breath of the cool sea air. 'That's better.'

Overhead a few squawking seagulls headed back out to the open sea. She wrapped a scarf around her shoulders and pulled on a pair of gloves. 'Warm enough?' she inquired, turning to her sister.

Queenie blinked for a minute in the sunshine. 'I'm fine. You were right; this is a good idea after all.' She breathed deeply. 'Very quiet now isn't it,' she mused, emerging from the passageway she gazed up and down the deserted street. 'Where is everybody?' Just as she said this, a face appeared in a little window in the adjacent cottage overlooking the passage down to the beach. She nodded politely to the elderly man who was gazing curiously through the dirty window pane. Sybil followed her gaze and waved at him.

'I wonder who that is?'

The face disappeared and within minutes the front door opened.

'Good afternoon,' they called politely, to the figure in the doorway. He leant heavily on a walking stick while holding on firmly to the door frame.

'You must be the couple who are staying with Beryl,' he muttered, in a tobacco roughened voice.

Sybil smiled at him. 'That's right, I'm Sybil and this is my sister Queenie.'

'Just two old ladies having a quiet seaside holiday,' grinned Queenie, winking at the elderly man.

He laughed, showing nicotine stained teeth. 'Ha, you can't fool me; I have been warned about you two already.'

'Oh dear,' Sybil looked at Queenie. 'Our reputation has preceded us!'

'It has indeed,' he shifted his weight and leant forward conspiritally. 'Not that I'm worried if you upset Serena.'

'You must be Albert,' Queenie guessed.

He nodded then looked down the street to the church. 'You watch yourselves.' He nodded a couple of times at the two old women and looked as though he would have liked to say more but instead closed the door.

Sybil raised her eyebrows. 'Okay,' she said slowly. 'Now we have met Albert.'

'Was that a warning, do you think?'

Her sister shrugged in response, 'Maybe,' she took Queenie's arm. 'Let's go, shall we?'

They sauntered slowly along the street avoiding the larger puddles that had formed on the uneven surface heading for the church at the far end of the village. From inside several of the white washed cottages snatches of music and laughter from a television wafted out but apart from that there was no sign of the residents.

Within a few minutes they were in front of the church gate. Queenie glanced across at the cottage. Although it appeared deserted she could feel somebody watching from one of the windows. She felt her sister chuckle silently.

'I'm expecting her to come bursting out of the cottage any minute.'

'Or the chimney, on her broomstick,' added Queenie. 'Now that would be a sight!' She pushed open the gate. 'Let's go and visit Thomas,' she suggested.

Sybil hesitated.

'What's wrong?'

'The grass will be wet and we'll get our shoes soaked.'
'Sybil Leavenham, I am surprised at you. I didn't realise you were such a wimp!'
'I'm not; I just don't want wet feet. Might get a chill,' she muttered defensively. She followed reluctantly through into the churchyard.
'Okay then, on your head be it.'
The grass was sodden and within minutes their shoes were soaked as they walked across to the fallen headstone.
'Told you!' muttered Sybil.
The posy of flowers still lay on the stone but with the rain it was looking rather worse for wear.
'All quiet,' Queenie looked around 'I thought we might see the young boy again.'
'Perhaps once was enough, he's got our attention after all.'
'But there must be more to his appearance than that.'
A few birds called from the dark wooded hillside behind them and with the wind soughing through the branches and whistling around the headstones it all added to the desolate feel of the spot. The constant dripping from the overhanging branches landing on their unprotected heads made the women shiver.
'What a miserable place to leave your bones. It's enough to make anybody walk.'
Behind them the gate squeaked on its wet hinges, they turned almost expecting to see Serena but it was just swaying in the breeze, creaking backwards and forwards as they watched.
'Come on; let's get out of this damp graveyard.'
Clods of wet grass stuck to their shoes and Sybil had to vigorously stamp her feet to dislodge it from the soles when they had regained the path. She sighed when she saw the water stains on her best pair of leather brogues. 'Soaked,' she said bitterly.' Told you.'
'Stop fussing. The shoes will dry off in no time.' Catching a movement in the corner of her eye Queenie grinned. Serena was watching them from the shelter of the cottage arbour.
Queenie couldn't resist, she raised her arm and waved. Although she couldn't see the young woman's expression, from the rigid stance she could guess Serena's annoyance at the sight of them.
'I was wondering when she would appear,' Sybil said calmly, pulling the gate closed behind them. She looked across at the beautiful cottage garden they had visited just a few days earlier. 'I think I would like to have a word with her about the cakes.'

'She'll deny it.'

'Of course.'

Keeping an eye on her they walked slowly to the front gate of the cottage and pushed it open. The squealing hinges left little doubt of their intent to enter the garden.

Serena came quickly into view from around the corner of the house, an expression of irritation written all over her face.

'The garden is closed,' she snapped.

'Oh, we know Serena.' Sybil followed her sister in and pushed the gate closed 'We just wanted to have a chat.'

Serena folded her arms and stared at them. 'About what?' she said coldly.

'Well,' began Queenie, smiling sweetly at her, 'As you know we are staying with Beryl.' She ignored the look of disdain that flickered over her face and carried on, the tone of her voice hardening. 'And we think it best if you left her alone. Your, shall we say misguided, interference in her guest house is causing her a lot of stress. Something that she doesn't need at the moment.'

Sybil nodded in agreement. 'We can look after her until her husband returns.'

Serena placed her hands on her hips and smiled. 'You think he will be back soon? I doubt that. He had a nasty fall. He could have broken his neck falling down those steps to the beach.'

'Is that what happened?' Sybil looked at her suspiciously. 'Just an unfortunate accident I suppose. I wonder if he remembers what happened; it will be interesting to hear his version of the 'accident'.'

Serena walked slowly across the grass to the two old women and stopped just in front of them. 'I'm sure a blow like that on the head would have erased any memory of it.'

'You're sure about that?'

'Oh yes.' She pointed to the gate. 'Now get out of my garden.'

'Your grandmother's garden,' Queenie reminded her pointedly.

'Grandmother won't be here forever then it will be my garden.'

'Oh dear, I hope granny isn't going to have an 'accident' as well,' Queenie said, in mock concern. She pulled open the squealing gate and ushered Sybil through. 'Just stay away from Beryl and the guest house. I think she has had enough of your meddling.'

The gate was slammed behind them and Serena gripped the metal, her knuckles whitening as she leant over it, glaring furiously at the sisters.

Sybil stared at her coldly. 'Beryl doesn't want to get the police involved in that act of vandalism so we told her we would deal with it. So just stay away.'

'Don't tell me what to do, this is my village and I run it.'

Queenie snorted. 'I doubt that very much.' She turned to Sybil. 'Come along dear, time to go.'

'Yes you should go, go and leave the village. Go home to where ever it is that you came from.'

'Ah but we haven't finished with you yet,' Queenie smiled and winked at the irate young woman. 'Have we dear?' she asked Sybil.

Her sister smiled coldly and slipped an arm through Queenies.

'We're just getting started.'

They waited until they were out of earshot before Sybil muttered, 'You don't think she really does own the whole village, do you?'

'No. Beryl owns Sea View. I saw that on the website. They retired from Weston and bought the property five years ago. And I bet she doesn't own the tea shop either.'

'Then why would she say that?'

'Because she's mad, dear.'

'Well, I suppose that's one explanation.'

Halfway between Serena's cottage and the guest house a stout middle aged woman was busy tying posters onto gateposts up and down the village street. She glanced up quickly as they came closer, a momentary look of suspicion crossed the woman's face and she gave an inaudible answer to Sybil's greeting. Sybil peered at the poster that she had just fixed to a gate. A photograph of a plump black and white cat filled most of the space with bold printing of LOST written above it.

'Oh dear,' she exclaimed sympathetically. 'Is it your cat?'

The woman nodded and looked at the handful of leaflets she was still holding. 'I'm putting them up everywhere. He never strays; I just can't think what's happened to him.'

'How long has he been missing?'

'Nobody has seen him for four days, he's very well known in the village. Bobby is in and out of my neighbour's cottages all the time.' she smiled ruefully. 'He's always looking for food, he's such as scrounger.'

'Thinks with his stomach, does he?' Queenie put out a hand for a leaflet. 'Well, we'll take one. We're going to be here for a few days and you never know, we might spot him.'

'Thank you, that's very kind,' she hesitated, and glanced over her shoulder towards the church. 'You're staying with Serena? It's just that I saw you coming out of Mrs Coppingers.'

Queenie sniggered slightly. 'No, we're at Sea View. We just needed to have a word with her.' She looked at the slightly mistrustful expression on the woman's face and smiled slowly.

'Queenie, no!'

'Nonsense. This young woman won't mind.'

She looked baffled, glancing from one sister to the other. 'Mind what?'

Queenie smiled, her pale eyes gleamed and she reached out and laid a hand gently on the woman's arm. She stared intently into her puzzled brown eyes. 'Now dear, you are going to tell me all about it.'

Her brow furrowed. 'What?' she mumbled, suddenly confused. 'I don't know...' Her arm began to tingle under Queenie's touch and a warm numb feeling slowly spread through her body. The old woman's voice seemed to come from far away and she had the strangest feeling as though she was on the verge of fainting.

'Yes, you do,' Queenie grip tightened and she stared unblinking into the woman's face. 'Janet,' she said quietly. 'Listen to me.'

The woman nodded, unable to take her eyes off of the old woman.

Behind her Sybil stirred impatiently, 'Really! Doing this on the street!'

'Shhhh!' Queenie turned back to Janet. 'Now, does Serena own this village?'

'No.'

'Does her grandmother own the village?'

'No.'

'Ha! That's what I thought,' she said gleefully.

'At least ask a few more pertinent questions now that you have hold of her.'

'I'm just getting to it. Now, listen to me Janet,' she gave her arm a gentle shake. 'Why is Serena trying to control everything?'

Janet sighed and blinked. 'The Coppingers, the family, they were in control for years. She wants to return to the old ways.' She swayed slightly and put out a hand to steady herself on the gate post. 'They controlled everything along this coast. Nobody was free of them.'

'I think that's enough Queenie, she is looking rather pale.'

'Just one more question Janet, how did they do that?'

'The Cunning Man,' she said faintly, and swayed. 'It was him.'

'That's enough Queenie! Let go of her.'

Queenie nodded and slowly released her grip on the woman's arm. 'Are you alright dear?' she asked calmly, watching Janet blink. 'You had a bit of a funny turn.'

The colour had flooded back into her face and a light sheen of perspiration coated her upper lip.

'Well, I don't know what happened. I felt most peculiar for a minute.' She rubbed a shaky hand over her face and took a deep breath. 'Perhaps I had better leave the rest of the posters for later.'

'I think that's wise.' Sybil patted her shoulder. 'Time to go home and have a nice cup of tea.'

Janet nodded and smiled slightly at them before walking shakily to a nearby cottage.

'Well! That was interesting.'

'Queenie, you are the limit! You shouldn't do that and here right in the middle of the street where anybody could see.'

'See what? We were just having a harmless chat.' She looked at her sister's outraged expression. 'Oh stop fussing; it's good to use a few of the old skills.'

'There is a time and place for that.'

'Which is here and now,' Queenie said firmly. 'We found out some very interesting information from Janet. The most significant is this character, the 'cunning man', who keeps popping up. We need to find out more.'

Chapter Five

It had been a tiring day but still Queenie was unable to sleep, she had tossed and turned for several hours trying to get comfortable and doze off but by the time the clock in the hall had struck twelve she had given up. So she slid quietly out of bed, got dressed and pulled the chair up to the open window. Pulling the cover off the bed she wrapped it around her shoulders. Behind her Sybil was fast asleep.

The half moon gave very little light and the shadows were deep and black down on the beach, just a few glints of moonlight on the soft rolling waves that slid up and down the beach. The boat moorings clanked in the stillness, nothing else broke the silence of this remote village.

Queenie sat and waited by the open window, for what she didn't know. But she had been doing this for so long now that she knew unseen forces were gathering at the edges of the mortal world, ready to spill over. Her fingers tingled and she rubbed them absently while waiting for events to unfold.

She pulled the cover tighter and peered out into the night, out over the shingle beach and Widbarrow Bay and as she watched a wall of sea mist blew steadily towards land, dark shapes roiling and massing within. Queenie leant forward straining to make sense of the noises coming from the mist. The sound of a boat grounding on the shingle, splashing and whispered voices reached the open window and she could just make out a handful of figures at the water's edge. For once she was uncertain as to whether they were of this world or the next. From under her bedroom window figures peeled off from the darker shadows formed by the guest house and hurried down the beach to join the figures by the boat. With stealthy movements they began to unload packages and barrels dumping them into the arms of the waiting men. The chill air forgotten she pushed the wrap onto the floor and hissed at her sleeping sister.

'Sybil! Wake up.' There was no answering stir from the bed. 'Sybil.' She tried again not taking her eyes from the beach. 'Sybil!' she hissed louder, unwilling to leave the window as the men started to file towards the narrow passage between the guest house and Albert's cottage. Their footsteps were oddly muted on the stone steps, all whispering had ceased as they walked in silence off the beach.

Queenie stood up quickly unwilling to lose sight of the men; grabbing her fleece she cast one last look at her still sleeping sister and hurriedly let herself out of the bedroom.

Pulling the front door closed behind her she gazed up and down the dark street. It was empty. Some instinct guided her towards the church and she walked slowly down the cobbled street cursing herself for not picking up the torch. As she inched her way forward a hand outstretched in front, dark figures appeared by the church gate. The closer she crept the more distinct the group became. Half a dozen roughly clothed men had halted in the shadow of the church wall, barrels and packages piled by their feet. Queenie slowed to a halt and crouched by the wall of a cottage listening as the muffled thud of hooves came from the steep lane between the church and the cottage. A few stones clattered down dislodged by the descending horses.

Just for a second a light was uncovered by one of the men and was instantly echoed by a pinprick of light from the lane. That second of light illuminated the features of the waiting men and Queenie's attention was drawn to the figure in the midst of the others. The thickset man who held the lantern; he waved the men forward as the horses emerged from the bottom of the lane. From where she stood she could sense the fear of the waiting men while the man with the lantern seemed confident and completely at ease. They quickly and silently loaded the goods onto the horses; as soon as the beasts started back up the lane the figures melted away into the night. She heard their footsteps scurry past her in the dark, none of them noticing the old woman crouching in the shadows. All except for the man with the lantern who paused until they had all gone then casually lit a cigarette from the flame; he drew a deep lungful of the smoke and extinguished the lamp. And then he was gone.

Queenie was alone in the street, no sign of the men or the horses. She shook her head unsure of what she had just seen. It seemed darker than before and unable to see a hand in front of her face she edged carefully out from the cottage wall her arms outstretched in front.

Taking a few cautious steps she began to head back towards the guest house when her hand brushed against something soft and warm. Withdrawing it sharply Queenie straightened and sighed. 'Good evening Serena,' she said quietly. She heard the young woman take a step closer.

'You should be careful,' Serena whispered in her ear. 'A fall on these cobbles could be very nasty especially to a woman of your age.'

'That could almost be taken as a threat, Serena,' she answered calmly, trying to judge how close she was. She heard an answering chuckle.

'A promise, yes. A promise of things to come. After all, out on your own late at night anything could happen.' She sighed. 'Your poor sister discovering you're missing in the morning and searching for your body. How distressing for her.'

Queenie's arm was suddenly grasped, finger nails digging through the fleece.

'I told you not to stay, you should have listened.'

A wave of dismay washed over Queenie. How she could have been so careless to have been caught unaware, she thought. She tensed, readying herself to pull from Serena's grasp.

There was a click in the quiet night and a bright light illuminated the two figures.

'She never listens. I should know. Now if you don't mind taking your hands off of my sister I'm sure she could do with a cup of tea.'

'Sybil! Good timing as usual.'

Serena swung around and stared unblinking into the torchlight, she pasted a smile onto her face. 'I was just explaining how slippery these cobbles are, your sister could have been hurt.

Queenie heard her sister snort in the darkness.

'Yes of course, you were just concerned for her safety. Well now I will just get my poor old sister back to her bed. So step aside and we will be going.'

Queenie shrugged off Serena's hand. 'If you don't mind,' she said acidly, and walked towards her sister's outstretched arm.

'Come along dear, Beryl has the kettle on for us.' Sybil turned back to the now quiet Serena. 'Good night.'

Chapter Six

There was a gentle tap on the bedroom door and Sybil opened it quickly with a finger pressed to her lips. She stepped out onto the landing pulling the door closed quietly behind her.

'Queenie is still asleep, she had a restless night.' Sybil smiled at Beryl who was neatly attired in a floral dress and matching cardigan, a splash of red lipstick on her smiling lips.

'You're ready to pick up Ralph?' she enquired.

'Yes, but I want to get your breakfast first. I have laid the table in the dining room so all I have to do is take your order for a cooked breakfast.'

'Cereal and toast will do for us this morning,' Sybil reassured her. 'So don't worry. I will give Queenie a nudge and we will be down in a few minutes.'

'Well if you are sure, I will just go and make some tea and coffee then.' Beryl nodded and smiled and trotted off happily down the stairs.

Sybil slipped back into the bedroom, walked over to Queenie's bed and looked down at her sleeping sister. Dark circles had appeared under her eyes and she frowned as she slept.

Sybil gently touched her shoulder. 'Queenie. Wake up. It's getting late.'

She groaned and rolled over, pulling the duvet up around her ears.

'Ten more minutes,' she mumbled.

'No. You have to get up now. Beryl is waiting to make our breakfast and we don't want to hold her up this morning. She is picking up her husband from the hospital.'

Sybil pulled a dressing gown from the wardrobe. 'Come on, off to the bathroom with you.'

Queenie sighed and pushed back the covers struggling to sit up. 'What time is it?'

'Past nine 'o'clock. You have overslept.'

'Huh! I wonder why,' she mumbled, sliding out of bed.

Within ten minutes they were sitting in the dining room pouring the fresh coffee that Beryl had just made.

'Now, toast?' she asked. 'Wholemeal or white?'

'White please,' Queenie said, stirring in a large spoonful of sugar.

'Would you like a cooked breakfast?' she asked politely, while taking a surreptitious look at her wristwatch.

'No, it's okay Beryl. You go and fetch Ralph. We'll sort out our breakfast and don't worry about the washing up, we can deal with that.'

'It's my fault for oversleeping,' apologised Queenie. 'I had quite a disturbed night.'

Sybil looked at her out of the corner of her eye. 'So unlike you, dear. You usually sleep like a log.'

'Yes,' agreed Queenie, keeping a straight face. 'I can't understand it.'

'I'm sorry to hear you didn't sleep well.' Beryl hesitated, fiddling with the coffee pot. 'I feel so guilty expecting you to sort out your own breakfast, after all you are our guests.'

'Serves us right for sleeping in,' replied Queenie. She waved a hand at her. 'Go on, off you go and don't worry. We'll see you later. We're looking forward to meeting your husband.'

'Well if you're sure,' she hesitated again, and started fiddling with the buttons on her cardigan. 'I must admit I will be glad to have him home.'

'Of course you will. Now we will see to everything and if we go out we'll lock everything up nice and tight.'

'Thank you. Well... I will be off then.' She walked to the door. 'Thank you for all your help; it's been a blessing to have you here.' She picked up a matching handbag and a set of keys and opened the front door.

Queenie waved her cup at her. 'Bye dear, drive carefully.'

'We'll see you later,' called Sybil, rising from the table. The door closed behind Beryl and Sybil looked at her sister. 'Now I shall go and make some toast.'

Queenie picked up the coffee pot and her cup. 'I'll come with you. It's more comfortable in the kitchen.' She followed Sybil into the back part of the guest house. 'That's better,' she exclaimed, plonking the pot down onto the kitchen table. 'Open the back door Sybil and let some of that lovely sea air in.'

It was a beautiful morning with not a cloud in sight and the sun was already hot enough to attract a few early bathers. From their position at the table they could see out across the beach and far out into the bay. A small family took up position in front of the guest house loaded down with bags and brightly coloured beach towels. The children were shrieking with excitement as they struggled into their swimwear.

Sybil smiled to herself as she buttered a slice of toast.

'Why don't you go and join them?'

She glanced up at Queenie. 'I would if I was a few years younger. It's lovely hearing children play.'

'Until they start screaming and having tantrums.'

Sybil shrugged and replied, 'I have heard adults making worse noise,' and stared out at the family again. The children were playing at the water's edge and squealing as the cold waves broke over their legs. Her attention was suddenly taken from the young family by the sight of Serena who was also sitting on the beach. She, unlike Sybil, was not watching the children; she was gazing moodily out to sea watching the many boats sailing across the bay.

'Looks like somebody else is enjoying the sea air.'

Queenie peered past her sister. 'Now I wonder what she is doing. Serena doesn't strike me as the sort of person who would enjoy cavorting on the beach.'

'Cavorting?' Sybil started laughing and then began to choke on a crumb. She wiped her streaming eyes and wheezed, 'Stop making me laugh. The idea of that woman cavorting or doing anything normal at all is ridiculous.' Sybil blew her nose and took a mouthful of cold coffee. Staring out at the solitary figure, her arms wrapped around her knees as she gazed intently out into the bay, Sybil declared, 'She's waiting for something.'

'Perhaps we could sneak up behind her and throw her in the sea.'

'What in front of the children? They would be scarred for life and have to spend the rest of it in therapy.'

'Murderous Grannies at the Seaside,' quoted Queenie gleefully waving a butter knife about, 'we could have a new career and become infamous.'

'The village would give us a medal for Services to the Community.'

Sybil took her gaze from the lone figure and started to pile the dirty dishes. 'Finished?' she inquired.

Queenie snatched the last piece of toast before her sister whisked it away. 'Nearly, is there any coffee left?'

'No.'

Sybil piled the dishes on to the work top and started to fill the sink with hot water. 'Come on let's get this done and then we can go and spy on Serena and see what she's up to.'

Queenie pulled herself out of her chair and pottered over to the window. 'Well, she has just moved and is walking along the beach to those boats that are parked at the end.'

'Beached.'

'Yes she is, dear.'

'No. Beached. The boats...'

'Whatever.' She leant forward peering out of the window. 'Ooh... she's talking to somebody.'

Sybil threw the washing up brush into the hot water and hurried over to the window.

'Who?'

'I can't see from here.' Queenie cast a quick look around the kitchen and caught sight of a pair of binoculars on a shelf next to a book on sea birds. 'Brilliant,' she exclaimed, snatching them off the shelf and raising it to her eyes. 'It's all fuzzy.'

'You have to adjust this.' Sybil reached across and fiddled with the focusing knob. 'Try that.'

'That's much better. I can see her. It's a man she is talking to, looks as though he is working on a boat. Bella Venture.'

'What?'

'The boat, it's called the Bella Venture.'

'Let me have a look,' exclaimed Sybil impatiently, taking the glasses from her sister. She quickly adjusted the focus and peered at the distant figures. 'Well, she is getting very animated down there. He looks a bit rough.'

'Rough?'

'Yes, you know. Rough.'

'A scallywag? A rogue? A ne'er do well?'

'Shut up Queenie, you know what I mean.' She handed back the binoculars. 'Look for yourself.'

Queenie raised the glasses and squinted through the lens.

'Well, she has finished talking to him and is walking back along the beach. Now she is sitting down on the sea wall.'

'What's he doing?'

'Not a lot, just polishing his rollocks. Now he's lighting up a cigarette and staring out to sea.'

'Exciting!' said Sybil, as she moved back to the sink and resumed the washing up. 'I'll just finish this and you carry on watching Serena.'

'Okay, I'll be the look out.'

The dishes were speedily washed and dried, the counters wiped down and the sink meticulously cleaned. Sybil picked up the place mats and wiped a damp cloth over the kitchen table.

'Anything happening?' she enquired of the silent Queenie.

'Nope, she is still watching and he's still fiddling about on the boat,' she sighed, and replaced the binoculars on the shelf. 'Are you ready yet?'

Sybil spread the dishcloth out onto the draining board and flicked a stray crumb into the sink.

'I'm done; do you think we should sweep the floor?'

'No! That's enough house work. We have some snooping to do.'

Outside the guest house the narrow street was busy with holiday makers, wearing brightly coloured t- shirts and shorts and clutching cameras. They had to weave their way through the crowds to reach the car park which was fast filling up. As they reached the end of the sea wall where Serena was still sat a huge bus rumbled down the hill and turned in.

'It's going to be a busy day,' commented Sybil. She glanced across to the young woman who had turned and was glaring at the passengers who were just starting to alight.

Queenie suddenly laughed. 'Now there's a face that would sour milk!'

'Good for business, though I'm sure Serena doesn't think about that. The pub and shops must rely on making enough in the summer to carry them through the winter.'

'Well it can't be easy now, I'm sure that fishing isn't the main income these days.'

They threaded their way through the parked cars to Queenie's little yellow car on the far side, Serena's four by four still tight in next to it.

'I'll just give the car a quick check, make sure she hasn't slashed the tyres or stuck a banana up the exhaust.'

'That's the last thing she would do, she wouldn't want to delay our departure in any way.'

'No, true,' Queenie sighed, and looked up from her examination of her precious car. 'It's fine,' she said relieved, and peered across the rows of cars to the beach. 'She's gone.'

Sybil pushed herself upright from leaning on the car and followed her sister's gaze. 'And the boat is leaving as well,' she pointed. 'Look, it's just being launched.'

'Where is she? Is she on the boat as well?'

'Nope. Well she must be here somewhere, perhaps she's gone home.' Sybil looked at her wristwatch. 'It's nearly midday and Beryl will be back soon. Let's not get caught in the car park, not that I don't want to meet Ralph but we can do that later. We have got a lot to do and we're only here for a few days.'

'You're right, let's get going.'

They walked slowly down the street following the groups of people who were busy snapping pictures of the floral displays in the picturesque village until they came to the small public house 'The Anchor' situated in the middle of the village. The chairs and tables outside were already busy with guests.

Sybil glanced at the facade of the building as they walked past and suddenly stopped.

'Let's pop in here and have a drink,' she suggested.

'What? But we have things to do!'

'I know, but sometimes it's a good idea just to stop and think. We need to plan a course of action.'

'Like a battle plan.'

Inside the small single bar was cool and reasonably quiet, the majority of its customers choosing to sit outside and enjoy the warm weather.

Two elderly men were sitting by the window engrossed in a game of dominoes. Sybil looked across the room and nudged her sister's arm.

'There's Albert, I thought I saw him in the window. I see he manages to make it across to the pub.'

Recognising her voice Albert raised his eyes briefly before fixing his attention back on the pieces.

Queenie snorted, 'He doesn't look pleased to see us.'

'We seem to have that effect on people.'

They approached the old wooden bar that dominated the tiny room; with the low beams it gave quite an oppressive feel to the room.

'What would you like to drink Sybil? I will have a small brandy please,' she said, addressing the young barmaid who had just appeared in front of them.

'And a sherry.'

She placed the drinks in front of them. 'Five pounds, sixty.'

Queenie looked staggered. 'How much?' she exclaimed. 'You can tell I haven't been to a pub for a while! It's daylight robbery,' she muttered, reaching for her purse. 'Have you got any money dear? I seem to be a bit short.'

Pulling out her handbag Sybil searched for her purse. 'How much do you need?'

'How much have you got?'

Sybil pulled out a ten pound note and offered it to her sister.

'That will do, thank you.' She looked at the barmaid who was impatiently tapping beautifully manicured nails on the counter. 'So sorry to keep you waiting,' she said icily.

There was silence in the far corner apart from the regular click of the domino pieces being placed into position.

'Let's go and join them, shall we?' muttered Queenie, before setting off across the uneven flagstone floor. 'Hello Albert, mind if we join you?' She pulled out a chair and sat down at the table without waiting for a reply.

His companion looked up in dismay and glanced across the table at Albert; standing up quickly he made to push past Sybil who was already pulling up a chair from a nearby table.

'Sit down,' she said firmly, 'and finish your game.'

He hesitated, looking like a rabbit caught in the headlights before reluctantly sitting down again. He gathered up his pieces in his gnarled hands, a scowl on his face.

'Nice to see you out Albert,' she smiled. 'I thought we might find some locals in here.'

Albert nodded, his crafty eyes examining the two elderly women.

'You're still here then,' he mumbled.

'Oh, we're not leaving yet, this village is just so interesting.' Queenie sipped her brandy while watching him over the rim. 'Who's your friend?' she asked, nodding at his silent companion.

'Duncan.'

'Hello Duncan,' she addressed him. 'Nice to meet you. I'm Queenie and this is my sister Sybil. We're staying at the Sea View.'

'I know,' he muttered. 'I have heard all about you.' Duncan raised his bleary eyes and glared at her. 'I hear you have been poking about. You should watch yourself.'

'Nothing wrong with a bit of natural curiosity,' she said calmly. 'Have you been friends long?'

'Grew up together,' answered Albert, before draining his glass, he wiped his mouth. 'Spent our lives here, only time me and him were away was during National Service. We came back though, never wanted to live anywhere else.'

'It must have been a close knit community then.'

'Still is,' muttered Duncan clicking a piece into place.

'So you still look out for each other?'

He lowered his head refusing to meet her inquisitive gaze.

Albert sighed and pushed his empty glass across the table towards her. 'If you're going to pump us for information you can start by buying a round. Just to wet our whistle, like.' He raised a hand to the barmaid. 'Two more Chloe,' and he pointed to Queenie, 'And she's paying.'

'Of course, I'd be glad to ply you with alcohol,' she grinned. 'But I am expecting oodles of dirt in return.'

Chloe plumped two brimming glasses down on the table and stared coldly at the two women.

'Anything else?'

'We'll make do with these, thank you dear. How well do you know the Coppingers?' she asked, after a few minutes of silence.

Duncan had just taken a mouthful of beer and Albert's face creased into a grin as he watched his friend start to choke.

'Everybody knows them,' muttered Albert.

'We have heard some interesting things about that family. How they ran the village.'

'Aye, they did that,' agreed Duncan, suddenly speaking up. 'They had their fingers into everything.'

'But that was a long time ago,' interrupted Albert. 'Long before we were born.'

'When exactly? We're very interested.'

'This all started back in the 1700's; a long time ago. Everybody knew him as Cruel Coppinger. You ever heard of him?' he asked. 'No? Well, the story goes that he was shipwrecked off the coast and swam ashore through the rough seas and landed up here. He married a local lass and to make a bit of extra money started a smuggling gang. We all did a bit of it of course, anybody with a boat did, but the Coppingers were different, they were ruthless. Anybody who got in their way was disposed of. They even killed a customs officer, threw him off the cliffs at Mupe Bay. That really brought the heat down on the village so he went quiet for a while but that didn't last. He was soon back at it.'

Duncan shuffled his feet and began slowly, 'My old dad used to tell me the story of when Cruel Coppinger was old and dying a big black ship sailed into the bay captained by the Devil himself, come to claim his soul.' He looked up and met the gaze of the two women, his eyes narrowed and he said firmly, 'And that's the tale of the Coppingers, it's all in the past.'

'But he left some descendants,' stated Queenie, staring thoughtfully at Duncan and Albert and feeling sure that they weren't telling the whole truth.

Albert sighed and took a sip from his glass. 'He left behind a son. My dad always said he was mad and every bit as bad as Cruel Coppinger.'

'Was he the Cunning Man?'

'Who told you about him?' Albert asked, raising his eyebrows.

'Oh, it just came up in conversation. So was he the Cunning Man?' Queenie asked again.

There was silence at the table for a few moments as Duncan shuffled the domino pieces on the table.

'It was a long time ago,' he muttered. 'And different times, fishing families are always superstitious.'

'Come on chaps, I bought you a beer. Who is the Cunning Man? Albert drummed his fingers impatiently on the table and stared at her through narrowed eyes.

'Absalon,' he said finally. 'Absalon Coppinger. It was him, he convinced everybody that the Devil walked the streets of the village and he was the only one who could hold him at bay. He reckoned he had special powers so everybody did what he told them.'

'And they believed him?'

'Some did, the ones in the know realised what he was up to.'

A light dawned in Sybil's eyes. 'So he was smuggling as well. And how long did all this go on?' she asked. 'For example is there smuggling going on now?'

'Absalon was the last smuggler,' Albert said, trying to sound convincing.

Queenie smiled, her eyes steely as she gazed across the table at him. 'And what about your own involvement in smuggling? Does Serena know about it? I bet she does,' she said, answering her own question.

'Me?' he answered, an injured tone in his voice. 'I don't know where you got that idea from.'

She grinned wickedly and leant across the table, fixing him with her pale eyes. 'I have a very good memory, and I quote... "We all did a bit of it of course, anybody with a boat..." and I'm guessing that you and your friend here,' nodding towards the silent Duncan, 'had a boat. So,' she continued, 'Serena knows about it and perhaps wanted you to help with her own little smuggling enterprise and that's why you won't open the door to her anymore. She's a real chip off the old block isn't she?'

His sallow cheeks flushed and he stood up, pushing his chair away from the table, the sudden movement spilling the domino pieces onto the floor.

'Smuggling is a thing of the past so just let it alone,' he snapped, and took his walking stick off the back of the chair. 'Come on Duncan, you can walk me home.'

Taking a sip of her brandy she watched the two old men struggle to their feet, she smiled coolly and nodded. 'Well, okay then, thank you for your help gentlemen, it's been very illuminating.'

Albert nodded at them and leaning heavily on his stick hobbled out of the pub; Duncan with a hand on his other arm steadying his tottering footsteps, he cast one last malevolent look at the sisters before pulling the door closed behind them.

'I think we have struck a nerve there, don't you?' said Queenie thoughtfully, her brow furrowed. 'And I think there is a lot they're keeping to themselves.'

Sybil nodded in agreement staring at the door.

'Good guess about Serena,' Queenie congratulated her sister. 'So you think that is what she's up to?'

'Well, it was more a stab in the dark but it does fit.'

Their half empty glasses sat in front of them forgotten while the sisters watched Albert and Duncan through the window. With their heads close together they looked as though they were having an animated conversation with Albert shrugging his head in the direction of the Anchor.

'Are your ears burning?' Sybil said smiling slightly. 'They were very unhappy about something, it's a shame we couldn't find out more.'

There was a sudden crash beside them making both women jump.

Chloe had emerged from behind the bar to collect the empty glasses and overhearing their conversation slapped down a tray on to the adjacent table, her expression frosty.

'Finished?' she asked, before whisking away their glasses. A damp cloth was briskly swept around the table and she stalked back to the bar without waiting for a reply.

'Well, it looks like it,' muttered Queenie at the retreating barmaid, she raised an eyebrow. 'I think it's time we left Sybil, we have outstayed our welcome.'

Outside the sunlight made them blink after the dim interior of the pub. Albert and Duncan had already disappeared presumably back to Albert's cottage, leaving the street to the tourists.

'That was a fortuitous meeting, don't you think?'

'It was a good idea of yours to pop in for a drink and now after that interesting conversation I really want to explore the lane near the church,' she turned to Sybil. 'Are you up for that?'

She nodded slowly although she looked slightly worried. 'I think we need to be careful though, we're used to dealing with the supernatural not smuggling gangs.'

Queenie looped her arm through her sisters and gave it a squeeze. 'It will be fine, after all what's the worst that can happen?'

'We end up face down in a ditch somewhere.'

'But it's so exciting; it's not every day that we get to tackle smugglers.'

'Keep your voice down Queenie!' she said quietly, looking around. 'We don't know how many people are involved and we have no proof.'

Just past the pub half hidden in a group of Japanese tourists busy clicking away with their digital cameras was Janet, busy fixing another of her Lost Cat posters to a telegraph pole.

The two women struggled through the crowd towards her.

'Hello Janet. No luck finding your cat?'

She looked up, her face creased with frustration. 'Oh hi. No, not yet. I have to replace all of these; somebody took the whole lot down last night.'

'Really?' exclaimed Sybil. 'How mean. I bet that was Serena!'

Janet nodded, her lips tightening. 'Probably. It's the sort of thing she would do.'

Hearing the squealing of the Coppinger's front gate she suddenly stopped talking and glared down the street. 'There! I have just put that one up!' she exclaimed 'Damn woman.'

Serena had stalked over to the church gate on which one of the posters was stapled and had ripped it down, she then screwed it into a ball and had stared up the street to where the three women stood watching her. Spotting another poster just farther up she began to walk towards it but recognising Queenie and Sybil with Janet she hesitated then headed back into her garden.

'Well,' a look of admiration came over Janet's face. 'I think you're getting to her.'

'We do our best,' Queenie said modestly, with a slight smirk. 'Keep putting up the posters and I'm sure Bobby will be found.'

Janet nodded and shifted the bundle under her arm. 'I've got another hundred to go up yet, she's not going to stop me.'

'Well, we'll leave you to it; we're off for a walk up the lane.'

A look of concern flickered over Janet's face. 'The lane next to Serena's cottage?' Seeing the women nod, she said, 'Be careful,' she licked her lips nervously and glanced towards the church. 'It's quite a steep lane and you could get hurt.'

The crowds had not yet reached the far end of the village, the church and graveyard was quiet with just a few birds singing in the trees and the sound of seagulls calling over the ocean. The sisters stood at the bottom of the steep lane and looked at the rough track full of boulders and gullies formed by falling rain.

Sybil gazed in concern at the steep gradient of the lane. 'You really want to go up there?' she asked in amazement. 'It's a bit steep for our old legs.'

'I told you I saw those horses the other night and I want to see where it goes. So come on.'

They walked slowly upwards, picking their way through the rocks until they reached the top gate of Serena's garden. There was no sign of the young woman outside although Queenie was sure that she would be watching from the cover of the house.

'Think we'll be able to sneak all the way up without her noticing?'

'No,' panted Sybil, pausing for a minute to catch her breath. 'And I can't believe horses could use this, it's far too rough.'

'Well, they were.' She looked back at her sister who was struggling to keep up, her face flushed and gasping for breath. 'Nearly there,' she said encouragingly. She paused; waiting for Sybil to reach her then offered her an arm. Sybil waved it away clutching at her side.

'You go on I would rather go at my own pace,' she gasped, and waved Queenie forward. 'Go on, I'll follow.'

'You're not having a heart attack, are you?'

'No I'm not, you daft bat. I have the stitch.'

'Just asking.'

They toiled slowly upwards in the hot sun, struggling on the rough track until they reached the seat built into the wall.

'Let's sit down for a minute,' gasped Queenie, wiping a trickle of sweat off her forehead. 'So you can catch your breath.'

Her sister was too breathless to reply and just sank gratefully onto the rough seat. She took out a delicate lace handkerchief from her handbag, wiped her face and took a few deep breaths as she gazed out over the clear waters of the bay.

'What a climb and what a view!' she said, after she had caught her breath. 'Almost worth the effort.'

'It's lovely isn't it?' agreed Queenie. 'I thought that the first time I came up here.' She nudged her sister's arm. 'And I also remember thinking what a good vantage point it would make.'

'The seat looks well used,' agreed Sybil. She looked across the bay with the bright sunshine it was possible to see for miles. 'I wonder how many men used to sit up here and watch for the smuggling boats.'

'I wonder.' Queenie's attention was caught by the sight of Serena in the garden below. She had appeared from under the arbour and was walking slowly up towards the vegetable patch, looking around her as she walked and peering over the hedge into the lane.

'I wonder if she is looking for us.'

'Looks like it.'

The two women settled back comfortably on the hard stone seat and watched as Serena halted and putting her hands on her hips, stared up the hill to the seat where they were resting.

'Oops, she has spotted us,' chuckled Queenie. 'Shall I wave?'

Her sister caught her arm and pushed it down. 'No. We'll pretend we haven't seen her.'

Seeing the impatient look on her face Sybil shook her head and repeated, 'No!'

'But she's going to hang around down there and watch us and I want to explore the path without her bothering us.'

'Well, waving at her and annoying her even more isn't going to help, is it? Just have a bit of patience Queenie, she will either get bored or we will wait until she is looking the other way.'

Her sister frowned impatiently and then her expression brightened suddenly. 'And then we will make a dash for it.'

'Speak for yourself dear. I don't think I am up to a dash, more a stumble.'

They sat comfortably in the sunshine while below Serena loitered in the garden, ostensibly pruning a few faded blooms from the rose bushes while she kept a close eye on the two women. After about twenty minutes she began to lose patience, her pruning became more vicious until she threw down the shears altogether and stalked off with the watering can.

Queenie gave her sister a sharp nudge in the ribs. 'Now! Quick move.'

The women were up out of the seat and half way to the tree line before Serena returned. They stopped in the shadow of the large pine trees gasping and laughing at their sudden dash. From their cover Sybil peered down into the garden where she could see Serena amongst the vegetable patch.

'She hasn't noticed yet.'

'Well, let's keep going while we can.' Queenie unzipped her fleece and wiped away a few beads of perspiration before leading the way further into the thick undergrowth of tangled brambles and waist high nettles. To the left and right small trails led off through the trees, one led back in the direction of the village while the left hand path hugged the edge of the tree line. The main track trailed off in front of them with long shoots of bramble growing across it making it difficult to make headway. Sybil unhooked a thorny shoot from her skirt.

'Nothing has been through here for years.'

Looking at the undisturbed ground underneath the trees which was thick with pine needles and dead leaves Queenie had to agree.

'There are no sign of horses passing this way at all but the track does lead straight on so it must go somewhere.' She turned back to her sister who was sucking a bloody finger. 'You okay to go a bit further?'

Sybil nodded. 'Now we are here,' she agreed. 'Lead on.'

The faint track led them further up through the trees until they reached the cut in the cliff. The narrow gully was completely choked with brambles; at the far end just barely visible in the undergrowth was an old wooden gate.

'Well, nothing has been through here,' Queenie sounded disappointed and slightly frustrated.

'We could try those other paths,' suggested Sybil, while she dabbed at the scratches on her legs from the bramble thorns. 'We could retrace our steps or we could go that way.' She nodded to the left where a small animal trail led off across the hillside following the line of a tumbledown wall. 'I vote we go that way to avoid the brambles.'

'Is it a path?' muttered Queenie, setting off down the well worn trail.

'It's a badger trail; so let's make use of it.'

Sybil followed her sister closely as they walked further into the dense copse. Underneath the canopy very little sunlight managed to penetrate and it was deathly quiet, all birdsong had ceased. They trod cautiously along the narrow path avoiding the large stones that littered the ground. Peering forward Queenie tensed and froze mid-stride, she motioned her sister to silence and pointed to a dark shape moving amongst the trees.

'There is somebody over there,' she whispered in Sybil's ear. 'I saw movement.'

'Is it Serena?' she asked quietly.

Queenie nudged her sharply. A figure was moving slowly away from them following the old wall. They inched quietly forward through the crackling undergrowth into the dark of the thick copse. Underneath the light seemed to fade until it was nearly dark and the silence was so deep that Sybil could hear the blood pounding in her ears. Whoever it was walked on, pausing every now and then as if aware that the sisters were following. A stray shaft of sunlight penetrated the trees and illuminated the person walking just in front of them. Queenie instantly recognised the thickset figure.

She halted and turned to her sister. 'It's him, the man I saw last night. He's the ring leader.' Although she had whispered, the sound of her voice carried through the clear air, for a minute he hesitated and almost turned to face them but then without a sound carried on walking through the woods.

'Are you sure?'

'Positive. It's him. Come on!' she urged, then looked around in surprise as Sybil grasped her arm.

'No. Let's get out of here.'

'What! What's wrong?'

With an expression of dismay Queenie realised that he had disappeared at the point where the wall had collapsed completely and all that remained was a pile of weed covered stones. The badger trail skirted this blockage to their trail and carried on in a straight line farther into the trees.

'Come on,' she urged again. 'We need to find out where he has gone.'

Sybil held her sisters arm firmly and said, 'No, we need to go now. We are in dangerous waters here and should leave well alone. Who knows what that man would do to us?'

'Well... I'm surprised at you Sybil.' Queenie looked angrily at her sister.

'Too bad! We need to be sensible and following a strange man through a wood is not a good idea!'

She looked around for the best route through the brambles and grasping her sister firmly by her sleeve pulled her back along the trail.

'We are going now, so stop arguing,' she said firmly, turning a deaf ear to Queenie's complaints until they had regained the main path.

Her sister's expression was still mutinous as they neared the lane leading down into the village.

'But we need to follow him!'

'No we don't and we're not going to and that is that. I will be sensible even if you're not.' Sybil drew a deep breath and gave her sister an irritable look. 'Sometimes you lose all common sense and go charging in regardless. Just stop and think occasionally!'

Queenie sniffed. 'And you're such an old stick in the mud,' she muttered and pushed past her.

They were just nearing the edge of the trees when Queenie suddenly dodged behind a large pine silently gesturing for Sybil to follow, just in time as Serena appeared from the top of the lane. She looked left and right along the paths not spotting the two old women hiding behind the tree and set off at a jog to the left which led away from the village.

'She's in a hurry,' said Sybil, peering around the trunk. 'She must think we went that way.'

Queenie didn't answer; she was carefully picking a few leaves off of her tweed skirt as she walked towards the lane.

'Let's get down to the village before Serena comes back, I don't want her coming down this steep lane after us.' Sybil glanced at her sister's frosty expression. 'Oh, stop sulking Queenie,' she said in exasperation. 'You're too old for that.'

'I am not sulking,' fired up Queenie. 'I just think we should have carried on. Who knows what we would have found out?'

'We are too old for a tussle in the woods with a strange man.'

'Huh! Speak for yourself,' Queenie muttered, stamping down the rocky lane.

'And slow down, you'll twist an ankle or something.'

The smell of roast chicken hung about the kitchen as Sybil washed the dishes. The room was quiet apart from the clink of the plates and the slow steady tick of the wall clock. Although Queenie had offered to help she had fallen asleep in front of the fire and Beryl had insisted on taking Ralph upstairs for a rest after their meal. The journey from the hospital had tired him and although he was obviously delighted to be home Sybil couldn't help noticing how pale and shaky he was at the meal table.

She moved to the table clearing away the place mats and wiping a few spots of gravy from the table. The last few rays of sunshine warmed the kitchen and glinted across the waves in the bay which at this late hour was nearly deserted, only a few boats bobbed at anchor in the calm waters. The visitors had gone and the beach was empty except for a lone man unloading his fishing gear from a boat. Recognising its bright paintwork Sybil straightened and quickly picked up the binoculars from the shelf. Fiddling to bring it into focus she trained them on the distant figure. It was Serena's friend from the morning, the owner of the Bella Venture; he was hurriedly unloading fishing rods and buckets from the now beached boat. She watched through the binoculars as he struggled off across the shingle heading for the car park weighed down with his kit. He paused for a minute to adjust a few of the rods that were slipping from his grasp; as he did so Sybil noticed something drop from under his arm.

I wonder what that is? she thought, slowly replacing the binoculars. She chewed on her lip for a minute before coming to a decision. Perhaps I will just take a stroll. She took off the borrowed apron, let herself out of the back door and climbed carefully down the stone steps to the beach. Walking slowly across the shifting shingle to the Bella Venture she kept an eye open for the owner but there was no sign of him and keeping her fingers crossed that he had already left the car park she approached the boat. The smell of fish and salt water greeted her as she peered over the side. A few inches of water lay in the bottom of the boat but apart from that it was empty.

The beach was still deserted as she headed towards the object lying farther up the shingle beach. It was a grey hessian bag, feeling slightly disappointed she picked it up. It was soaking wet and from one end a long blue rope dangled. Although she could see the bag was empty there was a thick deposit of a white substance on the inside. Sybil's heart suddenly thumped. This can't be drugs, she thought in alarm and fingered the substance before gingerly placing a bit on her tongue. The unmistakeable taste of salt made her laugh in relief.

'It's salt, that's all. Thank goodness,' she said aloud.

Coiling up the rope she placed it inside the bag and debated with herself trying to decide whether to return the bag to its owner or to keep it and show it to Queenie. As she mulled it over she heard footsteps on the shingle behind her.

'That's stealing.'

Sybil sighed and turned to face the young woman. 'Serena. You do have a knack for turning up when you're not wanted.'

Serena stared at the bag in her hand. 'What have you got there?'

'Your friend has just dropped it.'

'He's not my friend,' she said quickly. 'But give it to me; I will make sure he gets his property back.'

The old woman smiled calmly at her. 'Well, as he isn't your friend I will return it myself.' She looked across to the nearly empty car park and spotted him on the far side next to a beaten up old land rover. 'He's still here so I will just pop over and give it to him.'

With the speed of a cat that took Sybil completely by surprise Serena lunged forward and snatched the bag from her grasp.

'Why don't you stop poking your nose in, you old cow!' she hissed viciously, a few drops of spittle hitting Sybil in the face.

Sybil staggered back at the sudden onslaught, her foot twisting in the shifting stones of the beach. Seeing her wince in pain Serena smiled.

'Poor old thing,' she commiserated mockingly. 'Did you hurt yourself?'

'I'm fine,' Sybil said coldly. 'Do you really think you're going to get away with this? If you do you must be mad.' Then it was Sybil's turn to smile mockingly at Serena's expression. 'It's obvious what you're up to. How foolish you are.'

'You're foolish if you think you're going to stop me! Not that anybody would believe you,' she spat at Sybil. 'It would be just two stupid old women trying to get attention.'

'One phone call to Customs and Excise, that's all it would take Serena. So perhaps you should think about that and stop while you can.'

Serena stepped closer and pushed her face into Sybil's, she was now so angry that her whole body was shaking and a trail of spittle ran down her chin.

'Just stay out of my way and keep your bloody nose out my business,' she hissed, and thrust out an arm pushing Sybil to one side.

Losing her footing in the shingle Sybil staggered back and fell heavily onto her back. Without a backward glance Serena ran off up the beach to the car park leaving Sybil lying on the beach, winded and gasping from the shock.

Although shaken from the unexpected attack Sybil couldn't help feeling smug that she had guessed correctly about Serena's activities. As she struggled slowly and shakily to her feet she wondered exactly what it was that Serena was smuggling and how many of the villagers were involved. From the car park came the sound of raised voices as Serena caught up with the owner of the Bella Venture and threw the hessian bag into his face. He glared across at Sybil before snatching the bag from the floor and throwing it into the back of the land rover. With a few more angry words exchanged he climbed in and drove off, roaring up the steep road out of the village.

'Where have you been?' Queenie asked testily. 'I turn my back for five minutes and you're off.'

'You were asleep,' she answered indignantly. Sybil closed the back door and as an afterthought locked it. 'I have just had a close encounter with Serena on the beach.'

'And I missed it!' complained Queenie. 'So, what happened?'

Sybil sat down slowly at the table and gingerly rubbed her back. 'She knocked me over.'

Queenie hurried to her side and bent over her in concern. 'Are you okay?'

'I'm fine,' she smiled at her sisters worried face. 'Really. I'm okay. But I managed to upset Serena so it was worth it.' She smiled grimly, 'I was right about the smuggling though, that man and Serena are bringing something in, I found an empty bag that he dropped on the beach, it had some salt left in it. But I can't think that is what they are smuggling, after all you can get salt readily at the supermarket so that is a puzzle.'

'Another mystery for us to solve.'

The clock in the hall had just struck ten as they mounted the stairs. Queenie was yawning widely as they creaked up the stairs.

'I don't think you will have trouble sleeping tonight,' observed her sister opening the door and clicking on the light.

She yawned again and rubbed a tired hand through her pink hair. 'I will be asleep as soon as my head touches the pillow,' she continued sleepily, 'and then we'll see what tomorrow brings.'

Sybil closed the door and looked across at her sister who had flopped onto her bed in exhaustion. She hesitated before saying slowly 'I know you're not going to like it but I think we should go. We are in over our heads, Queenie. Smugglers are dangerous people and Serena is dangerous and mad.'

Queenie stopped mid-yawn and gazed in surprise at her sister. 'Are you serious?' she asked in disbelief. 'But we're really getting somewhere and to give up now would be terrible.'

'We're not getting anywhere, it's all guesses. Yes, there is a history of smuggling here and yes, we think that Serena is involved in it. But that's all we know. We should go home and perhaps inform the authorities,' she paused, 'although we have no proof.'

Queenie rubbed her face, staring at Sybil's anxious face. 'What about poor Thomas?' she cocked her head and looked accusingly at her sister.

'What about him? How could you walk away from a little boy who needs our help!'

'Don't try to make me feel guilty,' she snapped, throwing her cardigan on the bed. 'He's a ghost and maybe he doesn't have anything to do with this at all.'

'Rubbish,' began Queenie, meaning to say more but seeing the troubled expression on her sister's face she held her tongue. Her face softened and she rose from the bed to give Sybil a hug. 'Okay, let's not argue about this now, I can see you're worried. I tell you what we'll do; we will sleep on it and decide in the morning.'

Chapter Seven

It had been a busy day and unaccustomed to so much fresh air and exercise the sisters were soon lulled to sleep by the sound of the waves breaking on the beach. The bedroom curtains fluttered in the breeze from the open window and ruffled the sleeper's hair but they did not stir. Outside footsteps crunched across the shingle and began the steady climb up the stone steps to the village, whispering voices echoed against the buildings until they too were silent.

Down in the hall the clock ticked on, marking the hours until it struck twelve.

Queenie was roused from her sleep by a hand tapping her shoulder, still drowsy she mumbled, 'Ten more minutes,' and rolled over pulling the covers up over her ears.

Still exhausted she began to drift off again, only vaguely aware of somebody sitting on the edge of the bed. She felt a gentle tap on her shoulder again, the gentle touch quickly becoming a shake.

'Queenie, wake up.'

'What is it Sybil?' she mumbled, struggling to sit up.

The moon light was streaming in through the open window illuminating the figure sat next to her. It wasn't Sybil. The boy Thomas was perched beside her, his skinny legs clutched in his arms. His dark eyes gazed into hers, a slight smile crossed his face and he leaned forward.

'Come on,' he breathed. 'Come with me,' and gestured for her to rise. 'Come on,' he repeated and walked towards the door. As he walked past Sybil, still fast asleep, he raised a finger to his lips. He gestured again, impatient for Queenie to follow.

She pushed back the covers and struggled out of bed, slipping her feet into a pair of slippers she pulled Sybil's dressing gown from the wardrobe and prepared to follow Thomas; where she didn't know. Thomas's ghostly form moved silently down the staircase in front of her, the stairs creaking with her every step. She paused, listening to see if she had disturbed the sleepers but all was quiet and she followed the boy to the front door and out into the street. Outside a sea mist had blown in and had filled the village, the cold damp air swirled around her bare legs making her shiver. Droplets were quickly forming in her hair and she was soon soaked. It was so dense that the cottages, even though they were only feet away, were barely visible and for a minute she became confused and unable to get her bearings. Everything looked so different in the strange light.

She inched forward peering at the young boy who became more substantial with every step. He smiled nervously at her, revealing a missing front tooth and beckoned her on. His boots clattered on the cobbled street as he led the way, the sound echoing oddly off the walls. Wearing grey shorts and long knee socks his skinny legs were exposed to the chill damp air but he didn't seem to notice, unlike Queenie who was shivering violently, her damp clothes clinging to her body. With stumbling steps she followed him into the fog which swirled around them thicker and thicker as they approached the church. Strange whisperings and movement surrounded them and she swung round peering at the darker shadows trailing past.

Unable to see she crept forward following Thomas towards the end of the village where she could just make out tiny pinpricks of light. Hearing whispering voices her courage failed and she hesitated, hugging the wall of a cottage her foot bumped into a pile of old nets and wooden crates. Queenie froze, waiting to see if she had been heard. Thomas sidled closer to her and grasped her arm as the mist began to clear revealing the group of men gathered in front of the church. They were huddled around a familiar figure, the man that the sisters had seen earlier that day on the hillside. The lantern he was carrying illuminated his face, and for the first time Queenie could see him clearly.

The similarity between him and Serena was shocking. His hair, dark not blonde like his granddaughters was cut short with just a lock falling over his forehead, cold eyes glared at the group of men.

By his side stood one other, and from his appearance clearly not from the village. While the rest of the men, the ring leader included, were dressed in rough fishing gear he was neatly attired in a dark suit. The faint light from the lanterns reflected on his wire framed glasses casting strange shadows on his thin face. He was engaged in a fierce whispered conversation with the men who were showing signs of anger.

Queenie strained to hear what they were saying, her attention caught by the thin man who seemed so out of place; alien to the fishermen by clothes and manner. Unable to hear a word of the muttered conversation she inched forward, keeping close to the wall of the cottage. Thomas slipped a cold hand into hers as they inched nearer over the slippery cobbles. They were just in earshot when Queenie's leg slipped from under her, catching the edge of an old crate. It toppled forward and crashed on to the ground. The men's conversation came to an abrupt end and they swung round peering into the shadows towards the old woman and child.

She gasped in horror and urgently gestured for Thomas to go.

'Run,' she hissed. 'Go!'

He gave her a sad smile and just stood there as two of the men rushed towards them. In desperation Queenie tried to hide Thomas behind her but he slipped from her grasp and stood in front shielding her from the men. As he was dragged away he turned and gave Queenie one last gap toothed smile.

'Stop! No,' she shouted, trying to pull him free from their grasp. 'Leave him alone.'

Their hold on the small boy was too strong and they took no heed of the old woman, hauling young Thomas towards the waiting men.

Queenie stumbled after them, losing her footing she slipped again crashing down onto the cobbles.

'Thomas,' she screamed, struggling to get to her feet, her wet dressing gown clinging to her legs. One slipper was lost but she gave it no heed just hobbled towards the men waiting at the gate.

'Help!' she shouted, hoping that the residents of the village would hear and come to her aid. But the cottages remained dark and quiet. Apart from herself the only sign of life in the whole village were the men who had Thomas.

'Help,' she screamed again, watching in horror as the ringleader roughly grabbed a handful of the boy's hair and dragged him into the circle of light.

'Let him go,' Queenie demanded, pushing her way through the men. 'Or I'll call the police.'

Nobody looked at the old woman, their attention fixed on the scene before them as the thin man whispered urgently into their leader's ear; he grabbed at the man's arm but his clutching hand was thrown off with a curse.

One of the other men tried to pull the boy free as Thomas began to cry. Fierce whispering echoed around the circle of men as they drew closer around the frightened boy and his captor.

There was a sudden shriek and a strange gurgling noise that was drowned out by the angry howl of the men. Desperate to reach Thomas, Queenie pushed her way into the centre of the figures surrounding him. She slowed and stared in horror as the young boy swayed in the lantern light, a clutching hand to his throat as blood spurted from a deep slash. Blood bubbled from his mouth as he tried to speak and he cast one last look at Queenie before slowly slumping to the cobbles. There was a dreadful silence before Queenie started screaming; her legs, suddenly weak, collapsed beneath her and she crumpled to the ground inches from Thomas's dead body. Huge wracking sobs erupted from her mouth as she stared in horror at the fallen boy lying in a pool of blood. 'No! No! Thomas!'

As she lay there the cold sea mist rolled in and enveloped the small figure, cloaking the men and dimming the lights from the lantern until it was so thick she was unable to see and felt completely alone in the street. The cold from the cobbles quickly seeped into her bones and she began to shiver uncontrollably. Just as quickly as it had appeared the mist receded leaving behind an empty street; it was as though it had rolled in to wash away the terrible sight. She raised her head to look again at Thomas but he and the other men had all disappeared leaving the village as it had been earlier in the day down to the Lost Cat poster on a nearby gate post. She was the only thing moving in the street as she struggled to her feet.

No lights shone out in the cottages and there was no evidence of the men ever being there. She wiped a hand over her tear streaked face and stumbled back towards the guest house. Still weeping, she pushed open the front door and completely exhausted fell forward onto the floor. Queenie lay there for a minute unable to summon enough energy to move until hearing the stairs creaking she raised her head and peered into the dark hall.

'There you are. Oh my God Queenie, what has happened?' Sybil knelt stiffly next to her sister and pushed the wet hair from her face.

Queenie's eyes were closed and she was gasping for breath. Sybil gently shook her. 'Queenie!' she said, horrified at her sisters appearance. 'Are you okay? Are you hurt?' Sybil shook her again until Queenie opened her eyes.

'It's my fault,' she wailed. 'It's my fault, I killed him.'

'Killed who? What are you talking about?' She slipped an arm beneath Queenie and pulled her into a sitting position. 'You're soaked through dear; let's get you off the floor and upstairs.'

Queenie swayed in the hall light, holding onto her sister's arm she gasped out, 'You don't understand. It's all my fault.'

Alarmed at her appearance Sybil held her sister tightly and guided her towards the stairs.

'Shh, now calm down,' she said, trying to keep calm herself. 'Let's get upstairs before you get a chill and then you can tell me what you have been up to.'

Queenie dragged herself up the stairs now completely emotionally and physically exhausted, her thoughts in a whirl. As they reached the landing Beryl appeared from one of the bedrooms, turning on the light she gazed in horror at Queenie's bloodied and bruised appearance. 'What's happened? Is everything okay?'

'Everything is fine. Queenie has been sleepwalking again, that's all. Nothing to worry about, I'll just tuck her back into bed before she gets cold.' With a last reassuring smile at the landlady Sybil closed the door firmly in her astonished face and led Queenie to the bed where she collapsed onto the covers. Her feet, bare of one slipper, were wet and smeared with dirt and blood trickled down her legs from the many scratches and cuts. She raised her tear streaked face and sobbed, 'I killed him Sybil. You were right,' she went on. 'I rush in without thinking and I caused Thomas's death. He was just trying to protect me.'

Sybil gave her a worried look as she pulled the cover from her own bed and wrapped it around her shivering sister.

'Queenie, calm down,' she said gently. 'You're not making any sense, the boy died a long time ago. We know that. What you saw,' she said gently, smoothing the hair back from her sister's bruised face, 'was an echo of a past event.' She placed an arm around her sister's shoulder and held her tightly. 'It's not your fault he died. Perhaps this is what Thomas wanted to show you.' Sybil reached for a box of tissues on the bedside table and pulled out a handful. 'Here, now calm down and tell me what you saw and perhaps we can make some sense of it.'

Queenie blew her nose and nodded, trying to calm herself. She shivered and looked down at her wet clothes. 'I need to get out of these wet clothes first, I'm freezing.'

'Good idea.' Looking at her sisters hands that were grasping the cover Sybil gasped in dismay at the state of them. 'We need to clean these cuts as well,' she said in concern. 'And look at your legs Queenie! It's a wonder you haven't broken any bones.'

Her answer was muffled by the towel she was using to dry her hair. 'What?'

'I said I'm going to have a few bruises in the morning.'

'You certainly are. I'm wondering how we are going to explain them.'

'Nobody will notice.'

'They'll notice your black eye for sure. It's already a lovely shade of purple.'

Considering the situation Sybil couldn't stop herself from smiling at Queenie's dismayed squeak.

'A black eye!'

She hobbled to the dressing table and peered into the mirror; pressing the rapidly swelling eye with an exploratory finger.

'Ouch.'

'Don't poke it then.'

'Bother,' she muttered, turning back to her sister. 'I'm not going to be able to hide this.'

'I'll tell everybody I hit you, how about that?'

Queenie gave her a withering look as she pulled a clean nightdress over her head, on top of this she zipped her thick fleece then wrapped one of Sybil's scarves around her neck. Queenie perched on the edge of the bed again and looked soberly at her sister.

'I'm surprised you don't. How many times have you told me to stop and think first! I never listen,' she sighed, examining her bruised hands.

'Now don't get downhearted. Thomas needed to show you what happened. Perhaps it's my fault; if I wasn't trying to persuade you to go home he might not have felt the need to show you so vividly.'

There was loud sniffing as Queenie started to cry again.

'It was so real. I could even smell the blood. It was that man; he slit Thomas's throat and left him to die in the street, like an animal. How could anybody do that to a child?'

'What man? You haven't told me what you saw.'

'We saw him earlier on the hillside, it was him. The monster!' Queenie shook her head and pressed a hand over her eyes. 'It was awful,' she whispered. 'And there was nothing I could do to stop it.' She felt her hands being taken in a comforting grasp and opened her eyes.

'It was an echo, Queenie, a replay of things that happened years ago. You couldn't have stopped it. It's probably being replaying for years and only a few have been able to see it. And you were one of them. So the question is what are we going to do now?'

'We're staying,' announced Queenie. 'And we're not going until we find the truth.'

Her sister sighed and nodded slowly. 'I was afraid you were going to say that.' She rubbed a hand over her sisters back 'At least you are a bit warmer now. Why don't you get into bed and I will pop down to the kitchen and make some tea, and then we can discuss it.'

She pulled back the duvet and helped Queenie into bed, pulling the cover up she patted her sister on the shoulder.

'I won't be long.'

A chill breeze blew up the stairs from the open front door below. Sybil shivered as she crept down the creaking stairs intent on not disturbing Ralph and Beryl again that night and also wishing to avoid any awkward questions. The door handle was freezing to her touch and as she pushed the door to she glanced into the deserted street; the sound of hurrying footsteps reached her and dark shadows flitted up and down the street. The spirits were still restless she thought to herself; shivering and unable to deal with any more spectral encounters that night she closed the door firmly and headed towards the kitchen.

Outside, the wind, which had blown up since the afternoon was whistling mournfully around the seaward side of the guest house and the sound of the waves breaking on the shingle beach could be heard through the window, but inside the kitchen was still warm and cosy. Clicking on the bright overhead light the dark shadows receded into the corners of the room but she still felt uneasy. A prickling chill ran up her spine as she filled the kettle, the feeling of being watched gradually came over her as she took two large mugs out of the cupboard. Glancing out of the kitchen window she stared out over the darkened beach lit only by the square of light streaming from the guest house. The beach was empty. The skin prickled on the back of her neck, the feeling travelled down her spine to the palms of her hands. Absently rubbing them together she muttered to herself, 'By the pricking of my thumbs, look out evil this way comes.'

Still convinced that somebody was watching her she continued staring out into the dark night until a loud click behind her made her jump. The kettle had boiled and as she walked back to the waiting mugs she glanced at the back door. Her step faltered and her very breath seemed to freeze. On the other side of the glass panel stood the figure of a man peering into the brightly lit kitchen. His blue eyes, full of grief, bored into Sybil's and his thin lipped mouth twisted as he tried to speak. Shocked at his unexpected appearance Sybil staggered back, coming up short when her hip collided with the corner of the kitchen table; as she winced at the sudden pain the figure outside took one step closer to the door until his face was just inches away from the glass, his breath fogging the pane. Her throat tightened and all breath seemed to drain from her lungs as she watched the door handle slowly begin to turn. But the door stayed closed, the two stout bolts had been shot earlier that evening. An expression of frustration crossed his face and he raised a hand and slammed it against the door, leaving a dark handprint on the glass, a print that could only have been of blood.

For what seemed hours but could only have been seconds they stared at each other until with faltering steps Sybil made herself walk towards the back door, her knees trembling with each step she stumbled closer to the door until she was just inches away from the spectre outside. As she approached a change came over his face and a light gleamed in his eyes. Sybil's own pale almost colourless eyes met his defiantly as she reached out a trembling hand, she paused for just a second as more gaunt faced men stepped from the shadows in the passage and gathered outside the door. Drawing a deep breath she quickly pulled down the floral blind covering the glass panel. She jerked back as a deep groan echoed along the passageway and the door shook beneath a thundering blow.

Hurrying back to the tea cups she filled them with a trembling hand and gave them a brisk stir before hurriedly leaving the kitchen. Outside the back door the silent figure waited, for what Sybil wasn't sure, but she didn't intend to stay and find out; suppressing a shudder she hurried back upstairs to the bedroom and her sister. Pushing the door closed with her foot she sighed with relief and peered across the darkened room to Queenie's bed. Heavy breathing came from beneath the covers and she felt relieved that Queenie had managed to fall asleep.

'I'm not asleep.'

Sybil jumped at the unexpected voice and said in surprise, 'You sounded as though you were.'

Placing the hot tea on the bedside cabinet she carefully lowered herself on the side of the bed and peered at Queenie's face that was just visible beneath the covers. It was so pale that the bruises and cuts were livid against her skin; her eyes were still closed but a single tear trickled down the worn wrinkled skin of her face.

Sybil patted her gently and said, 'Come on, sit up and drink your tea.' She watched in concern as Queenie slowly pushed back the duvet and propped herself up on one arm. Sybil silently handed her the cup.

'I'm sorry. I just can't get it out of my mind. I keep hearing him scream,' she faltered. 'I felt so helpless Sybil.' She gazed at her sister, despair in her eyes 'What was I supposed to do?'

'Nothing. You just had to witness it.'

'Now what?'

'Well, I guess we're staying,' replied Sybil regretfully. 'You said we would decide in the morning and,' she glanced at the bedside clock, 'technically it is the morning.'

Queenie sniffed and wiped the tear from her cheek.

'Well, then it's decided. We're staying and we're going to find out what's going on. And God help anybody who tries to stop me.'

Chapter Eight

The sky was grey and overcast the next morning and a steady rain lashed against the bedroom window. Queenie rested her head against the glass and peered out over the choppy waters of the bay.

'This is not what I ordered for this morning,' she said, biting her lip in frustration. 'It's going to hamper us a great deal if this rain keeps up. Have you heard the weather forecast for the rest of the day?' she asked, turning to her sister who was combing her hair in front of the dressing table.'

'Not yet, we can find out at breakfast,' she glanced at her watch, 'and we are late again. Get a move on, Queenie.'

'I am ready,' she replied indignantly. 'I'm just waiting for you.'

'But you haven't combed your hair, it looks like a haystack.'

'I thought it would cover the bruises like this.'

'Well it doesn't; you look like an old bag lady!' She tossed over a comb. 'Here! Now hurry up, I can smell bacon and I'm getting very hungry.'

Queenie ran a comb gingerly through her hair, wincing as her sore hands tried to tease out the tangles.

'So do you think everybody is going to buy the sleepwalking story?

'Of course.' Sybil opened the bedroom door for her sister and watched as she hobbled through, wincing with every step. 'Well, maybe not. You look as though you have done a couple of rounds in the boxing ring.'

Pushing open the kitchen door Queenie limped in, hoping to sit down before Beryl and Ralph noticed the bruises on her legs.

'Good morning,' Beryl said cheerfully, turning from the cooker. Her mouth dropped open and she gasped, shocked at Queenies appearance. 'Good grief! I didn't realise you hurt yourself that badly last night. Do you need to see a Doctor?'

Ralph who was immersed in a newspaper looked up at the sound of his wife's astonished voice and peered over the top of his glasses.

'What happened to you?'

'I was sleepwalking last night; came a bit of a cropper,' she explained calmly, pulling out a chair opposite Ralph and sitting down gingerly, hoping he wouldn't notice her wince.

'I'm fine, it looks worse than it is.'

Sybil sat down next her and smiled at Beryl as she carried over two plates of bacon, eggs, fried tomatoes and mushrooms.

'I'm sorry we are late again for breakfast, the time just flew this morning.' Sybil looked at the mouth watering plateful that had been placed in front of her. 'A good breakfast will make you feel better Queenie.'

'Well, I hope so.' Beryl watched as Queenie gingerly picked up the knife and fork and began to eat, the cuts still red and angry on her hands. 'I will get the first aid kit after breakfast and we can see to your hands,' she hesitated, looking at her face, 'but I don't think I can do anything about your black eye.'

'Oh that's fine, nothing to worry about,' Queenie said, around a mouthful of egg. 'This is delicious.'

'You're going to need another holiday to get over this one,' Ralph said, as he carefully folded the newspaper and placed it on the table. He gazed at her, taking in the pale skin and the livid bruises on the old woman's face. 'It doesn't look as though it's turning out to be a nice break for you after all.'

She piled a slice of fried tomato onto a piece of bacon and popped it into her mouth. As she chewed she eyed him up. 'We're having a great time,' she mumbled. 'Aren't we?' she appealed to Sybil who was pouring herself a cup of coffee.

'It's been very interesting so far. We're enjoying exploring the area.' She put her cup down on the saucer and asked nonchalantly, 'I don't suppose you have any maps of the footpaths around the village, do you?'

'Of course, I have quite a collection of old maps, not that they would be of any use to you.' He pushed back his chair and stood up. 'But I do have an ordinance survey map which shows all the roads and footpaths around this area.

He pulled open one of the kitchen drawers and pulled out a well worn map. 'Here we are,' he said opening it and spreading it on the table. 'Which way were you thinking of walking?'

'We would like to explore the path by the church.'

Ralph smiled slightly and looked at Queenie. 'Not a good choice considering the state you're in this morning. It's very steep and it doesn't really go anywhere now. The path on the left is closed due to landslides; it leads to Mupe Bay and the cave but it's far too dangerous to use. And the way through to the downs is closed as well; it's all so overgrown now it's impassable.'

Sybil peered at the faded lines, tracing the route of the footpath. 'Mupe Bay,' she mused, 'where have I heard that name before?'

Her sister smiled slightly. 'Don't you remember dear, Albert was telling us about the customs officer who was thrown over the cliff there.'

'So you have been talking to Albert?' Ralph raised his eyebrows. 'You're honoured,' he joked. 'He can be a bit taciturn at the best of times; unless he's drunk,' he added, smiling ruefully.

'Well, we met him in The Anchor so he probably was. He and his friend Duncan were playing dominoes and we had a nice chat about the history of the village.' Queenie leant forward, assuming an innocent expression. 'There were smugglers here!' she announced. 'You wouldn't think it would you, such a quaint and peaceful village. Albert was telling us all about it.'

'I'm surprised he told you. Every time I have raised the subject he and everybody else in the village clammed up. I don't think they are proud of their smuggling past.'

Ladling a large spoonful of sugar into her cup Queenie asked carefully, 'So what's your interest in smuggling then?'

He shrugged. 'I found some old black and whites photos in the attic when we moved in, and I asked Albert if he knew anything about them. I think that sparked off my interest in the village and its history, that's when I found out about the smuggling.'

'Any chance of having a look at the photos?' Sybil inquired.

Looking from one sister to the other he said slowly, 'Sorry. Albert pounced on them as soon as I showed him and I haven't seen them since. I could ask him and see what he has done with them.'

'Oh, that's okay,' Queenie said airily. 'We can ask him.'

Ralph nodded and drummed his fingers thoughtfully on the table. 'I hadn't heard about the customs officer being murdered.'

'Ah well, we have ways of getting information out of people.'

'Information? You sound like detectives.'

Sybil smiled gently. 'Now really, do we look like detectives?'

'No,' he said slowly. 'But there is something about you both; I just can't put my finger on it.'

'Ralph!' said Beryl. 'That sounded very rude, you'll have to excuse my husband. He didn't mean it.'

Queenie scraped the last of the egg yolk from the plate and smeared it onto a piece of toast.

'It must be the bump on the head,' she smiled sweetly at him. 'How did that happen by the way?'

Hesitating, he glanced at his wife who was anxiously twisting a tea towel in her hands. 'Not too sure.'

'Really?' Queenie stared at him and reached across the table to take his hand. 'Perhaps I can refresh your memory.'

'I don't think so, dear,' Sybil put in swiftly and snatched her sisters hand away from Ralphs. 'He's just recovering from concussion so it wouldn't be a good idea.'

She sighed, 'Of course you're right, as usual.' Queenie stared across the table at his puzzled face; her eyes were steely and the smile had faded. 'Why don't you just tell me what happened Ralph? My sister will be very unhappy with me if I use other methods to find the truth.'

'What other methods?'

The two women remained silent and stony faced under his scrutiny. He shook his head confused by the change in the two old women and said defensively, 'I don't remember that much, the last thing I do remember was walking down the passageway to the beach.'

'Did you slip?'

His brow creased as he tried to remember. 'No,' he said slowly 'I think...,' he paused, a light suddenly dawning in his eyes, 'somebody was behind me.'

'So you were pushed,' stated Sybil.

'No! That's ridiculous,' burst out Beryl. Her lip trembled as she wiped a hand across her astounded face. 'Who would do such a thing?'

'Serena,' all three declared together.

Ralph looked shocked that the sisters had immediately come to the same conclusion as he had. 'No,' he said, trying to correct himself. 'That is ridiculous, why would she do that?' He suddenly closed his eyes and groaned. 'Of course.' He turned to Beryl who was hovering at his shoulder. 'I had an argument with her that morning; she wanted to buy the guest house. She said she was concerned that we weren't making a go of it and was very insistent that I accepted her offer. I told her that we were settled and very happy here and so I refused. And boy, did she get angry! She threatened me with all sorts of dire consequences if I didn't sell.' He shook his head in disbelief, 'But no, this is ridiculous. However much I dislike her I can't believe that Serena is capable of doing anything like that.' Ralph scowled at the old woman's bland expression. 'You're putting ideas in my head,' he accused her.

'Not at all. Just helping you to see the truth.'

'Oh really!' he snapped 'And how are you doing that? Mind control perhaps?' he added sarcastically.

'Something like that. Let's just say we have certain talents that enable us to see things that aren't usually visible'

'Oh God, I thought you two were weird! He shook his head in disbelief and inquired, trying to keep calm. 'And why are you using these so called talents of yours in our village?'

Queenie glanced at him dismissively before helping herself to another cup of coffee.

'You wouldn't believe us.'

'Really? Try me,' he waited for a minute before carrying on, 'You want to hear about weird? I have heard things the last year or so that has made my blood run cold, things that I can't explain.'

From behind him came a sound of distress from his wife. 'Oh, don't Ralph; we agreed you wouldn't say anything about that. Everybody will think you're mad.'

'It's okay Beryl,' he gave her a reassuring smile and turned back to the women. 'I think these two ladies know exactly what I mean.'

Queenie nodded as she wiped her mouth with a napkin.

'Yes, we do. We are here investigating the death of a young boy, and this activity that you have been experiencing is all bound up with his murder by the smuggling gang. Did you know,' she paused and looked at him inquiringly, 'that Serena's family, the Coppingers, were the instigators of all the smuggling here? There was a moments silence and she carried on, 'By the look on your face I guess that you didn't know,' she concluded.

'Which makes this all very interesting,' Sybil said calmly.

'Interesting is not the way I would describe it,' he said.

'No? Well, I find it very interesting that it is within the last year or so, about the time that Serena has been back, that you have been experiencing all this supernatural disturbance.' She stared around the table at their intrigued expressions. 'So is Serena the catalyst?'

Her sister rubbed a forefinger over her chin thoughtfully. 'That is an interesting thought,' she said slowly. 'Is it her attempts at smuggling that's causing the disturbance?'

'I really don't understand what you're talking about,' Beryl stared at the three of them. 'What has Serena got to do with smuggling?'

'She is in cohorts with the captain of the Bella Venture and is smuggling something into the country, although what it might be is anybody's guess,' mused Queenie.

'It involves salt,' put in Sybil.

'Salt?' Ralph looked baffled. 'Why would she be smuggling salt?'

'This is all ridiculous!' Beryl interrupted him and started snatching the dirty plates from the table and piling them in the sink. 'We may not like her but to suggest she would try and hurt Ralph and to be involved in smuggling is ridiculous. And,' she said turning fiercely on the sisters, 'you should be ashamed of yourselves for stirring up all this nonsense.'

Ralph remained silent during his wife's outburst and scrutinized his clasped hands on the table. He nodded thoughtfully. 'But they do have a point dear. There are strange things going on here, I know because I have seen it. And it can't be explained away that easily.'

There was a crash as Beryl threw a cup into the soapy water.

'That's enough! There is nothing going on here; it's a nice, normal little village and we are very happy here. I'm sure everything was fine until you two turned up,' she said accusingly. Beryl turned back to the sink and began to briskly wash the dishes, without turning she said slowly, 'I think it would be better if you left, after all you did only book for a couple of days. And,' she stammered slightly over the lie, 'we have other guests booked into your room.'

There was a moments silence in the room as the sisters exchanged glances before Sybil spoke, 'Well, if you wish us to go then we will. Will tomorrow morning be soon enough? After all we will have to arrange some other accommodation.'

Her husband stirred restlessly in his chair in front of the window. 'So you are not leaving the village?'

Queenie rose stiffly from the table and resting her hands on the top she leant forward and stared at him.

'We are not leaving until this has been solved; we owe it to Thomas. And if you or the rest of the village don't like it then it's too bad.'

'Well, that didn't go very well, did it?' muttered Sybil, as they walked slowly back up to their room.

'I suppose it's a bit much for them to handle and Beryl seems determined to explain it away even though Ralph has experienced it firsthand.'

'She's scared and I can't blame her.'

'It's a bit awkward that she wants us out; I suppose we could try The Anchor. Oh bother,' exclaimed Queenie in exasperation, 'this is a real nuisance. I just want to concentrate on solving the mystery not where I'm going to lay my head tomorrow night.'

She stamped over to the wardrobe and dragged out her case, throwing it onto the bed she tipped the contents out across the cover and started rummaging amongst the curious shaped bundles.

'What have you got there?'

Queenie looked up, a preoccupied expression on her face. 'What? Oh, I brought a few things just in case. I think this might be an ideal time to use one of my toys.' She smiled slightly and started to unwrap the silk from one of the packages, revealing a highly polished circle of obsidian. 'My scrying mirror.'

'You still use that thing?'

'Not very often.' She examined the surface of the black stone for any marks or imperfections and ran a gentle hand over the shiny surface. 'I hope I haven't lost the knack.'

'I doubt it Queenie; it's a bit like riding a bicycle.''

'Well, if you remember dear I was never very good on a bike, but still as we can't get out because of the rain I think I will blow the cobwebs off of this and give it a whirl.'

Sybil winced, remembering how good her sister was with this particular toy. Queenie had become very adept over the years with this method of clairvoyance and it was now second nature for her to use the black mirror as a portal to the spirit realm.

'I think I had better lock the door.'

'Good idea, and close the curtains as well.'

The grey rain filled day was shut out with the drawing of the curtains and the air in the room although warm at first became still and heavy; with the dimming of the light shadows began to appear in the corners of the room.

'Shall we begin?'

'Haven't you forgotten something?' Sybil enquired, raising an eyebrow.

'What? Oh Sybil I don't need to do that!' she said dismissively.

'We are not doing anything until you draw a circle of protection. You always told me it was the first rule of scrying; protect yourself first!'

'Alright!' she muttered, and delved in amongst the clutter on the bed to find four candles and a packet of sea salt. 'Are you joining me inside the circle?'

'Yes, I am!' Sybil said firmly.

Sprinkling a circle on the carpet with the salt she then placed the candles at equal distance around the circumference, lighting them before retreating to stand beside her sister in the middle.

Imagining a divine light surrounding herself and Sybil she channelled it through her hands and pointed to the circle, closing her eyes briefly Queenie began to chant in a low voice,

'I ask that the god and goddess bless this circle.

So that I may be free and protected within this space.

So Mote it be.'

Queenie looked at her sister inquiringly. 'Happy?'

She raised her eyebrows in exasperation. 'Was that the best you could do?'

'That will be fine, stop fussing dear. I know what I'm doing.'

'I have heard that before,' Sybil replied dryly, and handed her the mirror. 'Well, if you're sure.'

Queenie cupped it gently in her hands and peered into the black depths of the obsidian and as she did so the temperature in the room dropped dramatically. Sybil shivered and pulled the collar of her jumper up around her neck and watched as, with an ease that always astonished her, Queenie quickly dropped into a light trance.

Breathing rhythmically, she cast her thoughts deeper and deeper into the mirror. With her years of experience she swiftly visualised herself walking down an endless flight of stairs that led into a darkness that was blacker than night. Her body became weightless, all signs of age and weariness floated away as she descended.

Feeling strangely alone in the circle Sybil was very aware that the vessel that was her sister was empty and that everything that made Queenie who she was had gone to another plane of existence. She watched carefully as her breathing slowed, worried that her sister was in difficulties and readying herself to interrupt Queenie and draw her back.

Deep in her trance shadows paced alongside her sometimes murmuring softly in her ear, and at other times silent. While close at Queenie's feet padded an elderly grey cat with pale eyes, which kept her company on the journey to the gateway.

To her the journey seemed endless and the farther she descended the darker and heavier the atmosphere became. From the depths came the faint sound of many footsteps hurrying towards her, drawn to her strong aura. The footsteps became louder as they drew closer until she was surrounded by shadowy figures that clutched and tugged at her arm, their whispering voices echoing in the darkness.

A feeling of heaviness and oppression crept over her and Queenie began to feel dizzy. She swayed and staggered within the circle and would have fallen if Sybil hadn't tightened her grip on her arm. 'Queenie,' she murmured in her sister's ear. 'Come back.'

Deep in her trance Queenie heard her sister's voice faintly calling and turning to retrace her steps she shrugged away the suffocating shadows that threatened to overwhelm her. The cat ever present when she ventured into the spirit world gave a little meow of support and clung close to her legs as Queenie gathered her strength. She began to draw back to the mortal world and to the circle of protection pulling the spirits with her until she regained her body.

Queenie drew a deep breath and opened her eyes, blinking slowly she gazed around the room at the forms that were appearing in the dark corners. A more substantial form was manifesting from the swirling mist just in front of them. The features of Absalon wavered and flickered but his hooded bleak eyes remained fixed upon the two women safe in their circle. Sybil drew closer to her sister as his body solidified in front of them allowing them to pick out the tiniest details of his face and clothes. Figures appeared in the corners of the room, their whispering voices filling the air. Sybil clutched at her sisters arm. 'Shh, it's okay,' Queenie reassured her. She stared across the room at Absalon as he began to drift closer to the circle, all around the whispering shadows drew nearer to the two women, stopping short at the barrier of salt unable to penetrate their protection. Although at a loss to distinguish individual words the feeling of despair and grief coming from the long dead men of the village was unmistakable.

The smell of the sea and the sharp tang of blood filled Queenie's nose immediately taking her back to the night of Thomas' death. She shuddered, remembering the feeling of helplessness and horror. Recalling this she glared at the figure of Absalon floating just inches from her.

'How could you have done that?' she accused him in a low whisper. At the sound of her voice the whispering ceased and the shadows became still as though waiting for an answer.

From behind them came a low groan that grew in volume ending in a howl that filled the room, the hair rose on the back of their necks at the horrific noise and they turned to face the shadowy figure that uttered the heartrending noise. The man's anguished face was clear in the inky shadow and Queenie caught her breath.

'Are you Thomas's father?' she asked.

He nodded slowly.

'Help us,' she pleaded. 'Your son needs to be at rest. Help us,' she repeated.

His haunted eyes met Queenie's and he mouthed silently, 'Cave.'

'The cave? What's there?'

'The beginning of the truth,' a sibilant whisper echoed around the room. 'Find the truth then we will rest.'

The whispering swelled in volume until it filled the room and the women clapped their hands over their ears to shut out the heartrending noise.

'Stop!' shouted Queenie, 'That's enough!'

As she finished speaking all sound ceased in the room, she opened her eyes cautiously and peered around. Crouched next to her Sybil had her eyes screwed shut and hands firmly clamped over her ears. Queenie nudged her arm.

'They've gone.'

All except Absalon who still lingered at the edge of the circle, his eyes fixed on Queenie. She glared at him.

'I will find the truth, you monster.'

With this last scathing comment a flicker of emotion rippled over his blank face and he shuddered. With this trembling of his body the mist that made up his form began to slowly dissipate until the room was empty except for the two women.

With the last vestige of spectral mist disappearing the temperature of the room immediately returned to normal, and even though outside the rain still pattered against the window pane it quickly resumed its usual welcoming atmosphere.

Sybil straightened from her half crouching position behind her sister and sighed, at the same time releasing her vice-like grip on Queenie's arm.

'Thank goodness that's over.'

'You have just added to my bruises,' she replied, rubbing her arm. 'I have got enough already.'

'Sorry,' Sybil apologised. 'I wasn't expecting that at all, and I am really glad I insisted that you used a protective circle!'

'I wonder what is in that cave?' mused Queenie, walking stiffly to her bed. She flopped down on it in exhaustion and groaned. 'That was a bit tiring.'

'You weren't gone for that long.'

'Really? It seemed like I was there for hours.' She rubbed her hands together and smiled. 'Still, it worked out very well.'

Sybil sat next to her with a sober expression on her face.

'What now?'

Her sister glanced out of the window at the grey sky which threatened more rain.

'We need to get up that lane and across to Mupe Bay.'

'But Ralph said that the path was dangerous and we have had a lot of rain which will make it worse.'

'Oh, tish! Ralph says...' she said scornfully. 'Who cares what Ralph said.' Queenie stood quickly and taking her sister's arm tugged her upright. 'Come on, let's go for a hike.'

Chapter Nine

Armed with raincoats and brollies they ventured out of the guest house. Overhead heavy rain clouds hung over the village and a constant patter of rain beat down on their heads.

'We're going to get soaked,' complained Sybil. 'We should wait until the rain stops.'

'Maybe. Let's just have a look and see what state the lane is in. If it's not too bad we can have a go at getting across to Mupe Bay.' She opened her umbrella and gestured for Sybil to join her underneath. 'It's only rain,' she said, grinning.

The deserted street was slick with rain and the water gushing from the overflowing drainpipes lay in great puddles amongst the cobbles. Petals and wind damaged blossoms littered the ground at their feet.

They splashed along the street towards the church and stopped short at the sight of the rainwater gushing down the steep track; small stones, broken branches and leaves tumbled down in the torrent making it nigh on impassable. The water flowed past their feet, across the road and disappeared into a culvert in the sea wall.

They stood in the rain and gazed in dismay at the lane which had been temporarily transformed into a river.

'Bother!'

'So much for "it's only rain"!'

'It must be running straight off the hills,' Queenie sighed in exasperation. 'Well, we won't be walking up there today. Another obstacle in our path! I'm beginning to think everything is stacking up against us.'

Wiping a drip from her cheek Sybil smiled. 'That's just your imagination. It's only rain Queenie, after all this is an English summer.' She turned to face the village and gently patted her sister's arm. 'It can wait until the morning, the cave isn't going anywhere and neither are we.' Seeing the grumpy expression on her sister's face she made the one suggestion she knew would cheer Queenie up.

'Tea?'

The cloud disappeared from her face and she nodded. 'What a good idea, there's not much we can do here at the moment. I wonder if Jenny has any more of that lovely chocolate cake.'

Walking back along the village street towards the tea shop they had just drawn level with Albert's cottage when the front door opened and Duncan appeared on the step. Huddled deep in a thick overcoat he glared at the two women.

'Good morning,' called out Queenie, in her most cheerful manner. 'Been visiting your old friend? Talking about old times perhaps?'

Thrusting his hands deep into his pockets he stared through the driving rain.

'What's it to you?'

'You sound so defensive Duncan, why is that?' She smiled brightly at the old man.

'I'm surprised you are still here,' he scowled. His expression suddenly changed and a flicker of contempt crossed his face. 'I thought you would have had enough excitement and be running for home by now.'

She paused in surprise; understanding came to her as he pulled something from one of his overcoat pockets.

'Lose something?' he mocked. 'You shouldn't be interfering in things you don't understand.'

Queenie held out her hand for her wet and muddy slipper. 'Thank you Duncan, I wondered where that had gone,' she said politely.

He snorted. 'I'm sure you knew exactly where it was. In front of the church,' he reminded her. 'Where you were led.'

Her eyes narrowed. 'So you know about the ghosts, have you seen them as well?'

Duncan hesitated for a minute before replying gruffly, 'I've heard them over the years.'

'But never seen any of them?'

'No,' he said, quickly shaking his head. 'I wouldn't want to either. Hearing that scream is bad enough.'

An angry flush spread over Queenie's face. 'Then why haven't you ever tried to do anything you stupid man,' she snapped.

Duncan jerked upright, an angry light in his eyes. 'You don't know anything about it; you should leave well alone, you and your interfering sister.' He stepped back into the house and paused with his hand on the door. 'Just leave.'

The door slammed in their face, leaving them staring in silence at the house.

'Well, he was a bit touchy.'

'Stupid man.' growled Queenie. 'Those two old idiots knew about this all along.'

'Well, what could they do?'

'Something! They could have tried.'

'This sort of thing is beyond most people, Queenie.'

'That's no excuse,' she snapped. A gust of wind blew a shower of drops from a drainpipe soaking the two women. 'Oh great! Just what we needed.'

'I think we need to get out of this rain.' Sybil took a tighter grip on the umbrella which was in danger of taking off and started walking swiftly towards the cafe. 'And you need to calm down.'

'I am calm!' Queenie glared at the house for a minute before realising that Sybil had gone and she was alone. 'Wait for me!'

The little bell tinkled as Sybil pushed open the door, the smell of toasted teacakes wafted out on the warm air making Queenie's mouth water.

Jenny was reading a newspaper at one of the tables; she looked up on hearing the door open and smiled when she saw the two bedraggled women entering.

'Hello. Oh dear, you're soaked.' She stood up and hurried across to help them out of their wet coats. 'Let me help you with those, and I will hang them near the radiator to dry.'

'Thank you.' Sybil's fingers were so stiff from the cold rain that she was struggling with the buttons. She finally managed to extricate herself from the wet coat and sighed, wiping a few raindrops from her face. 'What a day!' she exclaimed, pulling off her damp scarf and handing it to Jenny as well. She looked around the empty room. 'It's very quiet in here.'

'It has been like this all day, in fact you are my first customers.'

Queenie threw her coat over a chair near the door and headed for a table near the window, she sat down saying with a slight air of smugness.

'Then we are in luck. There will be some of that lovely chocolate cake left.'

'I have been baking all morning and have just finished icing a chocolate cake. I must have known you would be in,' she smiled at them. 'Would you like a pot of tea with that or would you prefer coffee?'

'Tea, please. Nice and hot, as we are freezing.'

Jenny nodded in sympathy and looked at Queenie who was pushing a few strands of wet hair off her forehead.

'Goodness!' exclaimed Jenny, looking at her bruises, 'What happened to you?'

'Just a fall,' said Queenie calmly. 'Nothing to worry about.'

Sybil looked out of the steamy window and across to the beach, the visibility was very poor due to the heavy rain but she could just make out the row of fishing boats pulled up on the shingle. She leant forward suddenly and wiped her hand across the cloudy pane.

'The Bella Venture is not there.'

'Perhaps he is out fishing.'

'In this weather?' Sybil frowned. 'It's not a good day to be out at sea.' She stared along the deserted street. 'The village is very quiet today.'

'Good,' said Queenie. 'If I see any more locals I will probably wring their necks.'

From the kitchen came the sound of tinkling china as Jenny struggled out of the door with a loaded tray, she looked across at Queenie in bewilderment. 'Who's been annoying you?'

'Sorry,' said Sybil. 'Don't take any notice of my sister; it's just that we have had quite a trying morning.'

'I'm sorry to hear that.' She laid a piece of cake on the table in front of Queenie and handed her a fork. 'Here you are and if that doesn't bring a smile to your face nothing will.'

The sight of the large slice of gooey chocolate cake complete with a generous helping of clotted cream quickly cleared the gloomy expression from her face. She smiled. 'Now that is a sight to gladden the heart.'

Jenny laughed and handed Sybil her slice. 'Here you are, although you don't look as grumpy as your sister.'

Queenie paused, with a fork halfway to her mouth. 'It's not my fault,' she declared. 'There are some very annoying characters in this village.'

'Are you talking about Serena by any chance?' Jenny asked, with a slightly amused tone to her voice.

'Not this time,' replied Sybil. She pulled out a chair for her. 'Won't you join us?'

Jenny sat down; resting her elbows on the table she looked enquiringly at them. 'Well then, who are you talking about?'

'Those two old idiots, Alfred and Duncan,' grumbled Queenie.

'Queenie, don't be rude,' Sybil remonstrated with her. Seeing the surprised expression on Jenny's face she explained. 'They are being very reluctant to share some information with us; information that we need.'

Jenny looked a bit perturbed and said, shaking her head, 'I know Alfred can be a bit of an old so and so but I'm surprised that you're not getting on with Duncan, he's a sweetie.'

'Well, I suppose you know them better than we do.'

'Oh yes, I have known them all my life, they were friends with my parents,' she paused thoughtfully. 'What information did you need? Perhaps I can help.'

Pouring the tea for the three of them Sybil glanced at her and then quickly making up her mind said, 'Perhaps you can as you're local. How much do you know about the smuggling that went on here?'

The woman raised her eyebrows at the unexpected question. 'Oh that,' she said dismissively. 'That is common knowledge. Anybody could tell you about the smuggling.'

Placing her fork down on the plate Queenie wiped her mouth with the napkin and asked, 'And the murder of the little boy Thomas, is that common knowledge as well?'

Jenny's face dropped. 'Oh,' she said. 'How did you find out about Thomas?'

Queenie folded her hands on the table and fixed her with a stare. 'Well, I could lie to you and say that somebody told us but I won't. I saw the murder of Thomas by the man Absalon, the one everybody calls the Cunning Man.' She watched with interest as a variety of emotions flickered over Jenny's face. 'No, I'm not mad.' Queenie looked at her sister as if for approval of what she about to tell her. 'It's just that we come from a family that have certain talents which enable us to see things.'

'You mean you're clairvoyant?'

'Clairvoyant, psychic, medium, witchcraft, whatever you want to call it. But it's real.' Queenie leant back from the table and rubbed her forehead. 'What I can't understand is why nobody has tried to do anything or even acknowledge that this murder occurred. Duncan admitted he has heard the ghosts many times over the years, but has he done anything? No he hasn't!'

Jenny shifted uncomfortably in her chair.

'Everybody wants to forget it, it was an awful thing that happened but it was years ago. People move on.'

'Then why is Thomas not at rest? He hasn't moved on.'

Jenny shrugged. 'I don't know. I've never seen anything.'

'Ralph has.'

'Ralph, really?'

'Yes. He and Beryl are not happy that we are meddling and want us to leave the guest house.'

'That's a shame, When will you be going home?'

'We're not going,' Queenie replied sharply, 'not until we have solved this mystery, and,' she went on grimly, 'I'm sure Serena is the cause of the recent disturbances.'

'Serena? What has she got to do with Thomas's death?'

'It was her grandfather that murdered the boy. She is also involved with her own bit of smuggling.'

Jenny went quiet and glanced quickly out of the window towards the beach.

Sybil caught the involuntary movement and narrowed her eyes. 'But you know that already, don't you?'

She ran her fingers through her hair and groaned. 'Oh, dear. Yes, I had an idea she was doing something like this. She has been getting very friendly with Joey and he's notorious around here.'

Lifting the teapot Sybil refilled her cup and her sisters; she stared across the table at Jenny's embarrassed expression. 'Did you never think to report her?' she asked in disbelief.

Jenny looked horrified at the suggestion. 'I couldn't do that. Poor Mrs Coppinger, it would break her heart. She has had so much trouble with Serena over the years, I think this would be the final straw.'

'What sort of trouble?'

She sighed and looked uncomfortable but seeing the determined look on the old women's faces she knew she had no choice but to carry on, 'Well, Serena was okay when she was younger, always did very well at school then went onto university. Did really well there, she got a BA honours. That was a proud day for the family but it all went wrong when she went to Amsterdam to work. Well, anyway to cut a long story short her father had to bring her back; she was in a terrible state and spent the next year in a clinic. She had become addicted to all sorts of things when she was out there. Although she got cleaned up Serena was never the same after that; her mood swings were dreadful and she became obsessed with her grandfather.'

'Absalon.'

'Yes. Then a few years ago Mrs Coppinger told me Serena was getting married; she was so happy and relieved. I guess she thought it would settle Serena down.'

'But the husband died.'

Jenny nodded and took a sip from her tea. 'And then she came back here.'

'And started smuggling,' added Sybil. 'She seems intent on following in her grandfathers footsteps.'

Nobody spoke following this news while Queenie eyed up the piece of cake that lay untouched in front of her sister. 'Are you going to eat that?'

Sybil pushed it over wordlessly.

'I have plenty more out in the kitchen.' Jenny looked at Sybil who raised an ironic eyebrow and shook her head.

'That's okay. Let her eat it, chocolate cheers her up.'

'I hate to see good food wasted,' retorted Queenie. 'You will have to give my sister the recipe for this so she can make it for me at home. Otherwise we will be trekking back over here every weekend for a piece.'

'Well, I'm sure I will be very pleased to see you.'

Sybil smiled grimly, 'I wonder if you will be saying that in a few days.'

'So tell me Jenny,' Queenie pausing for a minute, fork in hand. 'This reputation that Absalon had powers, is there any truth in that or was it just smoke and mirrors?'

Jenny examined the intricate pattern on the tablecloth for a minute looking extremely uncomfortable and with a shaking finger traced the raised embroidery of a flower.

'My parents were convinced that he had them. It was always said that the Devil walks this coastline and it was Absalon that kept him out of the village. On certain nights when he was walking Absalon would visit every house in the village and mark the doors to keep everybody safe in their homes. My dad used to say that some nights the Devil managed to best him and get into the village, and in the morning they would find hoof prints where he had walked up and down the street. He would be looking for anybody who was not safe inside. I must admit after all these tales from my childhood I still get nervous going outside at night,' she laughed slightly. 'It's a bit ridiculous I suppose, a woman of my age still believing in this.'

There was a few minutes silence as Queenie became engrossed in scraping the last few crumbs from the plate then she asked suddenly, 'On those nights when the Devil was supposedly walking through the village did everybody stay inside?'

'Oh yes, nobody went outside at night.'

Queenie humphed. 'I bet those were the nights that Absalon and his cronies were landing contraband. Now Serena is trying to do the same thing.'

'Possibly. I know Serena has become obsessed with her grandfather recently. I saw Mrs Coppinger at the beginning of the week and she was really worried about Serena.'

Sybil stirred impatiently. 'Then why doesn't she just ask her to leave?'

'She couldn't do that, she adores Serena and anyway, where would she go?'

'I could think of a few places she could go,' muttered Queenie, before she leant forward and lifted the lid of the teapot. Peering inside she enquired, 'Is there any tea left?'

'I'll make a fresh pot,' Jenny jumped up and carried the pot towards the kitchen. 'I won't be a minute,' she said, over her shoulder.

Outside another heavy cloud appeared over the village, the heavens opened again and the rain began lashing against the window.

The sisters stared in silence across the grey choppy bay.

'Don't you just love English summers?' grumbled Queenie, breaking the silence.

'Perhaps it will be nice tomorrow.'

'Your optimism is sickening.'

Sybil laughed at her sister's surly expression. 'And you are such a grump!'

'I just need more chocolate cake.'

'I think two pieces are enough, even for you.'

Queenie grinned at her sister; her smile slowly fading as a figure appeared walking purposefully down the street towards the car park. A dark windcheater was pulled up close and tight around her neck but her head was uncovered, blonde hair darkened to black by the rain whipped around her head. She paused, leaning against the sea wall and gazed out across the choppy waves to the distant horizon where a heavy bank of rain clouds was rolling in towards the land. No boats were visible out in the bay; those at Bindon were all safely pulled up on the beach out of reach of the pounding waves. All except one.

Serena pulled up her sleeve and stared impatiently at her watch as the wind buffeted her making her rock back on her heels. The wind also brought the driving rain which soaked her clothes, turning her jeans black. Even from the cafe they could see the water running from her clothes.

'She must be waiting for Joey to return. With a cargo of what, I wonder?'

'And to go out in weather like this,' exclaimed Sybil. 'His idea or Serena's I wonder?'

'Well, if we sit here long enough we might see him return, and maybe get a peek at what he brings in.'

'Oh Lord!' gasped Jenny, from the kitchen door, nearly dropping the refilled teapot. 'What is she doing out there in the rain?'

'We think she's expecting the Bella Venture back soon.' Queenie eyed Jenny as she set the pot in front of Sybil. 'You didn't happen to notice when Joey left?'

She fussed about with the tea cups before answering, she didn't meet Queenies eye but answered brightly, 'Oh, I didn't see him leave this morning.'

Sybil lips twitched as she tried to hide her smile. 'So,' she said, 'If he left sometime this morning how far would he have been able to go and return by this time?'

Jenny's face fell when she realised her slip. 'I don't know,' she said simply, and gazed thoughtfully out of the window at the lone figure still waiting by the sea wall. 'Nobody knows where he goes or what he does.'

'Perhaps the weather is delaying him.'

As they watched, Serena, losing patience, turned to leave and as if aware of their scrutiny she stared across the street to the cafe. Seeing the three women sat at the table in the window she strode across and peered in through the cloudy glass at them. Although it had only been a day they were shocked by the change in her appearance; her face was chalk white and huge dark circles ringed her eyes which were curiously blank. Serena blinked against the rain which was running in rivulets down her face. By now her hair was soaked and was clinging to her head with spiderlike tendrils stuck across her face.

'She's getting soaked,' exclaimed Jenny, and hurried to the door to pull it open. 'Serena,' she called out into the rain. 'Serena come in, you're soaking wet.'

The young woman walked towards Jenny and stopped just inches in front of her. Serena pushed her face up close and hissed, 'What are they doing here? They are evil, servants of the devil.' Trembling with the cold she jabbed her finger into the woman's chest and stuttered, 'The devil will claim his own; remember that!'

Shocked, Jenny held up a calming hand and said soothingly, 'Now Serena, you're talking nonsense, come in out of the rain and have some tea.' The strange expression on Serena's face did not change, and seeing this Jenny pleaded with her again. 'Serena, you're not well; if you won't come in at least let me take you home.'

She jerked back at these words as if Jenny had struck her and glared at the shocked woman.

'Leave me alone! I don't need your help. Absalon aids me. His spirit walks beside me and guides me.' With these last words Serena began to sway and Jenny reached out a steadying hand towards her.

'But Absalon is dead, Serena.'

She slapped away the hand and staggered back, shouting against the wind that was howling around the front of the cafe. 'He is here with me; he will return and claim his own. And I,' she said, raising her head and staring fervently at Jenny, 'I will be here to aid him.'

Unable to think of anything to say to the distraught woman to diffuse the situation Jenny backed away until she was in front of the door. 'Oh dear, Serena, what will your grandmother say? She will be so upset with you behaving like this.'

Clenching her fist she waved it at Jenny. 'She does not understand, the blood of the Coppingers does not run in her veins. But when our family regains control of the village then she will understand and welcome her husband back from beyond the grave.'

Jenny's face dropped in appalled surprise and she hurriedly opened her mouth to remonstrate with her.

'Do not say another word woman!'

With this parting shot Serena staggered past Jenny and made her shaky way along the street back to her grandmother's cottage. Dumbfounded Jenny watched her until she was out of sight then pushed open the door to the cafe and walked back into the familiar warmth. Closing the door with a shaky hand she leant back against it and closed her eyes for a moment, Serena's words echoing in her mind.

'Are you alright?'

The words made her jerk upright and she looked across at the women still sat at the table quietly watching her.

'I'm fine, just a bit shocked,' she looked down at her clothes that had got soaked as she stood outside in the rain trying to reason with Serena. 'Now I'm wet as well,' she said dismally. Jenny walked slowly back to the table feeling shaken and sat down. Sybil silently poured out a hot cup of tea and pushed it in front of her.

'No wonder Mrs Coppinger is so worried,' Jenny said,' I didn't realise
Serena was in such a state.' She shook her head and gazed at the two
women in shock. 'The things she was saying; it was insane!' Jenny put
her head in her hands, her voice muffled as she asked for advice. 'What
shall I do? Do you think I should ring her grandmother and warn her?'
'Judging by her appearance there is no way that her grandmother hasn't
noticed her decline, there is such a marked difference since we saw her
last that I can't help wondering what has happened to cause it,' said
Queenie. She looked at Jenny's troubled face and said soothingly,
'There was nothing you could have said to her to calm her down, she is
past normal intervention. She needs specialist help now.'
Jenny stirred her tea slowly and nodded. 'You're right; I don't know
how to deal with somebody like that.' She looked at the women's calm
faces and said slowly, 'Perhaps it would be a good idea if you stayed
here. I have a spare room; it's nothing fancy. I just keep it ready in case
any of the family want to visit,' she paused uncertainly, 'It's just a
thought; of course you could stay at The Anchor; it would probably be
more comfortable for you both. I don't have all the amenities that they
have.'
Sybil interrupted her before she could say anymore. 'Thank you, we
would be very grateful.' She turned to Queenie who was nodding
thoughtfully.
'Does the room have a sea view?' she asked.
'Does it matter?' Sybil asked her sister in surprise.
Jenny smiled, 'Well as a matter of fact it does, right over the beach.'
Queenie stirred her tea in silence before answering with satisfaction,
'That's marvellous, then we will be able to see all the comings and
goings on the beach. We told Ralph and Beryl we would be leaving in
the morning so would it be alright to come round after breakfast?'
'That would work out very well,' Jenny nodded, 'It will give me a
chance to put a duster over the furniture and change the sheets.'
'Oh please, don't go to too much trouble for us, we will fit in with you.
We are just very grateful that you can offer us a bed.'
Jenny stood up and started briskly collecting the plates. 'It's no
trouble,' she reassured them and paused for a minute gazing at them
keenly, 'and I think you're right, this whole situation needs to be sorted
out for everybody's sake. We have closed our eyes to it for too long.'

Chapter Ten

By late afternoon the heavy clouds had blown over and a weak sun had just made its appearance for the first time that day and a growing chorus of bird song could be heard coming from the rain soaked trees on the hill behind the village. Slowly the puddles began to dry up in the gentle heat and the wind and rain damaged blooms from the village floral displays began to lift their heads in the welcome sunshine.

Sybil had pulled back the curtains and thrown open the bedroom window to let in the fresh sea air as they packed up their belongings in readiness for their departure in the morning.

Queenie put her hands on her hips and glared at her overflowing case. 'Now why won't this all go in?' She viciously jabbed at her wash bag trying to force it into the small space.

'Because I packed it for you in the first place,' Sybil said calmly, putting her sister aside she began to repack the case.

'You did not!' Queenie said indignantly, 'I distinctly remember packing it myself.'

'Yes, then I repacked it. As you made such a pig's ear of it the case wouldn't close.'

There was no animosity in this exchange; their good natured bickering had been a staple part of their relationship for most of their eighty plus years. They had never had a serious falling out and would probably never have but any bystander hearing this exchange would have found it difficult to believe. Which is how Ralph felt as he watched them from the doorway trying to decide whether he should interrupt or not. He coughed gently to gain their attention.

'Hello Ralph, what can we do for you?' asked Sybil, smiling politely. Behind her Queenie frowned at him and threw a pair of shoes on top of a neatly folded pile of clothes.

Sybil gestured around the room. 'As you can see we are getting ready to leave in the morning.'

He nodded looking uncomfortable. 'So I see.' He spread his hands apologetically. 'I am sorry about all this but what plans do you have for a meal tonight? I am only asking as Beryl has a migraine and won't be able to cook this evening.' Ralph paused, looking at Queenie's frosty expression, 'I could make a few sandwiches...perhaps?' he finished lamely.

Seeing his embarrassed expression Sybil took pity on him. 'Don't worry Ralph; I'm sure we will be able to get some food at The Anchor.' 'Their meals are very good; we often recommend them to our guests.' Ralph turned to leave then hesitated, ' I am very sorry about this but Beryl is quite upset about the whole thing, she's had a lot to put up with in the last few weeks and I don't want her worrying about this as well.' 'We understand,' Sybil nodded, 'Don't we Queenie?' giving her sister a sharp nudge.

She shrugged. 'Oh yes, we understand.'

'Good,' he said, rubbing his hands together, 'I will see you in the morning and have a good evening.'

The door closed softly behind him and the sisters stared at each other in silence for a few minutes.

'Well,' said Sybil eventually, 'I'm sure it will all work out for the best.' 'Huh! We shall see.' She slammed the lid of the case shut. 'Well, I'm finished,' she announced.

'Yes, but you will need a few things for tonight.'

'Well, why didn't you say that before I packed everything!'

Sybil smirked. 'And spoil your fun?'

The antique clock in the hall had just finished striking seven as they walked out of the guest house. It had turned out to be a beautiful evening, overhead the sky was a clear deep blue with hardly a cloud in sight. The wind had died down and the waters in the bay had become like a mill pond with the usual plethora of small boats magically reappearing out on the waves. This all boded well for their expedition the next day.

'Well,' Sybil said gazing up at the beautiful sky, 'after all that rain this morning, look at it now!'

'We'll be alright for tomorrow,' Queenie said in satisfaction. 'And I am determined to explore that cave.'

There were a few people still walking about the village but by their appearance they looked like residents returning home after work; some were already making their way to the pub which had its lights on, sending a warm welcoming glow out into the street. A low hubbub of voices came from the bar as Sybil pushed open the door and entered with her sister close behind. The voices slowly died away until there was complete silence in the room, every head had turned toward them and dozens of eyes watched their progress to a vacant table near the fireplace.

Seeing the frosty expression appearing on her sisters face Sybil reached out and took her arm, willing her to be calm.

'They are just curious, that's all,' she said.

Queenie stared back defiantly meeting their gaze until one by one they turned away.

'Really?' she muttered as she sat down. 'You would think they have never seen holidaymakers before.'

Sybil pulled a wry face. 'I think they realise we are more than tourists; courtesy of Duncan and Albert probably.'

'Are they here?' asked Queenie, peering around the crowded bar. 'Because if they are, I would like to give them a piece of my mind.'

'Oh hush Queenie, that's not necessary. We don't know the full story yet and I'm sure there is a reasonable explanation for the way they have behaved.' She stopped talking and quickly picked up the menu from the table. 'What are you going to have, Queenie?' she asked, as the young waitress bore down on their table. She met the girl's hostile look with a calm smile and a pleasant, 'Good evening. Do you think we could have a bottle of red wine to start with and,' she quickly consulted the menu, 'I would like the Salmon please. What about you Queenie?'

'Steak,' she said, fixing the young girl with a stony gaze. 'Rare and bloody, just the way I like it.'

Sybil closed her eyes briefly and nudged Queenie's foot under the table. 'What?' she asked indignantly. 'I'm just ordering a rare steak, that's all.' She looked inquiringly at the young girl silently scribbling down their order. 'Did you get that? Nice and rare.' Catching the cold look that the young girl gave her Queenie grinned and licked her lips. 'I just love the taste of blood.' She winced and glared at her sister. 'Stop kicking me!'

Without a word Chloe turned on her heel and walked off, heading for the kitchen. She passed close to the bar and leant across it to have a whispered conversation with the landlord. They looked over at Queenie and Sybil as they talked, the girl's expression speaking volumes of her opinion of the two women.

'I bet they are local as well, probably lived here for generations. And I bet there have been a few kegs of smuggled brandy in that cellar over the years.'

'I wonder what is down there now?'

Sighing in irritation, Queenie shrugged off her fleece and threw it over the back of a chair.

'I wish they would stop talking and get on with our order or we're going to starve to death.' She glared across the room at the waitress who was still leaning against the bar deep in conversation. She coughed loudly and on hearing this the waitress looked up to see Queenie elaborately tapping her wristwatch.

'You are being very rude,' said Sybil.

'I know and I don't care. I'm enjoying myself.'

'I'm glad you are having fun, I'm just worried that they will over salt our food, or worse.'

'They wouldn't dare; would they?' she asked, looking worried. 'I wouldn't like to think they're going to ruin a perfectly good steak.'

'Well, we shall see.'

The landlord broke off his whispered conversation with the waitress to serve a customer, as he pulled a pint he jerked his head impatiently in the direction of the kitchen. With a last cold look she disappeared through a door behind the bar.

'At last! She's taking our order to the chef; let's hope the food is worth waiting for.'

'Ralph did say The Anchor had a good reputation for food.'

'Ralph! Don't talk to me about Ralph. He seems quite happy to ignore all the psychic activity and if that's not bad enough he's turning a blind eye to the fact that Serena attacked him.'

'That can't be proved Queenie, it was just our theory. After all what can he do about it now? Watching Beryl's face this morning I think it was the idea that Serena might be responsible that upset her so much.'

Queenie shrugged. 'It couldn't have been pleasant to think that one of their neighbours had intentionally injured her husband.'

They were silent for a minute, an image of Serena that afternoon coming vividly to mind.

'She seems to have lost it completely,' Sybil said quietly. 'I wonder if her past history is affecting her behaviour?'

'Are you kidding?' scoffed Queenie. 'All that drug use had turned her whacko.' She leant towards her sister and drummed her fingers thoughtfully on the table. 'There is also the family's history of mental illness.'

'Oh, come off it! That was one member of the family, Cruel Coppinger's son. It doesn't follow that any mental problems have been passed down through the generations.'

Queenie sat back and looked a bit put out that her theory had been shot down.

'Well,' she carried on, 'it shows that there is bad blood in the Coppingers.

'I can't argue with that.'

As the evening wore on the noise in the bar rose back to its accustomed level with most of the customers all but forgetting the presence of the two women waiting for their meal.

Eventually the landlord lumbered out from behind the bar with a bottle of wine and two glasses clutched in his huge hands. 'Here you are,' he said, and placed a bottle of Merlot on the table which he deftly opened and poured out two generous glassfuls.

'Thank you,' Sybil took a tentative sip, expecting it to be of mediocre quality but was pleasantly surprised. She took a second larger sip and nodded. 'That's very nice. Try it Queenie,' and pushed over a glass for her sister.

She nodded, following a generous mouthful and catching the man's eye asked, 'Any idea how long our order will be?'

The man jerked his head in the direction of the kitchen. 'They're busy this evening but I will go and ask.' He nodded politely, threading his way through the groups of people stood in front of the bar to the kitchen.

'Oh well,' Queenie said drumming her fingers on the table, 'we can always go round to Jennys' and see if she has any cake left.'

'Just be patient, the food will be here in a minute.'

To take her mind off her growing hunger Sybil looked around the room at the other customers, some of which were involved in a very noisy game of darts at the back of the room. Another group arrived and pushed their way through to the bar; coming in behind them and on her own was Janet. Recognising Sybil through the throng she smiled and waved.

'Who are you smiling at?'

'Janet has just walked in; you remember Janet? With the cat.'

'Of course I do,' Queenie swivelled round and peered towards the woman who was pushing her way through the crowd towards them.

'Hi, how are you?' she called, when she was within speaking distance. 'It's busy tonight.'

'We're fine. Just waiting for our meal to arrive.

'It's taking ages,' grumbled Queenie.

'Oh, it always does. The chef is very good but very slow,' she grinned.
'But it's worth waiting for.' Janet looked around the room trying to spot
an empty table. 'Can I join you?'
'Of course,' Sybil said quickly, and pulled out the chair next to hers.
Janet shrugged of her jacket and draped it over the back of the seat. 'My
friend is supposed to be coming along in a minute but I hate waiting
around in a pub on my own even if I do know everybody.'
'Are you sure it's safe for you to be seen with us?' said Queenie, with
an ironic lift of an eyebrow. 'We're beginning to feel like pariahs here.'
Janet gave her a baffled look. 'Sorry?'
'We're not popular,' explained Sybil. 'I think Albert and Duncan have
been stirring things a bit.'
'Oh yes,' said Janet. 'I have heard that you have been asking questions.'
She leant back from the table as the waitress appeared at her elbow
bearing two generous plates of food. Janet touched the young girls arm
as she handed out the cutlery.
'Chloe, could I have a gin and tonic please?'
She glanced from Janet to the old women, an expression of surprise and
doubt on her face.
'We're friends,' Janet reassured her.
'Okay, I will bring it across.'
'Thanks.' As Chloe headed back to the bar Janet looked at her
retreating back and said, 'She's a nice girl, very helpful.
'Really? She has been a bit frosty with us.'
'I'm afraid that is down to Albert, he's a bit of a mischief maker. Chloe
is Duncan's granddaughter and she's worried you have been upsetting
him.'
'Well that explains it!' said Sybil, looking at Queenie who was too
engrossed in smearing a generous helping of mustard onto her steak to
pay attention to the conversation. She carried on in a low voice, 'I'm
afraid Queenie hasn't been that tactful with the two of them.'
Janet's lips twitched and she nodded. 'I guessed that. So I hear that you
have been asking about our history of smuggling.'
'Those two have been busy,' exclaimed Sybil. 'But yes, we have and
asking about other things as well.'
Chloe's arm suddenly appeared over Janet's shoulder making Sybil
jump.
'One G and T, Janet.'

'Thanks Chloe,' she said quietly, and waited until the girl had retreated behind the bar where she continued suspiciously watching the group by the fire.

Drawing a deep breath Janet began slowly, 'About the other things, it would be better if you left well alone. It's a very painful subject in the village.'

'I can understand that, it must have been an awful thing to have happened but it was a long time ago.' Seeing the expression of confusion on Janet's face Sybil asked puzzled, 'Are we missing something here?'

Taking a generous mouthful of her gin Janet nodded. 'I think you are. The other thing that I guess you are asking about is Tommy?'

'Who's Tommy?' Queenie asked, looking up from her meal for the first time.

'Tommy,' she stared at the sisters with a perplexed look. 'You did mean his murder didn't you? Or have I got the wrong end of the stick?'

'Thomas,' stated Queenie. 'You mean Thomas?'

'Yes, little Tommy Puckett, All these questions are stirring up painful memories.'

'Too bad,' Queenie said bluntly. 'We're more interested in the truth than anybody's feelings.'

'That was a bit brutal Queenie!' said Sybil, giving her an irritated look. 'We're not here to trample over everybody's feelings. It's just that,' she addressed Janet, 'the truth needs to come out and then,' she gestured vaguely, 'well, things will be resolved.' Sybil realised she was being a bit ambiguous but she wasn't sure how Janet would react to their real purpose.

On hearing this Janet snorted. 'Oh, I've heard about you two, and your clairvoyance. Jenny told me,' in reply to Sybil's questioning look.

'Of course, the village grapevine,' she smiled grimly. 'I live in a small village myself so I shouldn't be surprised.' Sybil smiled coolly at her and then looked down at her meal. 'Well, this does look delicious.'

'Yes and it will be getting cold,' warned her sister.

Shifting impatiently in her chair Janet watched them as they calmly carried on eating.

'You really should leave it alone,' she persisted. 'It will do no good, not now.'

Queenie picked up the bottle and offered it to her sister before refilling her own glass, without bothering to look at Janet she asked, 'So, who exactly are we upsetting with our questions?'

'Duncan.'

'What? Him? Why is he getting so wound up about it?'

Janet put her glass down sharply on the table getting very irritated with them. 'You see,' she snapped, 'this is the problem. You're interfering and you don't know what you're doing or whom you're upsetting.'

Holding up a soothing hand Sybil asked, 'Well, then enlighten us.'

Janet frowned, almost unwilling to help anymore but eventually said grudgingly, 'Tommy was Duncan's brother. That's why he is getting so upset with you; the whole family were devastated when they lost the little boy.'

Forks stopped midway between plate and mouth as they digested this piece of news.

'His brother?' gasped Sybil. 'Well that explains it. Why on earth didn't he say something?'

'Perhaps he thought it wasn't any of your business,' she replied bluntly. 'And it isn't.' Janet looked down at her empty glass and frowned. 'So you see what I mean? About leaving well alone?'

'Hmm,' Queenie nodded, waving the fork in her direction. 'Thank you for enlightening us. Have you found your cat yet?' she asked, bluntly changing the subject. Seeing Janet's mouth droop Queenie could guess the answer. 'Sorry,' she said. 'What a shame.'

'I have had him for such a long time that I am lost without him,' she sighed and looked around as a cheer came from the corner of the room. 'They are a good crowd here, in the village.'

'I'm sure they are,' agreed Sybil.

The door opened and a group of women came into the already crowded bar, Janet looked round and said quickly, 'There's my friend, I'll leave you to it.' She stood up and tucked the chair back under the table.

Looking at the two women she said quietly, 'You will think about what I said, won't you?'

Keeping her expression neutral Queenie nodded, 'We will give it a lot of thought, thank you Janet, you have been very helpful.'

She hesitated, unsure what to make of her seemingly innocent reply.

'Good, well I might see you again.'

'I am sure you will, good night.'

Her friends greeted her cheerfully as she threaded her way through the crowd to join them at the bar. One woman that Sybil recognised gave her a hug while staring curiously across the room at them. In answer to a question Janet just shrugged and they both turned to stare at Queenie.

'My ears are burning,' she muttered.

'It would appear that we have managed to upset her as well.'

'So, all in all it's been a good evening,' said Queenie, with a wink at Sybil. Pushing her plate to one side she sighed. 'That was delicious; Janet was right about the food.'

They sat in silence for a while as they finished off the bottle of wine, each busy with their own thoughts. Around them the pub got noisier as the evening wore on and the consumption of alcohol went up. The wine, constant hubbub and the warmth was beginning to make Sybil sleepy; she stifled a yawn and looked across the table to her sister whose eyes were also beginning to droop.

'Shall we make a move Queenie? It's getting late.'

Receiving a nod she fumbled in her handbag for her purse. 'I'll go and settle the bill,' Sybil looked across to where Chloe was busy behind the bar hoping to catch her eye; the purse dropped to the table as all thoughts of paying went from her head. She resumed her seat and hissed across the table rousing Queenie from her sleepy state, 'Look who's stood at the bar.'

Queenie half opened her eyes and looked blearily at her sister. 'Who?'

'Joey. He's drinking a pint with the barman. I wonder how long he's been there? I didn't see him come in.'

All signs of sleep disappeared as Queenie sat bolt upright and peered through the throng.

'So he's back.' She bit her lip for a minute as she thought. 'We could nip out and have a peek in his boat while he's busy in here.'

'What if he spots us?'

'From in here?' scoffed Queenie. She watched him for a minute. 'He's more interested in what's in his glass.'

He was leaning unsteadily against the bar, a half full glass cradled in a dirty hand. The old worn shirt had seen better days; the ragged sleeves were rolled up exposing his tanned and tattooed arms. Joey's brown corduroy trousers were in no better state, it looked as though he had stepped straight off the boat which the two women knew he had. Queenie eyed up the old rucksack at his feet wondering what it contained.

'I can't sit here for much longer Queenie. I need to get to bed, I'm exhausted.'

She nodded reluctantly. 'You're right; he looks as though he's going to be in here for a while. Right,' she said, pushing herself up from the table. 'You go and pay the bill and I'm going to go and find the Ladies toilet.'

Pausing for a minute, Sybil narrowed her eyes and said thoughtfully, 'Which is on the other side of the bar meaning you will be walking right past Joey or did you think of that?'

'Of course not,' she replied, doing her best to look innocent. 'I didn't give it a thought.' The smile didn't fade from her face as she pushed her way through to the bar, passing close to Joey. He paused, glass in hand when he recognised the elderly woman.

'Nice to see you made it back safely Joey,' she murmured.

A blank look came over his face as his alcohol fuddled brain tried to comprehend her meaning. His eyes followed her progress across the room until she disappeared from view; frowning he turned back to his pint to find that Sybil had appeared next to him. She nodded briefly to him while trying to attract the attention of the barman who was busy pulling pints. Looking up he nodded in her direction and said, 'I'll be with you in a minute.'

All chatter and the clinking of glasses made it difficult to hear but Sybil wasn't in any hurry as Queenie had not yet returned.

Joey shifted to one side as one of Janet's friends came to the bar with a couple of empty glasses and squeezed between them. Feeling he was no longer under the scrutiny of Sybil Joey relaxed, only to find Queenie had reappeared on the other side of him. He jumped and not daring to meet her cold gaze hunched over his nearly empty glass.

'Night, Joey,' she said, walking slowly past. 'Are you ready Sybil?

After the warm stuffy atmosphere of the pub it was a welcome relief to be outside in the cool evening air. Sybil, feeling the effects of the red wine, drew a deep breath and looked up at the clear night sky. 'What a beautiful night.'

Before Queenie could answer the door to the bar was thrust open and a group of very merry darts players spilled out into the street.

Sybil and Queenie quickly stepped back against the wall of the nearby cottage to allow them to stagger past; made friendly by the alcohol they wished the women good night before linking arms and swaying off down the street.

'Good night,' Sybil called after them. She yawned. 'That was a lovely meal but now I am ready for my bed.' As she spoke the door opened again and Joey appeared, he stumbled down the steps and staggered along the street heading for the boats, not noticing the women in the shadows.

'He's in a hurry,' whispered Queenie. Grasping Sybil's arm she pulled her in the direction that Joey had gone. 'Come on, let's follow him.'

'He's just going home, that's all.'

'I bet he isn't. I think he's looking for us, perhaps he thinks we have gone to look at his boat.' She linked her arm through Sybil's and gave it an encouraging squeeze. 'Come on, you can sleep later.'

Sybil sighed. 'You're impossible Queenie. Well, we will just have a quick look that's all. If you want to spend all night on the beach then you can but I will be tucked up nice and warm inside.'

Trying to be quiet and stop themselves giggling they stole after him; keeping to the shadows Queenie and Sybil followed him all the way down the street towards the car park.

At the last cottage before they reached the beach they stopped and stealthily peaked around the corner.

Sybil started to giggle.

'Shh...' whispered Queenie, whose eyesight belied her years could just see him in the distance staggering around the Bella Venture, seeing that nothing had been disturbed on board Joey then peered around the dark beach.

'He is looking for us,' whispered Queenie, 'and he will spot us if we stay here.' She looked over to the gift shop on the opposite side of the street where the awning over the door cast a deep shadow. 'Over here,' she hissed, trying to tiptoe quietly across to the doorway. They drew back into the dark and waited; although they could no longer see him they could hear his footsteps on the shingle and the low grumbling curses as he struggled drunkenly around the other beached vessels.

'He's not going to see us hidden in here.'

'Shh, he's coming,' warned Queenie.

Joey appeared from between two of the smaller boats and swaying gently began walking to the steps leading off the beach.

'I wonder what he's left in the boat?' breathed Sybil in her sister's ear, as they watched Joey struggling to gain the street. 'My goodness, he is pickled!'

Gasping for breath Joey swayed in the moonlight, staring towards the car park and then back towards the pub.

'When he leaves we can go and have a peek'

'Oh, now you want to go and have a look!'

'Shh... you're making too much noise,' giggled Sybil, as Joey staggered round to peer blearily across to the shop, he paused, head on one side as though he had heard something.

They held their breath.

Quickly losing interest Joey lurched towards the pub; he paused for a minute in the circle of light coming through the door but with a shake of his head changed his mind and continued down the street.

'It's lucky he didn't spot your fluorescent pink hair.'

'Don't be ridiculous, it's not fluorescent!'

'Of course it is, didn't you realise you glow in the dark?'

Her mouth dropped open and she gazed at Sybil in horror. 'What?' she gasped.

'Sorry, I thought you knew.'

Queenie tried to drag a lock of hair in front of her eyes but it was too short.

'You are joking, aren't you?' she appealed to her sister, but on hearing Sybil's muffled laughter she snapped, 'Oh for goodness sake! Stop being so ridiculous, you're giggling like a little school girl. I knew we shouldn't have had that wine; you always get silly.' She glared through the dim light to where her sister was leaning against the shop door.

'And don't go to sleep there, we will just go and have a quick poke about and then you had better go to bed.'

'That's what I've been saying, I need my bed.'

Queenie poked her head out from the dark doorway and checked that the street was clear; taking Sybil's arm she pulled her reluctant sister across to the steps leading down to the beach.

The moon was bright enough to enable them to see but Queenie had already pulled out her torch in readiness to light them down the steep steps. Walking carefully to avoid making too much noise and to avoid the risk of a twisted ankle on the shifting stones they picked their way across to the Bella Venture which was on the end of the row of boats nearest to them. It stood in the moonlight smelling strongly of fish and oil.

They stood on tiptoe and peered over the edge of the boat. Queenie directed the beam of the torch down into the bottom where a few inches of sludgy water lay, then peered into all the nooks and crannies. No bags or barrels had been left there; apart from a few odds and ends of rope it appeared empty.

'Nothing! Well, doesn't that beat all! Why did he come rushing back?'

Sybil peered down into the gloomy depths of the boat, straining to see in the poor light.

'What's that?' she said suddenly, pointing to the bow where a tatty life jacket was half hidden under a bench. She stood on tiptoe and tried to reach for it, the tips of her fingers just brushed the jacket but not enough for her to be able to grasp it.

'There is something in the pocket,' she tried again and groaned in frustration, 'but it's just out of reach. Damn!' she said in exasperation, and looked around for something to stand on.

'I can't see anything,' said Queenie, who continued peering into the boat as Sybil searched about the other nearby vessels for something to help her reach it.

'Found something,' a loud whisper came from behind a large fishing boat farther down the beach. There was a scraping noise and Sybil suddenly reappeared dragging a large boat hook. 'Look what I found.' She hauled the long pole over the edge of the Bella Venture and tried to hook the jacket, her first attempt failed and she was just trying again when Queenie who was getting impatient pushed her to one side.

'Let me try,' she demanded. 'Hold the torch.'

'I don't see why you will be able to do if I can't.'

'Because I am older than you.'

Sybil stared at her in exasperation. 'What a load of nonsense.' She held out the pole to her sister. 'Go on then smarty pants; let's see how you get on.'

Her sister silently handed her the torch and took the pole from her grasp; leaning forward as far as she could she slowly extended it until it was resting on the jacket. Then twisting the pole the hook caught on a strap. She grunted with satisfaction and slowly and cautiously began to drag it back towards them. 'There we are,' she said with a smug tone to her voice, seeing her sister's expression she grinned.

'You are so annoying Queenie.'

'With age comes experience,' she gloated, and gestured towards the jacket. 'Take it then, this pole is heavy.'

Sybil dragged the wet and smelly jacket out of the boat and dropped it onto the shingle.

'What is it?' asked Queenie, as Sybil pulled a plastic bag from one of the pockets. It was full of brightly coloured sweets. 'Sweets! Is that all?' she said in disgust. 'All this fuss for a bag of sweets.'

'Hold the torch still while I search the other pockets.' Sybil carefully and systematically searched the life jacket finding nothing of any interest. She hefted the plastic bag she still held and her brow furrowed. 'There is a lot in this bag, perhaps they contain something.'

'Like diamonds? Would they hide gems in sweets?'

She broke open the bag and poured a few into her hand, holding them in the torch light Sybil and Queenie peered at the small brightly coloured discs.

'Unless they are not sweets.'

Queenie tentatively picked one up. 'They aren't, are they?'

'I don't think so,' said Sybil quietly. 'Now we know what they are bringing in.'

'We do?' she asked, a puzzled frown on her face as she closely examined one.

'I think they are amphetamines.' Seeing the baffled look on her sister's face she tried to explain, 'It's what is known as a recreational drug. It has very strange side effects, mood swings, hallucinations, that sort of thing.'

'I'm none the wiser, Sybil,' complained her sister. 'How do you know about this?

'That's one of the benefits of having grandchildren, they seem determined to keep me clued up to the 21st century.'

Queenie handed the tablet back to her and asked, 'Now what do we do?'

'We have a choice,' she answered, pouring the handful back into the bag. 'We can, either put them back so he doesn't notice that we have been here and call the authorities, or take them away then make the phone call.'

Queenie shook her head, 'He needs to be found in possession, doesn't he?'

'But if we leave them, he or Serena might take them away before the police get here and then it will be our word against theirs.'

Pursing her lips Queenie turned to stare at the boat. 'Actually we have only got one choice. I dropped the boat hook into the bottom of the boat so we won't be able to get the life jacket back in its position.'

'Queenie!'

She shrugged. 'Well, look on the bright side, at least the decision is easy now.'

Her sister sighed in irritation. 'Oh well, that's all right then!'

'Don't be like that, things will work out, they always do.' She smiled and then stooped to pick up the life jacket, tossing it back into the boat. It hit the side with a thud, the sound echoing off the nearby buildings.

'Why did you do that?' Sybil hissed, jumping out of her skin. 'Somebody could have heard that.'

'Who?' scoffed Queenie. 'There is nobody here.' She quickly flicked the beam of her torch around the row of boats. 'See, it's all quiet.'

'At the moment. Joey left these in the boat for a reason, somebody is going to come and collect them and I would hazard a guess that it will be Serena.'

Sybil reached out and took the torch from her sister, turning it off she plunged them into darkness. They waited for their eyes to adjust to the dim light, at the same time listening. Over the sound of the waves breaking on the beach they could hear slow footsteps on the shingle. They stepped back quietly huddling against the side of the boat.

'What are we going to do?' hissed Queenie, looking around for somewhere to hide. Without a word Sybil grabbed her arm and pulled her to the stern of the boat away from the approaching figure, their hurrying footsteps sounding in the clear night air.

'Slow down Sybil, we're making too much noise,' she whispered.

'I know but we need to get out of here.'

They sheltered in the shadow of the boat and listened, the footsteps had slowed as they neared the Bella Venture and a dark figure appeared just feet away from the sisters. The faint light cast a shadow of her face but it was unmistakable, it was Serena. It was as Sybil had predicted she had come to the boat to pick up the bag. Serena peered around at the other boats to make sure she wasn't being watched and then nimbly pulled herself up and over the edge of the boat. There was a splash as she landed in the dirty water in the bottom. They could hear her moving about inside, there was a thud and a curse as she stumbled over the boat hook. Taking the opportunity of Serena being distracted, Sybil and Queenie slipped away to hide behind the next boat in the line.

'When she finds that bag is missing she will know it was us,' whispered Sybil quietly into Queenie's ear. 'We have to get out of here,' she said nervously, looking behind them into the dark shadows cast by the boats. 'And we don't know where Joey is.'

There was another crash as Serena pounced on the discarded life jacket which was quickly followed by a shriek of rage.

'She has discovered the bag is missing!'

'Come on,' whispered Queenie, heading for the far end of the line of boats. 'We will wait it out; she can't stay here all night.'

Looking back they could see her outlined against the night sky, she was prowling about the boat searching for the missing bag, then as if realisation had hit her Serena suddenly jerked upright and glared around the surrounding boats.

'Thieves,' she screamed, punching her fists into the air. 'I know it was you! I am going to kill you! Do you hear me? I am going to slit your throats!'

The women froze in horror at the ferocity of the young woman's words and watched as Serena dragged the boat hook from the bottom of the boat and grasping it in her hands jumped from the side of the boat.

There was scrunch as she landed in the shingle and then a rush of feet as Serena began running through the boats brandishing her makeshift weapon looking for the sisters.

They could hear Serena working her way along the row, the boat hook constantly being smashed against the sides of the vessels.

'I know you're here, old woman. I'm going to find you and cut out your heart!' she screamed, frustration becoming evident in her voice as she unsuccessfully searched for Queenie and Sybil. She was so close that they could hear her gasping breath as she drew nearer to the boat where they were hiding.

Sybil's legs began to tremble and her heart began to pound making her wheeze.

'Are you alright?' whispered Queenie, peering at her through the gloom, receiving no answer she reached out and grasped her arm making Sybil jump. 'It's okay,' Queenie reassured her. 'She won't find us.'

'She will,' a note of panic had appeared in Sybil's voice. 'She will find us, what are we going to do?'

Queenie bit her lip and thought quickly, she bent and scrabbled amongst the shingle for some large pebbles. 'Here goes,' she muttered, and threw a handful towards the sea wall. They clattered against the worn stones, the sound echoing around the beach.

Serena froze just feet from where they were hiding and turned in the direction of the noise, hefting the pole in her hands she began to run.

Watching her carefully as she disappeared through the boats Queenie placed an arm around her sister's shoulders and steered her back along the row of vessels.

'Time to go,' she whispered. 'I didn't think that would work but it will give us some time to get out the way.'

They headed down the beach towards the dark shore line, the noise of their struggling footsteps covered by the waves breaking on the shingle. Looking back Queenie could just make out Serena's figure standing on top of the wall; realising she had been tricked she was peering around trying to locate the sisters.

'Damn, she's figured it out already, we'll have to hurry.'

They struggled along close to the sea, the incoming waves breaking over their feet and filling their shoes. They had just drawn level with the tea shop when Serena furiously scanning the area spotted the two figures down by the water's edge.

'I see you!' she screamed, and jumped off the wall onto the beach. She started running towards them.

Sybil stumbled as the waves sucked the shingle from beneath her feet and she fell to her knees in the water; a large wave crashed over her soaking her and filling her mouth with salt water. She started coughing and spluttering as Queenie tried to pull her to her feet.

'What are we going to do?' she gasped, as Serena pounded down the beach towards them.

A few lights started to appear in the nearby cottages, seeing this Sybil began to shout.

'Help,' she screamed. 'Help us.'

Serena skidded to a halt a few feet away from them, a small hail of pebbles bouncing down the beach in front of her.

'Nobody's going to help you, why should they? You're outsiders.'

Queenie took a few deep breaths trying to keep cool and held out a hand. 'Calm down Serena, there's no need for any violence. We have already called the police,' she lied. 'So it's too late.'

Serena cocked her head on one side and listened for a minute. 'I can't hear any sirens,' she declared, a strange light gleaming in her eyes. 'It will be too late for you anyway, you'll be found floating in the sea. Oh dear, what a tragic accident,' she went on mockingly. Serena grinned viciously and brought up the boat hook level with Queenie's head. 'Who's first?'

'That's not going to happen,' Queenie said firmly. 'Everybody will know you were responsible, and your poor grandmother will be devastated.'

'Who cares,' she said. 'She's weak, she's not a Coppinger. When she's gone I will have everything.'

The boat hook was just inches from Queenie's face, one lunge from Serena and she would be seriously injured. Sybil clutched at her arm and pulled her sister backwards out of reach. They were now knee deep in the water and finding it difficult to keep their balance in the surging waves.

'That's a good idea, go for a swim,' she urged, a mad smile on her face and took one step closer and jabbed the hook into Queenie's chest pushing her deeper into the water.

'Go on,' she urged.

Queenie reached up and jerked the pole to one side. 'No thank you,' she said coldly, and kept a firm grip on it as Serena tried to pull if free from her grasp.

'Let go!' she panted, struggling to pull it out of the old woman's hand. Sybil floundered forward through the waves to grasp the pole as well and for a few minutes there was a mad tussle as the women struggled to wrest it from Serena, they dragged it and the young woman forward into the water.

'Let go of it,' she screamed. 'You evil creatures, you deserve to die.'

'You're mad,' ground out Queenie. 'You should be locked up.' She looked past Serena towards the top of the beach where a few people had gathered. 'Look Serena it's all over, people are coming to help us.'

A lone figure had detached itself from the watching crowd and was hurrying down the beach towards them.

'You fool,' spat Serena. 'That's Joey.'

'Serena,' he gasped, as soon as he was close enough. 'What the hell are you doing?'

The alcohol he had consumed earlier that evening was still racing through his system and making him unsteady on his feet, he lunged forward trying to snatch the pole and missed crashing into her back.

'You're turning on me as well?' she shrieked, and thrust him away with one hand.

Queenie took the opportunity to snatch the pole away from her slackened grip and summoning up the last of her strength hurled it over their heads into the sea.

Howling with rage Serena launched herself at Queenie. With the weight of the young woman and the shifting ground she lost her footing and fell backwards into the water with Serena still on top of her and her hands clutching her throat.

The waves crashed over their bodies; the swell pulled them down to the stony bottom and filled their mouths and eyes with gritty water. Unable to breathe Queenie struggled to push the young woman off and loosen the grip on her throat. The sound of muffled shouting came through the water and strong hands grasped her shoulders pulling her upright and into the air. Sybil had thrust her arms beneath Queenie's armpits holding her out of the water while Joey struggled to detach Serena's choking grip. Starting to see spots in front of her eyes she struggled to draw enough air into her lungs, with each gasp the sounds of the shouting and struggle became more distant as Queenie's heartbeat slowed and her thoughts began to drift. She found herself looking down at her own body lying in the surf. Her limp figure was being cradled by her sister who was desperately trying to keep her head above the water while Joey struggled with Serena. Queenie watched with a strange detachment as other forms started to appear on the beach, ghostly shadowy beings that had arrived to gather and watch the scene unfold. One figure that Queenie instantly recognised stood to one side impassively watching his granddaughter.

Sybil, feeling her sister lying so limp in her arms suddenly let go of Queenie's body and launched herself at the young woman.

'Let go!'

A strange feeling of satisfaction stirred in her breast as Sybil swung a clenched fist and caught Serena a resounding blow on the side of the head. The ferocity of the sudden blow caught her by surprise and she fell back, loosening her grip on the old woman's throat. Queenie drew a deep gasp, fighting for breath and as the fresh sea air filled her lungs she opened her eyes.

She was lying on her back above the water line where Sybil and Joey had dragged her; there was no sign of Serena. Sybil knelt by her side the anxiety apparent in her eyes.

'Are you alright? She put a restraining hand on her sister's shoulder as Queenie still gasping tried to sit up. 'Take it easy,' she warned.

'Where is she?' she asked, wheezing.

'She's gone.'

'You let her go?'

'We were too busy fishing you out of the sea,' scolded Sybil. 'You nearly drowned.'

'I'm fine,' she said weakly, wiping the stinging salt water out of her eyes. 'Help me up.'

'I don't think that's a good idea; you need to take it easy and catch your breath.'

'I'm not going to lie here like a beached whale,' she coughed, bringing up some sea water and held out her hand. 'Now help me up off this beach.'

Joey had collapsed onto the shingle with his head in his hands. Queenie looked at the shocked expression on his face.

'Well?' she wheezed. 'What have you got to say for yourself?'

A look of panic came over his face and he said hurriedly, 'This was nothing to do with me, I had no idea she was going to attack you.'
'Well she did, now what are you going to do about it?' she stuttered, swaying as she spoke. With the combination of the chill wind blowing off the sea, the shock and her wet clothes Queenie began to shiver.
'Never mind that now,' Sybil said bluntly. 'We need dry clothes and a warm drink or you are going to get hypothermia.'
Joey nodded, hopeful of a reprieve 'You're right. She probably needs some medical attention.'
'What a good idea Joey,' Queenie said. 'Perhaps you would like to phone for an ambulance and while you are at it phone the police as well.' She glared at him as he fell silent thinking about the consequences of the call. 'Exactly! Do you really want to explain why I was being throttled by a lunatic in the sea?'
'I think he should call the police. She tried to kill us, Queenie.'
'I know.' She grasped her sisters arm and steadied herself, 'But what you need to do first,' she glared at Joey, 'is to find Serena before she does anything stupid, well,' she paused for breath, 'even more stupid than what she has already tried to do. And we are going to go and dry off and have a very large brandy.'
He watched in amazement as the two doughty old women turned and staggered along the beach towards the guest house then shook his head and stared towards the sea wall where a few of the residents still lingered watching the events unfolding on the beach, none of which had come forward to help. As he walked towards them they melted away and in the few minutes it took to reach the steps the street was deserted. He spat in disgust and headed reluctantly towards the Coppinger's cottage.
The lights had been hurriedly extinguished in the nearby cottages plunging the beach into even greater darkness as the sound of their struggling footsteps echoed off the walls. They drew nearer to the back entrance of the guest house, by the time they had reached the steps Queenie's teeth were chattering and she was shivering violently. Unable to go on any farther she leant against the wall, a foot on the first step and gasped, 'You were right about getting mixed up with smugglers. I should have listened Sybil.'
'It's a bit late now,' she answered, laying a hand on her sister's shoulder. 'We are in it right up to our necks.' She peered through the dim light at Queenie who had her eyes shut. 'Do you want to leave?

'No!' she said sharply, opening her eyes and glaring at her sister. 'I will not give up.'

An icy breeze blew up the passage making her clench her chattering teeth against the cold.

'I won't,' she repeated.

A faint sigh floated around them and they froze as footsteps approached along the shingle beach.

'What now?' muttered Sybil.

Shadowy silent figures approached the steps and began to ascend, brushing past the two women who drew closer together against the wall. The footsteps reverberated against the stones so loudly that they wondered how anybody could ignore them. The cold these beings brought with them passed through Sybil's and Queenie's bodies, seeping through to their very bones and then trailed on following the ghosts up to the street.

'Don't even suggest that we follow them,' Sybil ordered, 'We have had enough for one night.' She took her sisters arm and began helping her up the steps to the door.

'Just for once I am going to agree with you,' Queenie said weakly, struggling to put one foot in front of the other.

They reached the door but found it locked.

'Let's try the front door,' Sybil suggested, putting her arm around Queenie's waist. 'Come on, we're nearly there.'

Stumbling up the last few steps they finally reached the front entrance of the guest house which was in darkness, the street was also pitch black, no lights shone out from any of the cottages or The Anchor. This door was firmly closed as well, no welcoming lights shone in the hallway.

'Shall we knock?' whispered Queenie.

'I have a feeling that they won't answer.' Sybil rattled the door handle in frustration and peered into the hall. 'We need to get out of these wet clothes,' she said angrily, 'and we need a warm drink. We will have to try Jenny; hopefully she will let us in.'

Behind her in the dark, invisible footsteps clattered over the cobbles, endlessly pacing towards the church and back. She peered over her shoulder into the shadows and shivered, the ghostly activity was growing in intensity with every minute.

'We really have stirred things up this time, Queenie.'

Her sister nodded, too tired and cold to answer.

'That's an understatement.'

The unexpected voice made Sybil start, Queenie however just opened one eye and blankly stared at Albert who was peering around the corner of his cottage.

'What do you want?' she asked weakly. 'Come to gloat?'

He grunted and jerked his head. 'You had better come in before you catch your death.'

'Huh! Now you want to help?' Queenie muttered, pushing herself away from the door frame against which she had been half collapsed.

'Suit yourself, I'm just offering you a warm fire and a drink, that's all.'

'And we are very grateful,' Sybil said quickly, pulling her sister out of the doorway. 'She's soaked through.'

'You don't look that dry either,' he grunted, eyeing her up.

'No, I'm not.'

'Well stop talking and come in then.'

He limped back to his front door, one hand steadying himself against the wall. The door stood open, a bright light flooded the small hallway which reeked of tobacco. Albert glanced back to check that the women were following and catching the movement in the shadows frowned.

'Come on, hurry up. Things are busy in the street tonight.'

Queenie asked, gasping with exhaustion as she entered the hallway, 'Does this often happen?'

'Sometimes; at certain times of the year.' He glanced up and down the deserted street. 'As you can see everybody stays in when they are active.' Albert frowned, 'It's not usually as bad as this.' He glared at Queenie who was tottering into his warm front room. 'I guess this is all down to you.'

She sunk down into his recently vacated armchair in front of the fire. 'Yes,' she said simply, 'It's all my fault.'

Albert closed and locked the door then followed the women into his small cluttered room.

'I expect you could do with a drink.'

'Brandy if you have any.' Queenie held out her shivering hands to the warmth of the gas fire. 'Or is that a silly question to ask an old smuggler?'

He grinned slightly, the first expression of warmth and humour that they had seen from him.

'We didn't smuggle brandy. It was just a few packets of cigarettes, that's all. Nothing serious; just Duncan and myself having a lark.'

He poured three tumblers of brandy and hobbled over to the sisters. Holding out a glass to Queenie he asked, 'So, now what are you going to do?'

'Get dry, warm and drunk, not necessarily in that order,' she answered drily.

He pushed a pile of old magazines off the sofa, settled down opposite the sisters and stared at them. Sybil was prising off hers and Queenie's soaked shoes and placing them in front of the fire. Feeling his gaze she looked up, 'They are soaked,' she explained, and gestured to Queenie, 'and we need some dry clothes.'

'I can lend you some pyjamas and blankets,' he frowned, 'You can't go out in the cold again so you had better stay here for the night, in front of the fire.' He took a mouthful of the brandy and coughed slightly over the fiery taste. 'I'll go and find them for you.'

'Are the pyjamas clean?' Sybil asked suspiciously.

Albert didn't bother to answer, he just lifted his eyebrows and stumped out of the room, they could hear his struggling steps on the staircase and within a few minutes he returned with an armful of towels, blankets and the pyjamas.

'Here,' he said brusquely. 'Change into these. I'll go and put the kettle on and give you some privacy.'

They waited until the door closed behind him before they started peeling off their wet clothes; Sybil gave Queenie a vigorous rub with one of the towels to get the blood back into her blue limbs before dressing her in a pair of Albert's striped pyjamas. A pile of wet clothes outside the door met his eyes when Albert returned with three mugs of steaming tea; he knocked cautiously before opening the door. 'Are you decent yet?'

'Yes, it's safe to come in,' she answered.

'Thank goodness,' he muttered, hobbling into the room. 'An old bachelor like me can't cope with having naked women in the house.' Queenie snorted, her face had nearly regained its usual healthy glow and the sparkle had returned to her pale eyes. 'Don't worry Albert you're safe enough.'

Sybil nudged her foot willing her to silence, the last thing she wanted was for Queenie to upset him and get them kicked out into the night.

'So you were never married?' she asked politely.

'No,' he answered shortly. 'Never felt the need.' He stared across the room at Queenie who had wrapped herself in a big blue blanket. 'Women are more trouble than they are worth.'

'How strange,' she replied, 'I always think that about men.'

Albert frowned as he stared at her. 'Why pink?' he asked suddenly.

Queenie took a sip of the strong brew and raised her eyebrows. 'This is my natural colour,' she said earnestly.

'Well it looks rather silly for a woman of your age,' he declared, enjoying the look of outrage on her face,

'And you look like a silly old...'

'Queenie!' interrupted Sybil. 'Please can we concentrate on the problems at hand and stop all this squabbling.'

The pair of them sat looking like naughty schoolchildren, eyeing each other up and waiting for the other to speak first.

'Well,' said Albert, breaking the silence first, 'you have stirred up a storm.'

'She tried to kill us.'

He shrugged. 'She's mad, everybody knows it.'

'And where has she gone?'

Albert shrugged again, unwilling to volunteer any information.

'For goodness sake,' snapped Queenie, struggling to push the blanket off so she could sit up. 'Don't you care?'

'About what?'

She gritted her teeth, staring at the old man in frustration. 'About what's happening in this village or more importantly what has happened.'

'Now that is a can of worms.'

'And why didn't you tell us that Thomas was Duncan's brother? Didn't you think it would be important for us to know?'

'All I could see was two old women poking their noses in,' Albert grinned and continued in amusement. 'You don't know much about human nature do you? This village is like a family, we have arguments and differences but somebody comes in and starts causing trouble then we all stand together. And,' he said, with a slightly satisfied edge to his voice, 'that's what has happened now, nobody will help you.'

'So you think we are on our own then?'

'Yep,' he declared.

'And if we call the police?'

'We will all deny it, after all where is your proof?'

On hearing this Sybil jumped and looked wildly around the room. 'What happened to the bag?'

Albert lifted an eyebrow, looking impassively at the sisters.

'It was a bag of drugs we found on Joeys boat. We must have dropped it in the sea whilst we were struggling with Serena.'

'There you go then,' he said with grim satisfaction, 'as I said no proof. And don't count on anybody backing up your story, all it will take is Bruce from the pub to mention that you had both been drinking... and well,' he held out his hands, 'what are the police going to think?'

'Okay,' said Queenie grimly, 'even if we can't rely on anybody else that is not going to stop us. As far as I am concerned, as long as she keeps out of my way Serena is your problem, all I am interested in is helping Thomas.'

A sad faraway look came over the old man's face at the mention of the young boy. 'Poor lad,' he murmured. 'Why does he still walk I wonder? I guess we will never know.'

'Oh yes we will, I am going to make sure of that.' Queenie sat back in her chair a grim look on her face. 'And if none of you want to know the truth then so be it.'

He cradled the warm mug in his arthritic hands and gazed at her, a slight look of admiration crossing his face. 'You're a tough old bird, aren't you?'

'Yes.'

The trio fell silent, each busy with their own thoughts while outside footsteps could still be heard on the cobbles and a distant shouting echoed up the street making them start. Albert braced himself; years of experience had taught him what was coming next. The sudden shriek made Queenie shudder, recognising that awful sound she was immediately transported back to the night of Thomas's death.

'Again?' she whispered.

'Yes,' Albert affirmed, he cleared his throat and carried on talking trying to keep his mind off what was happening outside. 'It's funny some of the older residents still believe that Absalon kept the evil spirits out of the village and now he's gone the spooks are free to walk the streets. They were great believers in his powers,' he snorted, 'they even believed he could cure their aches and pains.' Albert shook his head in disbelief.

'And could he?'

'I suppose if you believe something hard enough it will.'

'The power of suggestion,' mused Sybil.

'Whatever,' he grunted, 'I have no time for any of that nonsense. I do know however that he was a very clever manipulative man and he knew how to play everybody in the village.' He drained his cup and put it on the floor next to the sofa. 'That's enough talking, it's getting late and I'm off to bed,' he stood stiffly and looked down at the women. 'You'll be alright in front of the fire?' he questioned.

Receiving a nod from Sybil he walked slowly to the door, pausing with his hand on the handle, 'Stay inside tonight,' he warned. 'Tomorrow is another day, plenty of time for you to cause more mayhem.'

The door closed behind him and they listened to his slow footsteps on the staircase.

'Well, what a pickle we are in.' Sybil looked across the fireplace to her sister. 'Are you sure you are alright, after all you had quite a nasty experience.'

Queenie smiled slightly. 'As Albert said I'm a tough old bird.' She raised a hand and gingerly touched the bruising around her neck. 'This is a bit sore though, she had a really strong grip,' she said, trying to joke, but catching sight of the look on Sybil's face added swiftly, 'I'm fine really,'

'I hope so,' her sister answered grimly. 'We will see how you are in the morning and well...we'll see,' she finished lamely.

'I'm well enough to finish this,' Queenie declared, 'so no more discussions now, I think we need to try and get some sleep.'

The morning light coming in through the heavy curtains did nothing for the neglected appearance of Albert's cottage. It highlighted the layer of dust and tobacco ash on every surface and the cobwebs that hung from the ceiling, piles of old magazines and books cluttered every surface and more spilled out from under the furniture.

Sybil's fingers itched as she surveyed the mess. 'Do you think he would mind if I tidied up a bit?'

Her sister yawned and rubbed her neck, feeling rather stiff and sore from the combination of her adventure the night before and the night in Albert's armchair. She blinked sleepily and murmured, 'Probably.'

'But what a mess,' Sybil said despairingly. She caught sight of his mug on the floor and pounced on it. 'At least I can wash up the cups.'

'That would mean going into Albert's kitchen and judging by the state of this room it's not going to be pleasant.'

'I need a cup of tea,' said Sybil, 'and some breakfast so I am going to be brave and risk it.' She smoothed her hair, straightened the borrowed pyjamas and checking all the buttons were done up walked barefoot along the hall. 'Here goes,' she called. 'Wish me luck.'

'Shriek if you need me,' offered Queenie, settling back in the chair and closing her eyes, hoping the dull pain behind her eyes would ease. Her swollen throat which had kept her awake most of the night was by now so sore that she could hardly swallow. A small amount of brandy remained in her glass from the night before and she debated finishing it, reasoning that it might help. She opened one eye to locate the glass and found Albert hovering over her; she gave a start and glared at him.

'What are you doing?' she snapped.

'Morning to you too,' he grinned. 'Just checking to see if you were still breathing.'

'Very funny,' she said dryly. 'It will take more than Serena to finish me off and talking of which Sybil has ventured into your kitchen with the intention of rustling up some breakfast.'

'Has she now? I'm glad you're making yourself at home,' he said, mildly sarcastic, and shuffled off to the chair on the other side of the fireplace. He settled down and leaning forward examined her face carefully, 'So how are you this morning?' he asked, and noting the dangerous sparkle in her eyes he sat back reassured. 'You look very well, considering.'

'Thank you.'

'Is your sister a good cook?'

'Of course.'

They sat quietly glaring at each other, neither of them willing to speak while down the hall in the kitchen Sybil was preoccupied in clattering about in the cupboards; within a few minutes the smell of toast began to drift through the cottage.

'Hmm,' he grunted. 'At least she's not burning it.'

Queenie narrowed her eyes and determined to extract as much information from Albert while she could began, 'Ralph told me that he found some photographs in his attic.'

'That's right.'

'And you have them?'

'Right again.'

'Well,' she said, getting impatient with his ponderous manner, 'where are they?'

'Oh... you would like to have a look? Why didn't you say so?' he grinned, enjoying the look of frustration on her face.

'You are so annoying Albert!'

'I know. Aren't we alike?'

'Yes,' Queenie started chuckling, 'we probably are. That's why we are getting on so well,' she added, tongue in cheek. 'So... the photos?'

'Okay, if you insist.' He awkwardly levered himself out of the comfortable armchair and hobbled towards the cluttered cabinet; after much searching through the drawer, accompanied by inaudible mutterings he eventually pulled out a box overflowing with old black and white photographs. Albert placed the box on Queenie's lap.

'Here you are,' he said. 'They are in there somewhere.'

He settled down in the chair opposite her and watched as Queenie began to examine the photos.

'Who are all these people?' she asked, bewildered.

'Family, friends, anybody who used to live here,' he smiled slightly, 'There's years of history in that box.

Pulling out image after image and piling them onto her lap Queenie scanned each one quickly unable to see the one person she was looking for. The pile began to slide, spilling onto the floor.

'Damn,' she muttered, trying to grab them.

'Don't worry; I'll pick them up later.'

Getting frustrated as she had nearly emptied it Queenie pounced on a brown envelope which was the only thing remaining in the box. 'Ah...' she said hopefully, 'what's this?'

'Those are Ralphs.'

She closed her eyes for a minute in irritation and snapped them open quickly when she heard him chuckling. Biting back the comment that had immediately sprung to her lips Queenie decided to save her energy and began to examine the contents of the envelope instead. Inside were four small faded black and white images. One showed a group of men gathered around a fishing boat pulled up on a beach, which she recognised as Bindon, standing at the back towering over the others was the figure of Absalon frowning into the camera. One which caught her attention and made her pause was the image of a group of children playing in the street, she examined it carefully and although she couldn't be sure one child looked very familiar. Could that be Thomas? she wondered. The remaining images were of a portrait of a young woman; and a wedding group, again the image of Absalon loomed large in the background.

'Who is the woman?' she inquired, holding up the photograph.

'Don't you recognise her?' he carried on, in response to her raised eyebrows. 'It's Daisy, Mrs Coppinger.'

'Oh,' she said, then held up the street scene, 'and is this Thomas?'

Albert reached over and took it out of her hands, he sighed, 'That's the pair of them,' he said, 'Thomas and Duncan.'

'Has he seen this picture?'

'No.'

'Why not?'

'Why do you ask so many questions?'

The appearance of Sybil pushing her way through the front door carrying their bags prevented Queenie from giving Albert a pithy answer. Her sister's face was flushed with anger and she slammed the door with unnecessary force making the glass in the window frames rattle. An old jacket of Albert's was slung around her shoulders and she had pushed her feet into a pair of ancient black wellingtons.

'Can you believe it,' she began, incensed, 'they put our bags out on the front step! I was so angry I hammered on the door but they didn't even have the courage to come to the door. What a nerve!' She drew a few deep breaths trying to calm down. 'At least we have some dry clothes now.'

'The bags were outside?' queried Queenie in amazement. 'What were they thinking?'

Albert snorted. 'They must have heard what happened and decided to ditch you.'

'Or did somebody tell them to?'

'Maybe.' He looked at Sybil, a slight expression of sympathy on his craggy face. 'Don't let it worry you, at least now you have your belongings.'

'I suppose so,' she replied moodily, her face suddenly brightened. 'Don't we owe them for another night Queenie?'

Her sister nodded. 'They're not getting it though,' she croaked. 'Just let them dare ask!'

Chapter Eleven

There was an ominous atmosphere in the village as they left Albert's cottage, the street which had been busy with holidaymakers in the preceding days was deserted. The cottage doors were all closed and the curtains pulled tight across the windows, no visible signs of life anywhere. But still as the two women walked slowly towards Jenny's tea shop they had the uncomfortable feeling of being watched.

'This is very strange,' muttered Sybil, into her sister's ear. 'Where is everybody?'

'This reminds me of those old westerns we used to go and see at The Odeon. The lone gunmen walking down the street for a shootout at the corral.'

'Well, I will be John Wayne and you can be Eli Wallach.'

'No way, I'll be James Stewart.'

'Did he have any gunfights?'

'Gary Cooper then.'

'Gary Cooper didn't have pink hair.'

'He might have; the films were black and white so it wouldn't have shown up.'

'I doubt it, it wouldn't have done his image any good.'

This random conversation was one of many they indulged in and at this present time it had the added bonus of keeping their minds off the strange situation in which they had found themselves, it kept them occupied all the way down the street until they reached the cafe. Like all the other buildings in Bindon it was shut, the blinds pulled down and no sign of Jenny inside.

Sybil tapped on the glass; exchanging glances with Queenie as they waited quietly to see if Jenny would be joining the rest of the inhabitants in ostracising them.

'Well,' said Queenie, 'it looks like we will be sleeping in the car.'

'Perhaps it's time to go home.'

'No,' she said firmly, and with a mounting irritation rapped sharply on the glass door.

At the back of the cafe a light appeared in the dark interior and they could just make out Jenny hurrying towards the door. Her face brightened when she recognised the sisters.

'There you are,' she gasped. 'I have been so worried. Where have you been?' Barely giving them time to answer she pulled them quickly inside the cafe and shut the door.

'Jenny, is it alright for us to come in? Sybil asked quietly, 'we don't want to cause problems for you.'

She shook her head and took the bags from Sybil's hands. 'Bother him,' she said sharply. 'Nobody tells me what to do. I have been on the lookout as I thought you might come last night but Bruce said you had gone and then when I saw the car was still here I knew something must have happened.' Pausing for breath she pulled out a couple of chairs so they could sit down. 'Where have you been?' she asked curiously.

'We spent the night at Albert's.'

Jenny's mouth dropped open in amazement. 'Albert's? Are you serious?' She started laughing in disbelief. 'That old goat took you in... well I never!'

'We spent the night in front of the fire so we were warm enough. He even lent us some pyjamas,' grinned Sybil. 'Not quite my colour but we managed.'

'You poor things, have you had any breakfast?'

'Just toast, Albert's kitchen was a bit low on provisions.'

Jenny picked up their bags and started walking towards the kitchen. 'I'll show you to your room and while you're getting settled in I will make you some breakfast. How does that sound?'

'That is the best thing I have heard for ages,' wheezed Queenie, following Jenny through the door.

Although the room was very small, it was brightly decorated with old fashioned chintz wallpaper and matching bedspreads. A small posy of pinks had been placed on the dressing table; their spicy scent filled the room which added to the homely feeling. After spending the previous night in an armchair the beds looked very comfortable and inviting. Queenie headed for the nearest, stretched out and sighed. 'This feels so good,' she muttered sleepily, and within a second her eyelids had drooped and she was asleep.

Sybil grinned as Queenie's mouth dropped open and she began to snore. Sybil, not wanting to disturb her sister, decided to leave the unpacking until later and crept out of the bedroom and down the narrow cottage stairs to the kitchen to warn Jenny that only one breakfast was required. Queenie would have to have hers later when she woke which by the look of her would be a lot later.

She pushed open the door and walked into the small kitchen which unlike the cafe was spotless.

'How do you like your eggs, fried or scrambled?' Jenny enquired, her head in the fridge.

'Scrambled please.'

'And how about Queenie?' she asked, standing up and surveying Sybil.

'She will have to eat later; she lay down on the bed and went out like a light.'

Jenny nodded. 'She was looking very tired so a sleep will do her good.' She began beating the eggs and without raising her eyes from her task asked quietly, 'So what happened last night? Bruce told me that you both had got drunk and attacked Serena.' She whisked vigorously for a minute before adding, 'Not that I believed him.'

'Why is Bruce spreading tales like that? Is he friends with Serena? Oh...' said Sybil, 'of course, he's friends with Joey. I wonder,' she thought quickly, 'does he do business with Joey?'

Jenny gave her a strange sideways glance as she poured the eggs into a saucepan.

'Some,' she answered evasively.

'I suppose then it's in his interest to discredit us.' Receiving no response to this she watched her curiously as Jenny buttered the toast. 'I hope we are not putting you to too much trouble,' she asked politely.

'Not at all. It will give me something to do as it's going to be quiet today,' Jenny hesitated and looked uncomfortable as she informed Sybil, 'Bruce has closed the village.'

'How can he close the village?' Sybil asked, looking puzzled. She sat down at the table and pulled the teapot towards her. 'What about the visitors?'

'One road in and out,' she explained, 'it's easy enough, he's put a barrier across at the top of the lane just saying that the road is closed. That will stop any traffic.'

'And why?'

'As you guessed he does business, shall we call it,' she said scathingly, 'with Joey and I think his 'business' has gone missing. So he wants to find it. And Joey is missing as well so Bruce is livid.'

'All this time Serena had another partner as well as Joey, how could we have missed that!'

'Joey is just a pawn.'

'And Serena, where is she?'

'Gone.'

'Why do you all put up with this?'

'Because we have to live here.' she said defensively, and placed the plate of scrambled eggs in front of Sybil. 'Here you are.'

'Thank you,' and not wanting to provoke Jenny she changed the subject. 'I must admit to being rather hungry; we didn't eat much at Albert's as the bread was rather stale and I think I even detected a bit of mould on it.'

The worried look left Jenny's face. 'I'm always surprised he survives. Having seen the state of his kitchen I think he must have a cast iron stomach.'

'Well, he said Queenie was a tough old bird but I think he must pretty tough as well.'

'He said that? Albert must like her.'

'I doubt it; they seem to be at each other's throat every time they meet.'

'Sounds like true love,' Jenny chuckled. 'More toast?'

It was several hours before Queenie woke, she would have slept longer but the sun was high in the sky and pouring in through the small window directly onto her face. She opened one eye and blinked.

'What day is it?'

'Still today,' Sybil answered quietly, she was reading one of Jenny's magazines near the window and looking up from an article about decoupage she was encouraged to see that Queenie looked much improved by her nap. 'Feeling better?'

'Much,' she sat up and ran a careful hand over the bruising on her neck. 'This isn't so painful now.' She blinked and yawned, 'Has Jenny made breakfast yet?'

'You missed it.' Sybil chuckled at the look of horror on her sister's face. 'Don't worry; she is going to make you some lunch when you get up.'

'Lunch?'

'Yes, lunch. It's past one 'o'clock.'

'Why didn't you wake me?'

'You needed the sleep.'

'But we have things to do, Sybil.'

'I know but not if you're feeling exhausted. You'll need your strength if you want to continue with this.'

'I'm fine,' Queenie said, feeling a bit irritable, 'Do you know the more people want me to stop, the more I am determined to persevere.' As if to illustrate the point, she swung her legs off the bed and stood up.

'Mother always said you were stubborn.'

'Determined, Sybil.'

'No, stubborn. But I do have to fill you in on a few things before we go downstairs; it looks like Bruce from The Anchor is a silent partner of Serena's, who by the way is still missing. And so is Joey. And I found out why the village is deserted, it's because Bruce has closed it so he has enough time to find the drugs, which by the way he's convinced that we still have.'

Queenies mouth dropped open in surprise. 'You have been busy.'

'All this came from Jenny over breakfast.'

'So...' she said thoughtfully, 'things are not as simple as we thought.'

'You thought it was simple?' Sybil said, 'simple?' she repeated, shaking her head. 'Let's get some lunch. If I can't persuade you to be sensible and go home you're going to need all the energy you can get.'

A table was already set for lunch, a bright spotlessly clean, Sybil noted with relief, red and white checked table cloth was spread out covered in Jenny's best china. Plates of buttered bread, cheeses, ham and salad waited for Queenie. She sighed in satisfaction when she saw the spread and headed without a word for the nearest chair.

Jenny appeared in the kitchen door carrying a tea pot. 'There you are, how are you feeling now?' she asked, looking at the bright colour in Queenie's cheeks.

'Fine,' she replied casually, reaching for the plate of meat. 'This looks delicious Jenny.'

'Well help yourself to whatever you want.' She poured the tea for the sisters and sat down at the table with them, cupping her chin in her hand she surveyed her battle worn guests. 'So what are you going to do now?' she enquired.

'Well,' began Queenie cautiously, after the events of the past few hours she was reluctant to confide in anybody, 'We're just going to ask a few more questions and see if we can find Joey. I hope he's okay, after all he did help us last night.'

'If I know Joey, he's fine. He's probably holed up somewhere, he will turn up again like a bad penny when things have calmed down and gone back to normal.'

'Back to normal? What's normal for this village?'

Chapter Twelve

'You were very reticent with Jenny earlier,' noted Sybil. 'Don't you trust her?'

Making sure the bedroom door was shut Queenie whispered, 'I'm not sure I can trust anybody here, not after last night.' She shrugged, looking a bit defensive. 'Well, do you?'

Her sister frowned as she buttoned her coat and said slowly, 'I think you're right to be cautious but let's not antagonise Jenny as well. We need at least one friend here.' She looked in concern at Queenie as she struggled with the zip on her fleece. 'Let me help you with that.'

The exertion was making her wheeze and two bright red spots had appeared on her cheeks.

'You don't look well Queenie, sensible counsel would suggest that we postpone this trek up the lane until you're feeling better.' Receiving a vehement shake of the head Sybil sighed, 'I didn't think you would listen but I felt duty bound to say it.'

Spread out on the bed was all of Queenie's little toys as she called them and she started rummaging amongst the packages selecting a few to put in her pocket.

'You're not taking all of that, are you?' Sybil asked in disbelief.

'No, not all of it. I just wanted to check nothing was damaged. But I am going to take this with me.' She popped a large black tourmaline crystal in with the bundle of sage and agrimony, then as an afterthought slung a rosary around her neck. 'There, that should do it.' She handed Sybil the torch, 'We will need this for the cave,' and stood for a few minutes mentally reviewing all of the items then said finally, 'I think we're ready.'

They let themselves out of the cafe while Jenny was hard at work baking in the kitchen and began the walk along the deserted street to the church. A few curtains twitched as they passed but none of the residents appeared. The sisters walked in silence until they reached the steep lane.

'At least this time we will be able to walk up there without Serena following us.'

Sybil stared at the rough path and then looked at her sister who was already gasping from the short walk from the cafe.

'Why don't you stay here and let me go?' she suggested, but realised her mistake when a fierce spark appeared in Queenie's eyes.

'If you think I am going to let you go on your own you must be mad,' she declared, and without another word began walking up the hill.

They were both breathless by the time they reached the seat in the wall. Sybil squeezed in next to her sister on the worn stone.

'I'm sure that lane is getting steeper,' panted Sybil, leaning back against the stones. Receiving no answer she opened her eyes to check that Queenie was alright but she needn't have worried. She was leaning forward and peering down the hill.

'It looks like we have company,' she grunted.

Sybil jerked upright and following her sister's gaze peered at the figure toiling up the stony track.

'Who is that?' The figure raised his head and she suddenly recognised him. 'He's following us! He must still think we have the bag of amphetamines.' She plucked nervously at Queenie's sleeve. 'We need to hide.' Sybil looked wildly around but seeing nothing but the trees for shelter was at a loss. 'What shall we do?'

'Stay calm, that's what we'll do.' Queenie rose and led the way through the gate into the trees. 'Come on,' she gasped, the sudden exertion making her cough.

The sound echoed around the hill and down the track, Bruce raised his head and looked searchingly towards the tree lined hillside. Sybil was close on her sisters heels as she struggled farther up the path, they pushed deeper into the bramble undergrowth following the path they had discovered earlier in their stay. Pausing to catch her breath Queenie leant against the trunk of a pine and gazed behind them.

'He's still coming but I don't think he can see us. If we keep quiet we might be okay.'

'Just don't cough,' Sybil whispered.

Below them Bruce had reached the point where the path divided, he paused trying to decide which path the women would have followed. Decision made, he plunged along the path to the left which led to Mupe Bay.

'Damn,' Queenie grumbled. 'Why did he have to choose that way? I don't want to run into him at the cave.'

'He might not know about the cave.'

'I have no doubt that all the residents of this village know about it, but we are not going to be able to find out much if Bruce is skulking about.' From their vantage point on the hillside they watched in silence as Bruce disappeared from view along the narrow path.

Beneath the trees where they stood quietly waiting, the shadows began to grow engulfing the women in darkness, all insect sound faded from the undergrowth and the birds, one by one slowly fell silent. The women froze in the oppressive atmosphere and as one turned slowly. Standing just feet away in the deep shadow cast by a large pine was Absalon.

Sybil drew in a jerky breath and shuddered at the bleak expression on his face.

His gaze travelled slowly from one to the other; lingering on Queenie's pale and bruised face. Satisfied that he had the sister's attention he turned and moved off into the woods.

'Shall we follow him?'

'No!' said Sybil, shrinking from any further contact with the menacing figure.

But feeling that the women were not following he halted and turned, gesturing slightly to encourage them forward.

'Look,' Queenie whispered. 'He wants us to follow.'

Grasping Queenies arm Sybil tried to restrain her sister. 'It's a trap,' she warned, 'or maybe he is trying to distract us.'

Watching from a distance he smiled mockingly recognising the women's reluctance, but never one to resist a challenge Queenie pushed off her sisters restraining hand and stepped forward, following the path that Absalon took.

'He's laughing at us, the devil,' she growled, and marched forward pushing her way through the dense growth of nettles and brambles oblivious to the stings and thorns. Reluctantly Sybil struggled after her. 'Wait,' she pleaded. 'Just slow down Queenie!'

However quickly they tried to follow Absalon always remained just out of reach on the narrow trail that followed the line of old wall. He paused on reaching the spot where he had disappeared previously, where the wall had collapsed into a pile of stones. The air was chill beneath the trees, very little light seeped through the canopy but Sybil could see quite clearly the unsettling gleam in his eye as he watched them struggling towards him.

Queenie halted, swaying and exhausted just feet from him and glared at his impassive expression.

'Well?' she growled.

His lip curled and with one last unfathomable look the figure of Absalon began to slowly fade away.

'What!' she squealed. 'Oh, for goodness sake.' Feeling suddenly faint she hobbled forward to perch on the ruined wall. 'What was all that about?' she asked her sister weakly. 'Dragging us through this wood for what?' She shifted, uncomfortable on the sharp stones and as she did so the pile moved beneath her.

'Careful Queenie.'

'It's fine, stop fussing. This pile of stones has been here for years and my weight isn't suddenly going to make it collapse.'

Another stone slid down taking with it a small avalanche of soil. Sybil quickly pulled her up.

'Get off Queenie, the whole thing is really unstable and you don't want any more injuries.'

They hopped quickly out of the way as another shower of stones slid down, the larger stones bouncing off into the nettles close to where they stood. Underneath the old wall and now exposed was a mound of earth, hard packed after years of weight from the stones. This too began to move, large slabs of compacted earth rose as though pushed from beneath and slid down and into the undergrowth, followed by more dirt and a shower of smaller stones. The soil beneath the hard packed crust was much looser and sticking out from the earth were a few shreds of tattered cloth.

'What's that?' Queenie croaked. 'I wonder...' she nudged her sister. 'Go on Sybil, have a look.'

Looking less than enthusiastic at the suggestion she took a step closer and peered at the remnants of cloth.

'I don't see why I have to do this,' she complained. 'You're supposed to be the expert.'

'I'm delegating because I don't feel well,' Queenie said pathetically. 'So get on with it and let's find out what is under all that earth.'

Picking up a fallen branch Sybil began to scrape away the soil around the material exposing what lay beneath. Hearing the sudden intake of breath Queenie hurried to her side. They stared down at the greying bones and the shreds of tattered clothes that still clung to its owner.

'I suppose there is no doubt that it's a body,' Sybil said quietly, looking for confirmation from her sister who nodded.

Sybil suddenly jerked back as more soil slid down, this time exposing the remains of a skeletal hand poking from the earth, the bony fingers reaching out to the two old women as if in supplication. A heavy gold ring adorned one of the digits; as the supporting soil slid from the hand the bones collapsed upon themselves and the ring slid off and rolled down towards them ending in a patch of nettles.

'So this is where he ended up,' Queenie said, and kicked a clod of earth back over the exposed bones. 'And as far as I am concerned he can stay here.'

'But we should inform somebody that we have found a body.'

'Why? ' Queenie grunted. 'I bet the residents of this village already know he is here.'

'Do you think it was revenge, perhaps?'

'Could you blame Thomas's father for that?'

'No,' said Sybil slowly, 'But it's our duty to inform the authorities.'

'Oh, tish!' Queenie said in disgust. 'Let sleeping bodies lie, that's what I say. And if Absalon isn't happy because he is buried up here instead of the churchyard then too bad!'

She turned her back on the mound of earth and its occupant and began to retrace her steps along the path, she paused realising that Sybil was not with her. She had stayed looking down at the fragments of bones with a worried expression.

'We can't leave it like this Queenie, it needs covering. A hiker might find it or a child. That would be awful.' Without waiting for an answer or any help Sybil bent to pick up one of the fallen stones.

'You'll hurt your back, you silly woman.'

'Come and help then.' She peered at her sister who was waiting impatiently in the shade of a tree. 'I'm not leaving until it's done,' she warned.

After a few minutes of watching her sister struggling to move the heavy stones Queenie reluctantly came forward to help and with both of them working they managed to replace enough of the soil and wall to conceal the grave.

'That's better,' Sybil said in relief.

'We should have put a stake through his heart.'

'Shush Queenie, let him rest in peace.'

'But he's not, is he? And that's the problem.' Queenie straightened her back and winced. 'Can we go now? We are wasting time.'

Sybil hesitated, then bending quickly retrieved the ring from the undergrowth and poked it back into the loose soil covering the body.

'There,' she said finally. 'Now we can go.'

Overhead the sun reappeared from behind a dark storm cloud and flooded the clearing with dappled light, and as they walked slowly away from the hidden grave birdsong once again filled the glade. But unseen by the women and standing in the deepest shadows where the sunlight could not penetrate a silent figure watched them go.

Approaching the point where all the paths joined at the top of the lane Queenie hesitated.

'I wonder where Bruce is?' she whispered. She crept forward and peered down through the trees to the village. 'There's somebody at the bottom of the lane,' she said, gesturing to her sister to take a look. 'Is that him?'

'Maybe, I can't be sure from here.'

'If he stays down there and doesn't bother us that will be fine.'

Keeping a wary eye on the figure below they walked quietly down the left hand path; the damp grass had already been beaten down by Bruce's hurrying footsteps. One side of the narrow path was covered in tangled undergrowth, on the other it was a steep drop to the beach. Small scrubby plants clung to the side of the cliff and in some places the path had disappeared, sliding down onto the rocks below. Queenie led the way scrambling carefully around these places, the soil still dribbling over the edge warning of imminent landslides. Roosting birds flew up from under their feet and small rabbits popped up in front of them then ran for cover in precariously dug burrows.

They were now out of sight of the village and had drawn level with the old iron cross fixed on the outcrop of rock; the tide had risen and the waves were crashing over its rusty foundations. Just past this was the start of a path descending to the beach, it scrambled down through the rocks of the cliff and in some places crude steps had been roughly chiselled out of the stone.

Queenie halted and stared down in consternation, below she could just see a small rocky cove.

'Is this the only way down?' Sybil moved to her side and cautiously peered over the edge.

'It looks like it.' Disliking heights Queenie wavered, indecision written on her face. 'Oh dear.'

'This looks very precarious,' muttered Sybil, moving closer to the beginning of the path, she leant out inspecting the route down.

Queenie, her heart suddenly thumping, grabbed her arm and dragged her away from the edge.

'What are you doing? You could fall,' her voice suddenly shrill.

'It's not as bad as it looks,' Sybil said encouragingly. 'I can see where somebody has been using it recently.' She looked at Queenie's pale face and grinned. 'You wanted to do this, remember? It's not that steep,' she added, trying to coax her sister.

She sniffed, 'I didn't realise I would have to go rock climbing.' Then watched in horror as Sybil began the descent. 'Be careful!' a note of hysteria entering her voice as she watched her sister disappear from view.

Sybil's voice suddenly echoed back up the cliff. 'Come on Queenie, it's okay. Really, it's easy peasy.'

Gritting her teeth Queenie edged closer and peered over, just below was Sybil slowly working her way down through the rocks, a hand on either side to steady her descent. She paused and looked over her shoulder grinning. 'This is fun.'

'You're mad Sybil!' she said in disgust, and took one tentative step down, clutching desperately at the woody roots of the heather growing from the cliff as the loose soil dislodged by her feet spilled down onto Sybil.

'Are you okay up there?'

'Fine, just fine,' Queenie replied testily. 'Loving every minute of it.'
With every step more soil showered down the precarious path.

Sybil had already reached the small beach and was watching in trepidation as Queenie inched her way down the cliff face.

'You're doing really well,' she called encouragingly.

'Shut up Sybil.' She paused for breath and lifting her gaze looked around to see how far she had come. Everything started swimming before her eyes and she groaned. Leaning back against the rocks she quickly closed her eyes and waited for the world to stop spinning.

'Oh dear,' Queenie muttered to herself, 'you do get yourself into some pickles.'

Hearing Sybil calling from the beach she opened her eyes and quickly fixed her gaze on the path and taking a few deep breaths began the descent again. Placing one foot slowly in front of the other she managed at a snail's pace to finally reach the beach. Wiping the perspiration from her face she glared at Sybil and said firmly, 'I am not doing that again!'
Foregoing the pleasure of pointing out that she would have no choice as it was the only way off the beach, Sybil simply smiled and pointed over her shoulder.

'There's the cave.'

Turning slowly Queenie gazed at the opening in the cliff face. A small sandy beach sloped up to the dark entrance.

'Shall we?' said Sybil, slipping an arm through her sister's. Surprised to see the reluctant expression on Queenie's face, she asked in concern, 'Are you alright?'

'I'm scared.'

Sybil looked shocked. 'You? You're not scared of anything.'

'Well I am this time. I am scared of what we will find in there,' Queenie shook her head and carried on resolutely, 'but we can't stand here all day so I suppose we had better go in. But,' she said, firmly grasping Sybil's arm, 'stay close. I have a bad feeling about this.'

Arm in arm they approached the mouth of the cave and paused just inside while Sybil pulled the torch from her pocket and turned it on. The air was chill and damp; water was seeping down from the cliffs above staining the walls of the cave with bright red and orange mineral deposits but as they ventured farther inside the first thing they noticed was the smell.

It was so bad they began to gag.

'What is that stink?' gasped Sybil, her voice muffled from the sleeve she had pressed over her nose and mouth. She panned the torch quickly over the rocks littering the floor of the cave. In the middle was the remains of a fire pit, a few charred lumps of wood still lay in the ashes. Sybil trod over to it and in the torchlight peered at the cinders.

'Somebody has been here recently,' she said, her voice still muffled. Behind her Queenie who was remaining close to her sister stiffened. Reaching forward she redirected the hand holding the torch to the wall of the cave. They had found the origin of the smell. Silently they gazed at the gruesome sight. Hanging on the wall of the cave were half a dozen crudely made crucifixes but this wasn't what made the sisters pause.

On each cross spread eagled and nailed were the decomposing remains of a cat, their dead glassy eyes reflecting back the light from the torch. Queenie and Sybil stood and gazed in horrified silence at the dreadful sight, now realising the significance of Janet's missing cat.

'So this is what happened to Bobby.'

'Poor cats. Why would anybody do this?' Sybil said, tears welling in her eyes. 'Poor little things.'

Queenie shook her head in disgust and took the torch from Sybil, pointed it at the fire and began raking about in the ashes. She grunted, under her foot was a charred jawbone.

'So she has been trying to raise the spirits of the dead; her grandfather I suppose,' she sighed. 'Stupid woman just doesn't have a clue, does she?'

Sybil bent and picked up the small bone. 'Poor little puss. I wonder if this was Bobby?'

She froze as a pebble clattered in the farthest corner of the cave.

Queenie quickly pointed the light into the shadows, and was not surprised when it picked out Serena crouching in the shadows.

'There you are,' she said calmly. 'We were wondering where you were hiding.'

Serena stood up slowly blinking against the bright light.

'I am not hiding. This is my cave and you have no right to be here. You're trespassing and interrupting my work.'

The women turned to stare at the sorry specimens fixed to the cave wall.

'This is work?' Sybil said angrily. 'What's wrong with you!'

'It was necessary. I needed sacrifices for Absalon to return.'

Stirring the ashes with her foot Queenie smiled grimly. 'And you thought this would work? That an ignorant nobody like you could summon spirits and bind them? You have no idea of what you're doing,' she said scathingly.

Serena stepped forward into the circle of light. 'I will summon him; Absalon will return and the Coppingers will control everything as they should.'

'Those days are gone Serena,' said Sybil.

'I have power,' she said firmly. 'He will come to me.'

'He's already here,' Queenie said sharply, 'and not because of your antics.'

The young woman stumbled across the rough floor of the cave towards the sisters, a triumphant smile on her face.

'Then I was successful, he has answered my summons.'

Queenie shook her head and kicked the ashes. 'Not by doing this,' she said angrily, 'meddling like this when you don't know what you are doing, anything could happen.'

Serena came to a stop, just feet from the angry women; placing her hands on her hips she sneered, 'You know nothing old woman.'

'Really?' Queenie said in a dangerous voice. 'I do know the ritual for summoning and it doesn't need the slaughter of innocent animals. We have already seen him and it wasn't the result of your efforts.'

'No,' said Serena, scornfully, 'he wouldn't reveal himself to you. Not to you!' she spat, 'You are evil; he protected the village against creatures like you.'

'It was a trick, you fool,' she answered derisively. 'He pulled the wool over everybody's eyes so that he could land his cargo in secrecy. You didn't know your grandfather at all, did you?'

Flinching at the contemptuous tone in Queenie's voice Serena clenched her fists and raised them in front of her and began trembling with fury. Expecting an attack at any minute Sybil moved closer to her sister.

'I did know him,' she shrieked. 'He would have seen you for what you are and driven you out. Devil worshipers!' She leant towards them, glaring at the elderly women. 'You should die!' she screamed, her voice echoing around the cave

'Devil worshipers. Us?' Queenie said furiously. She jabbed her thumb angrily into her chest to illustrate the point, 'Let me tell you Serena, the Devil worships me! And don't you forget it! I can do things to you that would make you weep blood,' she growled.

By this time Queenie's rage was so incandescent that the very air in the cave began to vibrate, thrumming in their ears while behind her the charred fragments of wood in the fire pit suddenly burst into flames sending up a shower of sparks. She held out a hand and pulling out a penknife from her fleece pocket laid the blade against her wrist and grimly looked Serena in the eye.

'Just one drop of my blood is all that is needed to summon a spirit. Perhaps Absalon will come, perhaps not. I might just open the gates to Hell and unleash the Devil's Hounds,' she paused, a chill smile playing on her lips. 'I could summon a demon and it would do my bidding and rip you to shreds and you, Serena, would cease to be a nuisance to me.'

Queenie leaned towards Serena who had recoiled from her and had retreated in alarm to the rear wall of the cave.

'Do you understand what I am saying? I could destroy you Serena and it would be so easy.'

The light surrounding Queenie began to ripple and flicker while the flames flared up, higher and higher until they were licking the roof of the cave. At the heart of the fire a dark spot began to grow and expand until all the flames were burning black. Dark shadows flowed towards the old woman and wrapped around her like a cloak; strange lights flickered over her face and the darkness was reflected in Queenie's eyes, transforming her into a thing of nightmares.

The knife was lowered over the paper thin skin of her wrist.

'One drop,' she repeated grimly.

Serena's eyes grew wide with fear as great black wings expanded out of the shadows that had become part of Queenie and trembled in dreadful anticipation. With a hiss the wings began to reach for her. Serena cowered back, her hands frantically scrabbling at the rough rocks behind her as the blackness threatened to engulf her.

'Queenie.'

'Well Serena?' she asked, with a dreadful menace in her voice. 'It's your move. Shall I open the gates?'

'Queenie!' Sybil thundered.

'What?' she snapped, turning to her sister.

'Stop!' she said firmly. 'You need to calm down.'

With Queenies attention taken from Serena the shadows retreated slightly from the terrified young woman and seizing her opportunity she rushed towards the entrance. She staggered, arms flailing and crying with terror down the beach and splashed through the rising tide to the path.

'Damn!' Queenie said furiously. 'She's getting away and it's all your fault! Sybil, you... You're... You're such a party pooper!'

'Stop it!' Sybil ordered. 'You're getting out of control.' She gestured to the roaring inferno in the middle of the cave. 'And get rid of that. Now!'

Sybil glared at her, furious that Queenie had allowed her anger to overcome her common sense, knowing from past experience how dangerous that could be. They scowled at each other for a minute until Queenie's face suddenly cleared and she grinned.

'But I was having fun,' she said plaintively.

Her sister was relieved to see that the black look had been replaced by Queenie's usual mischievous twinkle. The enveloping shadows reluctantly slid away from her body as she regained control and dissipated into the farthest corners of the cave, and the flames behind them slowly subsided into a few smouldering embers leaving just a smog of black smoke hanging above their heads.

'That wasn't fun Queenie; you were getting nasty, which didn't help us at all. You have driven Serena off and we are back at square one.'

'No we're not,' answered Queenie indignantly. She gestured around the cave. 'We found this.'

'Half a dozen dead cats; very useful,' Sybil grunted in disgust, she frowned, still angry with her sisters behaviour. 'Now what are we going to do?'

Queenie shrugged and coughed suddenly, 'Can we discuss this outside? I need to get away from the smell,' and holding a hand over her face she tottered to the entrance.

'Don't think I'm letting you off that easily, Queenie Beresford!' warned Sybil, following her outside.

In comparison to the cave the air was warm and fresh. Queenie drew a few deep breaths, blinking in the sun and waited for Sybil to join her. Hearing an exclamation of dismay she swung round quickly and saw Sybil staring out into the cove. Sybil had seen what she had not; the tide was rising quickly and had already covered the bottom edge of the cliff path cutting off their only route out of the cove. The waves were rolling up the gently sloping beach and were already at their feet as they stood just outside the cave.

'How are we going to get out?' Queenie said in alarm.

'We're not.'

'But we'll drown.' Queenie staggered back as a wave broke over her feet.

Sybil caught her arm as she slipped on the shingle and said, trying to keep calm, 'We'll just have to wait it out in the cave.'

They stumbled back a few paces as the incoming waves raced up the beach forcing them to retreat.

'What if the cave floods? We're trapped Sybil!' She looked around wildly, scouring the cliff for a way out of their predicament. 'There must be another way out,' and stepped a few paces into the swirling water to peer up at the cliff top. 'Hey!' she suddenly shouted, waving her arms over her head. 'Hey! Help. We're stuck down here!'

Way above them somebody was peering over the cliff edge.

She waved again, desperate to get their attention. 'Hey! We're trapped!' Sybil struggled through the waves to her side and looked up; shading her eyes she peered at the figure looking down at them.

'It's Duncan.'

'Hey, Duncan! Down here,' shouted Queenie. 'We're trapped.'

He stared down at the two tiny figures on the beach below and without a sign or acknowledgement stepped back disappearing from their view.

'What!' squealed Queenie. 'The old devil... He's left!'

'I'm sure he's gone for help,' soothed Sybil.

'We will have drowned by the time anybody gets here.'

'No we won't!' said Sybil firmly. 'We'll just have to wait for the tide to go out.'

The swirling waves were making it difficult to keep their balance on the shifting sands so they hurriedly waded back to the entrance of the cave.

'What a choice,' groaned Queenie, 'we either drown or we get stunk to death.'

'We are not going to drown,' said Sybil impatiently. She pointed to the irregular line of flotsam that lay before them. 'The sea only comes up to there so we will be safe enough inside.'

'What if it's a really high tide?'

'What if I just throw you in and hold your head under the water, you annoying old woman,' she replied, losing patience.

'Okay,' said Queenie, looking startled. 'Now who needs to calm down?'

'I am doing my best to stay calm but you're not helping!' Sybil turned away from her and squelched back into the cave, once inside she hesitated for a while before hurriedly walking back to stand silently by her sister.

'Bit pongy in there, is it?'

'Very.'

They stood silently surveying the cove and the rising water.

'So, how long is this going to take?' Queenie asked mildly, after a few minutes.

'What?'

'For the water to go down.'

'It usually takes about twelve hours for the tide to come up and go out again but it was already on the way in, so,' Sybil thought for a minute, 'maybe about six hours for it to turn.'

'How long?' she exclaimed in dismay, 'We are going to be stuck in that horrible damp cave for hours. Huh,' she grumbled, 'if I had known I would have brought some sandwiches.'

Sybil pulled a face. 'We should have checked the tide times before we set out but I just didn't think about it. Oh well,' she sighed, 'nothing we can do about it now.'

A sharp wind blew off the sea swirling into the cove and bringing the smell of rain; the white horses topping the waves rose and swirled higher up the beach towards them. A few drops began to fall.

'That is all we need.'

The few drops became heavier, blowing into the entrance and forcing the sisters farther back into the dark interior.

Holding their hands over their noses they peered with watering eyes at Serena's handy work.

'Could we put the remains outside?' suggested Queenie.
'The tide will carry them off and wash them up on the next beach and some poor little kiddie making sandcastles will have a dreadful fright.'
'Burn them?'
'Be sensible Queenie, that will make the smell worse.'
She sniffed. 'Just trying to be helpful.'
Feeling chilled Sybil stared towards the fire pit where a few embers were still glowing in the darkness.
'We might as well be warm,' she said, in a muffled voice and turning on the torch peered about the floor of the cave for driftwood.
They were in luck, tucked up against the back wall was Serena's store of firewood. She pounced on it and dragged it back to the fire. Feeding the embers with slivers of wood she carefully coaxed the fire back to life. The flames began to lick at the driftwood sending up showers of blue and gold sparks as it caught and began to burn.
Sybil held out her cold wet hands to the blaze and sighed, 'That's better, come and sit by the fire,' she encouraged her sister who was staring moodily out into the pouring rain. 'At least we will be warm while we wait.'
Surveying the now roaring fire Queenie nodded, a pensive look on her face. 'I have made a right mess of this,' she declared. 'I let my anger get the better of me.' She shook her head in disgust and moved to Sybil's side. Enjoying the warmth of the fire for a minute she went on moodily,' I should have been calmer with Serena and now she has scuttled off to goodness knows where. And we still haven't nailed this mystery.'
Watching her carefully Sybil couldn't help but agree, inwardly at least, but said soothingly, 'But we were right about Serena being the cause of the increasing psychic disturbances.'
Brushing away a few of the larger stones Queenie settled down near the fire; taking off her sodden shoes she emptied the water and set them in front of the pit. Clasping her knees she stared pensively into the flickering flames.
'We're missing something Sybil, I know we are.'
The fire popped and crackled in the following silence as they mulled over their situation.
'Perhaps she did bring them,' offered Sybil, as an explanation.
Queenie gestured behind them at the crosses. 'By doing that?' she asked in scorn. 'She didn't even get that right.'
'Have you ever...?' Sybil asked tentatively.

'No.'

'Good,' she replied, greatly relieved.

They huddled closer to the fire as the wind blew harder and waves boomed around the entrance, a gust suddenly swirled in and around the cave. The fire flared up scattering a shower of sparks into the farthest corners of the cave. Sybil idly followed the trail of a glowing ember as it was carried up to the ceiling and then began to fall. It flickered and finally went out as it landed on something half hidden behind a rock. 'What is that?' she said, sitting forward and peering into the now dark area.

'Go and have a look.'

She hesitated, before rising stiffly and walked slowly towards it. It was an old cardboard box bound up with string. Sybil stretched out a hand to open it and then paused. 'Shall I?' she appealed to her sister.

'I bet it's Serena's. Bring it over to the light and we'll have a look.' Undoing the string she opened the cardboard flaps and peered in. Two glowing eyes peered back at her and she squealed. Slamming it shut, she backed away and hissed to her sister, 'There is something in the box.'

Hearing her voice a little furry head pushed its way out through the flaps and gave a plaintive meow. Blinking in the dim light from the fire, it meowed again.

'It's a cat!' she exclaimed, and carefully lifted it out of the box. 'Look Queenie.'

She carried it gently back to the fire. Glad of a bit of warmth the cat snuggled its head under her chin as she gently held it, and it began to purr.

'Poor pussy cat,' she murmured.

By the light of the flames they could see the sad state it was in, painfully thin and its black and white fur was wet and matted with urine.

'That is Bobby,' said Queenie, peering at it. 'He's a bit thinner but I'm sure that's him.' She tickled the cat under the chin and grinned. 'Janet will be pleased; she might like us again now we have found her cat.'

'I bet he's hungry.'

'So am I. I wonder if he is any good at catching fish?'

'Don't be silly, poor iddle puddums,' Sybil cooed, wrapping her jacket around its shivering body. 'Is u cold?'

'Do you know how ridiculous you sound?' said Queenie, looking at her in disgust.

'Don't be so grumpy. We found Bobby; that's one good thing that has come out of this mess.'

Queenie sighed and lifted an eyebrow. 'When they find our poor drowned corpses,' she said sarcastically, 'they can put that on our gravestones "But they found Bobby".'

'We saved him from a horrible and gruesome death, so I for one am feeling very pleased with myself.'

Leaning back against a rock Queenie sniffed. 'That's good. Now put another piece of wood on the fire.'

'We ought to ration the wood as we don't know how long we are going to be here.' Sybil looked in concern at her sister as she shivered. 'And I wouldn't want to run out later when it gets really cold.'

'I suppose you are right,' she sniffed, pulling the collar of her fleece tight around her neck, she shifted uncomfortably, pulling a few sharp rocks out from under her bottom. 'But it's getting colder,' she complained, 'Look, I can see my breath.'

'I know it is.' Sybil peered at her watch in the fading light. 'It's not that late either.'

She looked towards the entrance where huge banks of grey clouds were piling up over the bay, reducing the light to a dismal murk. 'There's a storm blowing up.'

She threw another stick on the fire as the first rumble of thunder echoed along the coast. Queenie shivered again and suddenly sneezed making the cat jump in Sybil's arms.

'Bless you,' Sybil said automatically.

A flash of lightening filled the cave with an eye watering glare quickly followed by another clap of thunder. The sudden flash revealed the huge waves pounding up the beach and the great mounds of sea foam blown by the fierce winds piling up just inside the cave. Farther out in the bay the huge waves rose and fell, battering the coast line and almost hidden by the swell a small speck appeared almost dancing over the water as it ploughed through the turbulent waters towards the beach. Behind it piled black storm clouds lit by great sizzling bolts of lightning. The rowers, head down in the lashing rain and backs bent against the straining oars skilfully manoeuvred the small craft towards Mupe Bay.

Spotting the small boat Sybil couldn't believe their luck; she squealed and quickly nudged Queenie who was hunched over the fire.

'Look! A boat.'

Queenie raised her head and gazed blearily out across the water to the approaching craft. She blinked and stared.

'I told you we would be rescued,' Sybil said in relief, struggling to rise from her spot near the fire.

'Sit down Sybil,' said Queenie, reaching for her arm. 'It's not what you think.'

Another flash of lightening filled the sky. Bright enough for Sybil to see it was no rescue craft. Strange lights flickered around the phantom boat and its occupants as it skimmed across the surface of the water towards them. In the stern Sybil could just make out the figure of a man, lashed by the wind and rain, with his hand steady on the tiller guiding it through the pounding waves to the beach and the smugglers cave.

In her arms the cat began to growl.

Sybil huddled closer to her sister.

'Who are they?' she whispered, her eyes wide with alarm as the boat slid silently up the beach.

Without a splash the sailors jumped ashore carrying bundles and small kegs under their arms heading silently to the rear of the cave. One of the men hesitated on the beach fumbling in a pocket, and a light unexpectedly flared in his cupped hands illuminating a thin and haggard face. Sybil stared at his threadbare clothes as he raised the lantern and hurriedly followed the men inside. Not one of the gaunt men cast a shadow in the pale light.

'Sit tight and keep quiet,' muttered Queenie, still hunched over the flames.

They watched intently as the ghosts piled their contraband against the back wall. None of them looked familiar to the two women and but gazing at their rough clothes Queenie quickly realised that they were from an earlier century.

'Who are they?' whispered Sybil again, into Queenies ear.

She shook her head frowning, and muttered in Sybil's ear, 'Those aren't Absalon's men,' and continued watching as they took more from the boat. The pile of smuggled goods grew quickly. 'I wonder if this is Cruel Coppinger?' she whispered.

Her murmuring voice hovered in the air and the name Coppinger echoed clearly around the cave. It reached the ears of the man pouring over a parchment, he paused, lifting his quill from the list and peered into the darkness searching for the owner of the whispered voice. Queenie and Sybil froze.

Holding up a lantern he stepped forward towards the centre of the cave. Queenie's mouth dropped open; the weak light was just enough for her to see his face. Although it wasn't Absalon the resemblance was enough to confirm her suspicions of the man's identity.

So this was one of his ancestors, thought Queenie grimly. Cruel Coppinger himself.

He had the same bleak look to his eye as his descendant. An old flintlock pistol was thrust into his waistband and she had no doubt that it had seen some use during his smuggling career.

'Nice family,' she muttered, then bit her lip as he turned towards her. Standing just feet away from them he scanned the cave searching for the intruder in his hideout. The man's gaze passed straight over the women and the blazing fire unaware of their presence.

From behind the two women a pebble clattered. Coppinger stiffened and peered over their heads into the shadows, his hand clawing at the pistol then froze as a man stepped forward.

'Coppinger, stand fast!' he commanded, covering him and the crew with his own weapon. 'You are all under arrest for taking part in this illegal trade and cheating the Government of their lawful taxes.'

Coppinger's crew grew quiet and cast fearful eyes around searching for more revenue officers hidden inside.

'Ridout, you maggot!' called out one of the men. 'You'd turn us in?'

'For a twenty pound reward,' he sneered, 'I'd sell my own mother for that.' He grinned at the angry faces. 'Of course if you made it worth my while,' he suggested craftily, 'I'd be willing to look the other way, say half the profits?'

His smile faded as a shot rang out and a bright spreading stain appeared on his tunic.

Acrid smoke plumed up from one of the men as he threw down his weapon and lunged towards the injured man who had fallen to his knees. Ridout stared down at his chest in disbelief as the blood seeped through his waistcoat; he cast one last puzzled look towards Coppinger before falling forward onto the sand.

The noise of the gunshot, magnified by the close confines of the cave, had stunned the women momentarily but as the smoke cleared and all became quiet around them, Queenie opened her eyes and looked over to where the men had been stood.

All had disappeared, the mortally wounded officer had also gone, and no blood remained spilt on the sand. The cave was empty apart from the two women and the cat.

The flames from the fire puttered in the silence, the light flickering over the sister's worried faces.

Queenie sneezed, breaking the spell.

'It's getting busy in here,' she paused and blew her nose, 'this cave certainly has a bloody history.'

'So much blood has been spilt by this family,' said Sybil. 'For what...just a few coins?'

'It must have been worth their while, more than a few coins,' Queenie pointed out. 'It seems they have been using this cave for years. I suppose that's why Serena thought it would suit her purposes. I doubt that she realised that caves are gateways to the otherworld and with all this blood that has been spilled here she has unwittingly brought forth more spirits than she had intended. They would have been drawn like bees to a honeypot.'

Heads close together they talked quietly still unnerved by the sight of another murder. Drips began to fall with increasing speed from the ceiling spattering into the fire and making it hiss.

'How much longer?' said Sybil. 'I thought help would be here by now.'

'I told you Duncan wasn't going to help.'

She didn't reply as inwardly she was beginning to believe Queenie but with a sigh shifted closer to the fire. The cat disturbed from its contented doze by the movement slowly stretched and yawned. Sybil stroked it absentmindedly as she watched the steam rising from her wet shoes and it started to purr.

The wind whistled in and around the rocks in the cave; small eddies of sand blew up forming into little whirlwinds hovering just inches over the floor of the cave. More sand blew in with each gust until there was a thick haze hanging in the air.

The cat ceased its purring and stiffened.

On the other side of the fireplace, just outside the circle of light, the hanging cloud of dust grew thicker. It ceased to move in the wind blowing off the sea and grew with each passing second; slowly it swirled higher into a pillar of blackness. Dark shadows spilled from it and spread outwards while inside the swirling cloud the figure of a man began to manifest.

Bobby began to growl; his bulging eyes were fixed on the opposite side of the wall.

Behind the appearing figure the very rocks seemed to ripple; shadows slid from the cave walls and moved forward to stand behind him.

Stepping into the firelight Absalon was before them. With his arms folded he stared across the fire at the two women, the flames dancing across his bleak hopeless face. The same expression was echoed in the faces of the men behind him.

'Look who's here,' grunted Queenie, glaring from under lowered brows at the unwelcome although not entirely unexpected visitor. 'Come to look at your grand-daughter's handiwork?' she said loudly. 'You must be very proud Coppinger.'

Several of the men started forward angrily at her words but one gesture from Absalon was enough to stop them.

'That's right, control your dogs,' she sneered.

Sybil plucked at her sleeve. 'Queenie watch what you say, don't antagonise him.'

'Or what? What's he going to do, he's a ghost.' She glared at the dark figure. 'Do you hear me Absalon? You're a ghost, you don't belong here anymore.'

He stepped closer and stared down at Queenie.

'You can't control the village from beyond the grave and Serena can't do it for you. Give it up and go back to the spirit world.'

He shook his head and stared intently at her.

Queenie shook her head angrily. 'No, stay out of my head! I can feel you trying to get in but I am not interested in anything you have to tell me. Not after you murdered poor Thomas.' Queenie stood up and scowled at him. 'You monster! That poor little boy. I hope his father took his revenge on you.' She clapped her hands over her ears and shouted, 'No, I won't listen to you! You should be burning in hell with the rest of your family.'

His face twisted with rage at these words and he suddenly reached out for Queenie; shadowy fingers flowed forward clutching at her throat and she staggered back to escape the freezing touch. A wave of dizziness came over her and she reached blindly for her sister.

'Calm down Queenie, you need to keep a clear head.'

Sybil put a steadying arm around her waist and looked nervously at Absalon who had momentarily checked himself and withdrawn to the other side of the fire; he was still staring coldly at them.

From behind him more shadowy figures arrived to stand by his side until the cave was full of men, crowding around the women on all sides. The cat, still held firmly under Sybil's arm, struggled and growled desperate to escape. Its claws dug into her arm but still she kept a tight hold knowing that there was nowhere for it to hide.

'What are we going to do?' she whispered, on a rising wave of panic.
'Serena's blood sacrifices have drawn them through the gate so I will
have to send them back,' Queenie gasped weakly. 'If I have the strength
to do it,' she added, and began searching in her pockets.
Her fingers closed on the bunch of agrimony. Queenie pulled Sybil
closer to her side and with her foot traced a circle around them both in
the sandy floor and staring defiantly at the ghostly figures watching her
she began to chant, 'Thrice around the circles bound, sink all evil to the
ground. Within this circle we are safe; against spirits that threaten us I
stand. Banish their souls and remove their powers and let these evil
beings flee through time and space. So Mote it be!'
Hearing these words and realising what Queenie was about to do
Absalon leapt forward, a look of rage contorting his features as he tried
to grasp Queenies hand before she dropped the herb onto the glowing
firewood.
'Begone,' she ordered, as the agrimony began to burn releasing its foul
smell. 'Return to the otherworld where you belong.'
The smoke billowed up from the fire obscuring the men beyond from
their sight but as the fumes touched their astral bodies the ghosts
wavered like a heat haze on a summer's day and with one last
despairing howl Absalon and the rest of the men vanished. Coughing
from the acrid smoke Queenie dragged her sister back from the
fireplace and the fumes.
'Gods,' she gasped, her eyes watering. 'I had forgotten how awful that
stuff is.' Holding her chest Queenie slumped against the wall gasping
and coughing; eyes streaming and unable to see she asked Sybil, 'Have
they gone?'
'Yes,' she answered thankfully. 'They have.'
Queenie leant her head back against the cold rock and groaned, 'At
least I did that right.'
'You have done really well,' said Sybil, kneeling next to her. She
placed a hand onto her sister's forehead and flinched; it was burning.
'You have a bit of a temperature,' she said, trying to stay calm. 'Can
you get up and move nearer to the fire?'
'Let the herb burn out first,' she replied weakly, and took a few gasping
breaths before stiffening. 'Now what?' she asked in despair, as a few
rocks rattled in the far corner of the cave. 'Sybil, I can't deal with much
more,' she wheezed, fighting for breath. 'I haven't the strength.'
'Don't worry,' Sybil said firmly. 'Anything else dares to enter this cave
and I will deal with it.'

A dim light appeared in the corner of the cave; echoing footsteps shuffled closer scrunching over the rough floor of the cave. Sybil watched in trepidation as the back wall of the cave lit up with a soft glow. She clenched her fists realising it was up to her protect them both as Queenie had slumped against the wall in a dead faint.

A figure appeared at the back of the cave and Sybil, with a quaking heart, readied herself. Suddenly a dazzling light shone in her face and she flinched, holding up a hand to shade her eyes.

'Are you alright?' asked a gruff voice.

'Who's that?' she said, surprise making her voice shrill.

He lowered the torch to the floor and walked forward.

'Duncan!' she exclaimed.

'Well,' he asked, 'are you alright?'

'Yes...no,' she replied hurriedly. 'Queenie is sick.'

Duncan trained the torch on Queenie's slumped body at the side of the cave. 'She doesn't look too good,' he muttered.

'How did you get here?'

Duncan shifted his gaze from her sister to Sybil and frowned. 'Through the tunnel,' he replied shortly. 'Can she walk?' he asked, turning back to Queenie. 'It's the only way to get out of here. Well?' he asked Sybil sharply, who was staring at him completely bemused.

Pulling herself together she hurried over to Queenie and gently patted her cheek. 'Queenie,' she said gently, 'Queenie, wake up. We have been rescued. Come on,' she urged, 'you need to get up.'

Her sister's eyelids flickered for a minute and finally opened. Queenie looked blankly at her.

'What?' she mumbled.

'We are being rescued.'

'Who is it this time? The Four Horsemen of the Apocalypse?'

'No, it's Duncan.'

Queenie gave a weak cackle. 'Of course it is.'

'Really...it is! Come on, you have to get up Queenie.' Wrapping her arm around her sisters waist Sybil began to heave her upright; looking over Queenie's head at Duncan she asked acidly, 'Some help would be good, I can't manage her on my own.' Between them they managed to pull the limp Queenie upright and supporting her on both sides guided her to the back of the cave. Behind them the cat hesitated and gave a plaintive meow. 'Come on puss,' encouraged Sybil. 'We're going home.'

Hidden behind a large rock was a narrow fissure.

'It's a bit of a tight squeeze,' he muttered, shining the torch into the dark passage. 'But you should be able to manage.' He stared at Queenie, 'Not sure about your sister though.'

She raised her head and glared at him. 'I am not staying here a moment longer,' Queenie said weakly. 'So let's get moving.'

Leading the way Duncan squeezed through the jagged opening, Queenie grasping his arm for support as she followed. Close behind came Sybil with the torch and following her trotted the cat. Just a few feet in and the passage opened up enough that they were able to stand side by side. Sybil slipped an arm around her sister's waist for support. 'Okay?' she asked quietly.

Queenie nodded, unable to speak.

'Come on,' said Duncan, picking up the cat he lead the way farther into the dark and damp tunnel. Water dripped continually from the roof and down the walls flooding the floor, in some places it was so deep that it was over their knees. The water was also freezing; it was so cold Sybil had to grit her teeth to stop them chattering but she was more concerned about Queenie as they struggled on.

'How much farther, Duncan?'

'A way,' he muttered, pausing to catch his breath. 'This is the first time I have been through here for years.'

'You used this tunnel? For what?'

He raised an eyebrow and gave her a scathing look. 'What do you think?'

Sybil looked shocked then asked, 'Who else knows about it?'

'Not many now; it's best forgotten about.' Duncan shrugged impatiently and took Queenie's arm. 'Stop talking and come on. Your sister needs to get out of here.'

'So do I,' she snapped. 'It's been a very trying day and I can't wait to see the back of this damn cave.'

'Well, you know what I'm going to say to that, don't you?' he muttered, carefully leading Queenie around a rock fall. Receiving no answer he looked back at Sybil's angry face.

'You should have minded your own business,' he said slowly and clearly. 'And that goes for you too,' he muttered at Queenie.

'She's not listening.'

'Yes, I am,' she said weakly. 'I just can't understand why you are all in denial.'

'It's complicated,' he replied tersely, and paused. 'Take a minute,' he ordered. 'We are about half way.'

'Is that all?' asked Sybil, wiping a cobweb from her face. 'Where the hell does this tunnel come out?'

'You'll see,' he smiled grimly, and suddenly turned off the torch leaving just Sybil's to light the tunnel. 'I need to save my batteries, they're getting low. Of course if I had known I was going to mount a rescue I would have replaced them.' The following silence was only broken by the constant dripping and Queenie's ragged breathing. Sybil shivered. A stone clicked in the distance.

'What was that?' she whispered, peering into the dark tunnel behind them.

Duncan sighed. 'Nothing.' There was rasp and a match flared and the aromatic fragrance of a cigarette filled the tunnel.

Queenie coughed. 'I've given up,' she said faintly, leaning against the wall. 'Haven't I Sybil?'

'Yes dear,' replied her sister, patting her gently on the shoulder. 'Mostly.'

'Father smoked,' continued Queenie, 'twenty roll ups a day. Survived two world wars and was killed by a collapsing wall.' She laughed weakly. 'Ironic isn't it?'

The end of Duncan's cigarette glowed brightly in the darkness and his eyes caught and reflected the red light as he stared thoughtfully at her. 'We had better move on; she sounds feverish.'

'Good idea,' Sybil nodded firmly, although in the nearly pitch black of the tunnel Duncan would not have been able to see her. She pulled Queenie upright and slipped her arm around her waist again.

'Come along dear, time to go.'

'Are we going home now?'

'Yes, we're going home,' she replied, trying to keep calm.

Queenie was shivering violently in the damp and bitterly cold tunnel, her clothes were already soaked with sweat and her breathing was becoming more laboured the deeper they went into the passageway.

'How much farther is it?' demanded Sybil.

'Not much,' he replied, flicking on his torch.

Their splashing footsteps echoing along the tunnel was the only thing punctuating the silence, that and a few plaintive meows from the cat tucked under Duncan's arm.

'It's alright puss,' encouraged Sybil. 'Nearly home.'

'Are we home?' wheezed Queenie.

'Soon,' encouraged her sister, guiding her stumbling steps forward into the darkness.

After what seemed an age the tunnel started to slope upwards and the floor became dry and sandy. On either side the tunnel walls and ceiling were supported by old wooden prop shafts; piles of loose soil had slipped from the roof forming small blockages in their path. Queenie stumbled against one of the rickety posts as they were struggling past and started a mini landslide of soil and rocks that quickly filled half of the tunnel behind them.

'Is this tunnel safe?' Sybil whispered, envisioning all the weight of the cliffs over their heads and beginning to panic.

'No.' Duncan trudged on slowly, the circle of light from the torch trained on the ground just in front of him. 'All right back there?' he inquired suddenly.

'Oh yes,' she said witheringly, 'we're just fine,' and took a firmer grip around Queenies waist and jerked her upright as her legs began to sag. 'Come on not much longer,' she encouraged, 'then we can have a nice cup of tea.'

'Tea.'

'That's it, tea.'

Chapter Thirteen

A current of fresh warm air blew down the tunnel and wafted across their faces, and in the distance a dim light outlined the shape of a door. Duncan slowed and turned off his torch. 'We're here, just keep quiet,' he ordered, 'and turn off that light!' Sybil quickly did as she was told, unnerved by the fear in the old man's voice and pocketed the torch. He moved slowly and quietly to the door and stood for a minute with his ear pressed to it listening. He nodded to the women and whispered, 'All clear, but keep quiet.' The dry rusty hinges squealed as he pushed it cautiously open and peered in. Satisfied that the room was empty he opened it wider and stepped forward gesturing for them to follow. Sybil and Queenie stumbled over the threshold into what looked and felt like a cellar. The cat slipped through after them and scurried behind a box as Duncan began replacing the lumber and old bits of furniture that had hidden the door. 'Are we home?' wheezed Queenie, and as she spoke her legs buckled and would have fallen to the floor but for Sybil's strong arm about her. She and Duncan half carried her limp body to a pile of crates near the wall and lowered her down.

'Sit here for a minute Queenie,' said Sybil, peering into her pallid face. 'Get your breath back.'

Queenie laughed weakly, 'Where's it gone?'

'Shh!' said Duncan tersely. He pointed to the ceiling above where the sound of footsteps could be heard pacing backwards and forwards.

'Where are we?' hissed Sybil.

'Shh!'

Murmuring voices filtered down into the underground room and they waited scarcely breathing as the conversation above grew heated. Strain as she might Sybil couldn't make out individual words or identify the speakers apart from being certain that one of them was a man. A door banged overhead and the slow pacing resumed.

'We'll have to wait until the coast is clear,' Duncan breathed in Sybil's ear, 'and it's better if we're not seen coming out of here.' He gestured to the pile of crates where Queenie was slumped. 'Wait there.'

Sybil nodded and sat down on the creaking boxes. 'We have to wait for a minute,' she whispered to Queenie, putting an arm around her sister trying to keep her warm. Queenie was still shivering and Sybil looked about desperate for something to wrap her in. Next to the boxes was a pile of old hessian potato sacks, she bent down and pulled a handful towards her disturbing years of dust and cobwebs. Sybil sneezed. 'Shh!'

'Sorry,' she sniffed, and carefully placed a sack around Queenie's shoulders and another over her knees. 'There you are,' she said quietly, 'that will help.'

Above them the pacing continued effectively trapping them down in the cellar. Minutes ticked by while they waited in the darkness.

'Is there a light down here?' she asked quietly, moving nearer to Duncan. 'A candle, lantern or something, I'm sure that would raise Queenie's spirits, mine as well to be honest.'

Duncan grunted and started poking in amongst the clutter stacked on the many shelves around the walls. 'There might be something here,' he muttered. Every now and then he would pause and listen intently while the sounds overhead continued. He went back to his search, pulling out old paint encrusted jamjars, dried up brushes and other long forgotten items that should have been thrown away years ago. Behind one tin was an old Tilley lamp and as he pulled it out the shelf collapsed spilling all the old rubbish onto the floor. He froze and looked at the ceiling waiting to see if anybody had heard the crash but the footsteps continued pacing backwards and forwards. Little chinks of light spilled down between the cracks in the floorboards and they could see the shadow of the walker flickering across the gaps. Duncan blew out a relieved breath and gently shook the lantern; he nodded satisfied when he heard the paraffin sloshing about in the base. He opened the glass mantle, struck a match and the lantern flared into life sending its bright bluish light into all the dark corners of the cellar. The whitewashed walls reflected back the flare of the Tilley lantern and illuminated the flight of stone steps leading to a small door.

'Can't we just slip out?' pleaded Sybil.

He shook his head. 'No. We would be spotted and we don't want that.' Duncan sat down next to them on the old crates; he reached across and carefully adjusted the sack around Queenie's shoulders. 'Sorry,' he muttered, 'we'll just have to wait.' The lid of the crate creaked ominously and he shifted his weight cautiously, with this last movement the rotten lid snapped in two pitching him onto the floor. Duncan's grunt of pain was quickly choked back and he struggled to his feet looking fearfully at the door.

'Are you alright?' whispered Sybil, lifting the lantern.

The light shone on the old man as he gingerly rubbed his leg. Duncan grunted, 'I'm fine.'

The bright light shone into the crate and Sybil peered in at the contents. 'A coat!' she exclaimed, and pulled out a dark tweed jacket. 'Just the thing Queenie; this will keep you warm.'

She shook it out and wrapped the fusty smelling coat around her sister's shoulders then pushed the lantern into Duncan's hand. 'Hold this while I see if there is anything else in there we can use.'

Balanced on top of the suitcase jammed in the bottom of the crate was an old leather satchel. Sybil stared at it thoughtfully for a minute until curiosity got the better of her and struggling a little with the stiff leather buckles she opened it. Inside was a notebook and two rolls of old white banknotes. Beside her Duncan stepped forward and peered at the contents, he quickly put the lantern next to Queenie on the crate and reached into the bag.

'It's money!' he said quietly, and flicked through the notes rapidly counting. 'There must be about a hundred pounds here in five pound notes.' He took the other roll from the bag and examined it. 'One pound notes, another hundred pounds.'

The large white notes issued by the Bank of England had the date mark 1935.

'Those are old,' exclaimed Sybil. 'What are they doing down here?'

Duncan didn't answer, he frowned staring down at the satchel and putting his hand in pulled out the notebook, as he did so something fell onto the floor. A small piece of card folded in two lay at their feet. On the cover printed in black were the words National Registration Identity Card. Inside was the owners name, Stephen Jones, 13 Mayhew Terrace, Oxford.

'Who is that?' asked Sybil, peering over his shoulder. 'Do you know him? Was he from the village?'

Duncan shook his head. 'Never heard of him.'

'What is the identity card of somebody from Oxford doing in a little fishing village in Dorset? And why did he leave all this money down here?'

'Dunno,' he grunted, before plunging his arm inside the crate for the suitcase.

'And what's that?' Sybil pushed the rolls of money back into the satchel and moved to help Duncan pull the heavy case from the crate. They dropped it on the box next to Queenie, flung back the lid and gazed at the contents. She blinked slowly and peered at the grey metal box it contained.

'That's a transmitter,' she wheezed.

'A what?'

'A radio. It's for transmitting messages,' she coughed and carried on breathlessly, 'Very old and not much use now.' Queenie coughed again. 'Uncle Bob had one, don't you remember? He brought it back at the end of the war in 1945; we used to play with it in his attic until one of the crystals burnt out.'

Standing close to Duncan Sybil suddenly felt him stiffen and he quickly slammed the lid of the suitcase and threw it back into the crate, followed by the satchel and the money. 'Forget you saw this!' he hissed, turning to glare at the women. 'You hear me?'

'Okay,' Sybil said slowly, exchanging puzzled glances with her sister. Duncan threw the broken lid back on top of the crate and banged it down with his fist. 'We shouldn't have been poking about,' he muttered, before hurrying to the foot of the stairs. Obviously rattled by what he found in the crate he was impatient to be gone, he opened the door a chink and squinted through the gap.

'What was all that about?' croaked Queenie, when he was out of earshot.

'I have no idea,' admitted Sybil, but her mouth dropped open as Duncan slipped out through the door closing it softly behind him. 'He's gone,' she gasped. 'He's left us again!'

Her sister laughed weakly, 'He's good at that,' she gasped, fighting for breath. 'Sybil, we need to get out of here.' Queenie staggered as she stood slowly and grasped Sybil's arm quickly before she fell. 'Come on.'

With her sister's arm around her they staggered slowly to the steps, the cat following them and seeing the door bounded up the stairs in front of them and started clawing at the wood eager to be out in the fresh air.

'That's it,' Sybil encouraged. 'Just a few more steps,' as Queenie struggled up the first few but then stumbled and pitched forward cracking her knees on the stone. Biting her lip to stop the yell of pain she collapsed on the stairs. Unable to go any farther she rested her head in her hands. 'I can't,' she said weakly. 'I just can't go any farther, I'm sorry.' She raised her head and looked pitifully at her sister. 'You will have to go on without me,' Queenie half smiled, 'I never thought I would be saying that.'

Looking from her sister to the door Sybil quickly came to a decision. 'Right,' she said. 'Sit tight here and I am going for help. You need an ambulance,' she said firmly, expecting protests but none came confirming her worst fears about Queenie's condition.

She nodded and whispered, 'Okay.'

Patting her sister on the shoulder Sybil hurried past and up the stairs to the door where the impatient cat was beginning to meow loudly. 'Shush,' she said, picking it up and stroking its head. 'Be quiet now,' before pushing the door slowly open. Sybil peeked out of the gap into a small hallway. It was empty so she sidled out holding her breath. Casting one last look at her sister still slumped on the stone stairs she carefully closed the door, which to her surprise came out under a staircase. The flagstone hall led to a front door; at the other end was a kitchen just visible through a half open door. The door that led to the room directly over the cellar was closed and Sybil could hear the restless footsteps behind it. Opposite the cellar was the living room which was also empty. Spotting a phone on a small table near the window and cradling the cat under her arm she hurried over to the table, just as she reached to pick up the phone Sybil glanced out of the window. Her hand froze in mid air; the garden outside the window was all too familiar. It was Mrs Coppinger's cottage. Of course, she thought, the pieces falling into place, it was the logical place for the tunnel to emerge. Realising where she was Sybil glanced nervously around the room; her attention was immediately caught by an old photograph hanging over the fireplace. Dressed in his best suit and tie and posing in front of that very fireplace Absalon stared down at her. Irritated by the cold look Sybil turned her back on the picture but even then she could still feel his eyes on the back of her neck. Picking up the phone she began dialling the emergency services. Talking in a low voice not to be overheard Sybil quickly gave the details of Queenie's condition and the address. She was just replacing the phone when a hand gripped her shoulder.

Sybil jumped and turned around expecting to see Mrs Coppinger. 'What are you doing?'

She sighed in relief. 'Duncan!' then asked suspiciously, 'Where have you been? You left us again!'

'Did you call the police?' he asked, ignoring her questions.

'I called for an ambulance. Queenie is really ill.'

Duncan nodded. 'How long?' he asked brusquely.

'About twenty minutes.'

He looked around the room. 'Where is she?'

'She is still in the cellar. Queenie couldn't make it up the stairs and I couldn't manage on my own,' Sybil said pointedly, glaring at him.

'So?' she said, grabbing his arm before he walked away. 'I want an answer Duncan, where have you been?'

He pushed her restraining hand off in irritation. 'I was making sure it was safe to come out,' he paused and looked at her suspicious face. 'I was coming back.'

'Really?' Sybil looked sceptical.

'Of course,' he said looking rather offended at her obvious lack of faith in him. 'I didn't struggle all the way through that flooded tunnel to rescue you both to abandon you now.'

'I'm sorry,' said Sybil, suddenly feeling guilty, 'but it has been a difficult time.'

Duncan grunted, 'I guess so,' he said grudgingly. 'Come on, let's get your sister out of the cellar before she gets pneumonia.' He stepped cautiously to the door; satisfied the hallway was empty he pulled Sybil behind him and hurried to the cellar door. Queenie was still where Sybil had left her and looked up when she heard their step on the stairs.

'Back again?' she croaked at Duncan.

'Of course, you silly woman,' he said gruffly, helping her to her feet. Between the two of them they managed to get Queenie to the top of the stairs and out into the hall. A few more steps and they would have made it to the front door but the kitchen door slowly swung open and framed in the doorway was Mrs Coppinger. She gazed at them in surprise and looked from Duncan to the sisters taking in their dishevelled appearance.

'Good Evening,' she said, regaining her composure.

'Daisy,' said Duncan, holding up a calming hand. 'We're not here to cause any trouble.'

She smiled. 'I'm glad to hear it.' She looked at Sybil and Queenie and her smile faded. 'And why are you in my home?'

'It's a long story,' said Sybil bluntly, 'and one I don't have time for now. I just need to look after my sister.'

Mrs Coppinger calmly looked from them to the cat that was weaving in and out of Sybil's legs. 'A cat?' she asked.

'Yes,' Sybil said gruffly. 'Another part of the story and one you really don't want to hear about.'

'Well,' Mrs Coppinger said, with a faint smile on her lips. 'You look as though you could all do with a cup of tea.' She turned stiffly leaning heavily on her stick and walked back into the kitchen. 'Duncan,' she called over her shoulder. 'Come and help please.'

He hesitated for a minute and gestured with a nod of his head for the sisters to wait in the living room then followed Daisy into the kitchen. Sybil helped Queenie to the chair near the fireplace where she slumped, gasping for breath.

'Don't worry Queenie,' she said, hovering over her in concern. 'An ambulance is on its way and then we will be out of here.'

'Good,' she replied weakly, leaning back with her eyes closed. A worrying blue tinge had appeared around her lips and she grabbed at Sybil's hand. 'Sorry, this is all my fault. I could have got you killed,' she said, a tear running down her ashen face.

'Oh Queenie, we're a pair of tough old birds as Albert said, it will take more than a few ghosts and a mad woman to finish us off.' She bent over her sister and gave her quick hug. 'Everything is going to be fine,' she said, trying to reassure Queenie.

A tinkle of china came from the hallway as Duncan slowly walked in bearing a tray closely followed by Mrs Coppinger.

'Mad woman?' she enquired, pricking up her ears. She looked suspiciously at the pair of them. 'And who is that?'

'Just gossiping Mrs Coppinger, that's all,' said Sybil, watching her carefully.

The old woman hobbled over to the fireplace and looked down at Queenie. 'She is in my chair,' she announced, and gestured to the sofa positioned in front of the window. 'Let her sit there.'

'Daisy,' protested Duncan. 'She's ill, leave her alone.'

Her mouth thinned and she glared in dislike at Queenie. 'So what have you been doing?' she asked, looking at her wet and dirty clothes. 'You're filthy.'

Queenie returned her cold look and said in scorn, 'Your tunnel is rather dirty.'

'Tunnel?' What tunnel?'

Duncan half closed his eyes in exasperation at Queenie's slip. 'There's a tunnel leading from Mupe Bay.'

'Why didn't I know about it?'

'There was no need for you to know.'

The sudden look of anger on her face was swiftly replaced by a look of calm cunning. 'So there's a tunnel,' she said slowly, 'Well, well.'

Turning away from them she hobbled to the table and pulled out a chair and sat down. 'Tea?' she inquired, holding up the teapot. Beneath the table the cat smelling the milk began to meow and rub itself against Mrs Coppinger's legs. She glared at it, pushing it away with her foot. 'And where did the cat come from?'

'That is Janet's cat, Bobby. He went missing a few days ago,' volunteered Duncan, still watching the old woman carefully.

Her hand paused for a minute, 'Oh,' she said, then handed a cup to Sybil, 'Here you are. Sugar?' proffering the sugar bowl.

'No, thank you. I should take him back.' She looked across at Duncan. 'Can you look after Queenie for me while I return Bobby to his owner?' Sybil stared at Mrs Coppinger and pointedly said, 'The ambulance will be here in about five minutes.'

Her calm gaze met Sybil's for a brief second before she nodded. Sybil stood and quickly scooped Bobby from under the table.

'Come on cat, let's get you home.' The front door slammed behind her as she half ran down the path to the gate, the hinges squealing as loudly as ever as she pushed her way through. Bobby, recognising the familiar street, started to struggle in her arms. 'Just wait a minute,' she scolded. 'I want to make sure you get home safely. You have already used up enough of your nine lives.'

Reaching Janet's house, she adjusted the cat under her arm and hammered on the front door, hoping that the woman would be in. Sybil didn't have long to wait, the door swung open and Janet stood there looking at her coldly.

'What do you want?' she asked, before spotting Bobby tucked under Sybil's arm. The frosty expression disappeared as she reached for her precious cat. 'Oh my God! Bobby!' she squealed, crushing him in an embrace. 'Where did you find him?' she called after Sybil, who was already hurrying back along the road.

She paused for a minute. 'You don't want to know Janet,' she said, over her shoulder.

Sybil had just reached the cottage when the ambulance appeared at the end of the street inching its way down through the narrow space between the cottages. A wave of relief swept over her making her feel suddenly weak. Sybil raised a hand and waved at the driver and stood back quickly as it drew to a halt outside the cottage.

Chapter Fourteen

Queenie lay on the stretcher with a blanket tucked up under her chin, an oxygen mask strapped to her face.

'You will be fine now,' reassured Sybil, as the paramedics wheeled her carefully out of the living room. 'And I will be right behind you so don't worry.'

Queenie half opened her eyes and nodded weakly. Duncan patted her arm as she was wheeled past him.

'You'll be fine, old girl,' he said.

Sybil winced, expecting a sharp retort from her sister but apart from a flicker of an eyelid she didn't appear to have heard or cared about Duncan's comment. Sybil looked across to where Mrs Coppinger was pouring a fresh cup of tea. 'Thank you for letting us wait here,' she said politely, before following the stretcher from the house.

'Are you going? Don't you want to finish your tea first?' she asked, suddenly standing and hobbling over to Sybil. She took her arm, her grip surprisingly strong for a woman of her age. 'I think you should sit down, just for a minute and calm yourself,' she looked at Duncan. 'Don't you agree?'

'Well...' he said slowly, 'I'm sure Sybil would rather go.'

'Nonsense,' she said briskly and led Sybil back to the chair near the fire. 'Sit down and I will pour you a fresh cup of tea.'

'Thank you but no,' Sybil said impatiently. 'I would like to be there when the Doctor examines her.'

Mrs Coppinger smiled. 'It's not going to make any difference if you are there,' she said calmly, pouring the tea. 'She's going to die.'

Sybil's mouth dropped open at the callous statement. 'Of course she's not,' she said angrily.

The old woman smiled as she spooned in some sugar and stirred it. 'Oh, she will, I will be surprised if she makes it to the hospital.'

'Daisy!' What an awful thing to say.' Duncan stood up and walked swiftly over to Sybil's side. 'Come on,' he said. 'I will take you to your car.'

'Sit down.'

'Daisy!'

'Sit down Duncan and you too.' She placed the cup carefully into its saucer and stared thoughtfully at the old man. 'Why are you helping them?' she appealed to him. 'You, of all people.'

'This has to stop,' he said angrily. 'Serena has gone too far this time.'

'Ah Serena,' she said sadly. 'My beautiful granddaughter.'

'She is ill,' said Sybil. 'She needs help.'

'She gets all the help she needs from me.'

Sybil banged her fist on the table in front of the old woman. 'Do you know what she has been doing in the cave? ' she asked angrily.

Daisy shrugged uncaring. 'No. But she is special,' she smiled fondly, 'just like my husband. He was special.'

'Your husband was evil,' said Sybil.

A clock ticked loudly in the silence while Daisy looked blankly at her.

'He was a good man.' she said sternly.

'He was smuggler, and worse!'

Daisy looked away from her furious gaze towards the photo of Absalon hanging over the fireplace. His grim face stared down at the tableau before him. 'It was necessary,' she said, smiling slightly at his picture.

'What is wrong with you all?' Sybil shook her head in disbelief then started as Duncan began to speak haltingly beside her.

'You have to understand Sybil, this was a poor village and times were hard, very hard.'

'Yes,' said Daisy, nodding in agreement. 'And the men did what was necessary to provide for their families,' she shrugged, 'and if that involved a little smuggling then that is what they did. Nobody got hurt.'

'But Thomas did!' shouted Sybil. 'Your husband murdered him.'

Mrs Coppinger slammed her hand down on the table making the china jump. 'My husband wouldn't hurt a fly,' she said hotly.

'Daisy,' remonstrated Duncan. 'That's enough said.'

Sybil looked at him in disbelief. 'Why are you protecting him? It was your brother that was killed.' She shook her head by now totally confused and very tired. Tired of the whole village and just wanting to be away.

Mrs Coppinger rose stiffly from the table and walked slowly to an old dresser, she pulled open one of the drawers. 'They are so keen to know Duncan.' She turned around holding an old pistol. 'I think I should satisfy her curiosity.'

Sybil's heart froze as she looked at the gun in her hand.

'Do you know what this is?' she asked Sybil.

'Yes, it is an old German Luger.'

'Well done,' she murmured and hobbled back to the table. 'You see, it was just a terrible mistake,' she said calmly.

'A mistake!' shouted Duncan. 'That was my brother!'

'Calm yourself Duncan. It wasn't Absalon's fault.' She turned back to Sybil, 'You see,' she continued, ignoring Duncan's outburst, 'he was offered a lot of money for a special cargo but it wasn't what he and the men were expecting.' She looked down at the gun in her hand. 'This was the first thing that gave him away. Silly really; to bring this.'

Sybil, her thoughts reeling, looked at Duncan who was staring sadly at the floor.

'The war had just started,' he said slowly, 'and it was becoming more and more difficult to make any runs. And with the rationing any extra income was always needed.' He walked slowly to the sofa and sat down, his hands rubbing the rough material of his trousers. 'They didn't realise,' he said quietly, 'not until they brought him ashore.'

'Who?' she asked wildly. 'What are you talking about?'

'He killed Thomas, not my husband,' said Mrs Coppinger coldly. 'My Absalon was a good man.'

Duncan snorted. 'He was a clever, grasping bugger but,' he hesitated, 'he wasn't a murderer.'

Her legs suddenly weak Sybil collapsed onto the sofa next to him. Outside the birds were singing and the fragrance from the roses drifted in through the half open window but none of that seemed to matter. Inside, the room was thick with death and intrigue. 'So what happened to this man?' she asked weakly.

'He was in the cellar for days while they tried to decide what to do. The men beat him half to death; they wanted to kill him. But Absalon stopped it; he wanted to do the right thing and hand him in to the authorities.'

Sybil shook her head confused.

A slight smile played over Daisy's lips as she looked at the gun in her hand. 'But I couldn't let him do that. If they had handed the man in they would all have been arrested. It was treason to smuggle in a German spy. My Absalon would have been hanged as a traitor.'

'And father, and the rest of the men,' put in Duncan.

She carried on, ignoring Duncan again and said softly, 'And I couldn't allow that, could I? I couldn't let them take my husband. So I waited until they were asleep and I went down into the cellar,' she looked at Sybil, blinking slowly remembering the scene. 'I shot him,' she said simply.

Duncan groaned and put his head in his hands. 'Why did you have to tell her?'

'You killed the man in the cellar?'

'Yes... His name was Kurt, he begged me to help but of course I couldn't,' she paused and looked at the photo. 'I did it for my husband,' a troubled look came over her face and the gun wavered in her hand, 'but he didn't understand.' She looked appealingly at Duncan. 'Why? Why didn't he? The way he looked at me...'

'Daisy,' he said gently, moving to her side, 'let me have the gun.'

'No,' she said, looking past the old man to where Sybil was still sitting speechless on the sofa. 'Everything I did will be for nothing if she leaves this house. It will all come out and my husband will be branded a traitor, and I couldn't bear that.' Her mouth trembled and a single tear ran down her cheek, she brushed it away absently as she continued to watch Sybil. 'Why couldn't you just mind your own business, always poking about and asking questions,' she cried out suddenly. 'And now I have to stop you taking Serena from me as well.'

As if she had been waiting outside, the young woman suddenly appeared, sidling in through the door and blinking vaguely at the angry trio of people. 'Grandmother?' she asked, her face pale and anxious. 'What is she doing here? And where is the other one?' Serena scurried to her grandmother's side and gripping her arm hissed in her ear, 'They're evil, grandma, they will bring death here. I have seen them, they summoned evil things.'

Her grandmother nodded, not taking her eyes from Sybil. 'You're right dear,' she said comfortingly. 'Now don't worry, Duncan and I will deal with her.'

A sudden image of her sister lying on the stretcher appeared in front of her and a wave of rage swept over Sybil and she bounced to her feet. 'Aren't two murders enough for this village?' she shouted, and glared furiously at the old man. 'And you,' she spat, 'what is wrong with you. Your poor brother can't rest in peace because of this family. Are you going to help them commit another murder, how many more people are you going to hurt? Because we won't be the last to ask questions.'

'Grandma,' whimpered Serena, retreating from Sybil's fury. 'Stop her.'

Daisy raised the gun and pointed it at Sybil's chest. 'Whatever it takes to keep the family's reputation intact I will do it.'

Sybil gazed into her eyes and seeing the cold determination braced herself, but the shot never came. Duncan had placed himself in front of the old woman and held out his hand again for the gun.

'That's enough Daisy. She's right, all these lies have to stop and if the truth comes out then so be it.' He carefully reached forward and took the gun from her slackening grip then quickly placed it in his pocket. 'It was a long time ago and it's time we buried our ghosts.' Duncan's voice broke as he said this and he looked at Sybil. 'And,' he said sadly, 'the thought of poor Thomas still wandering about the village instead of being at peace breaks my heart. So I would like the truth to come out so that all of them, Absalon included, are at peace.'

They both jumped as there was a crash behind them, Daisy had swept the china teapot to the floor in a fit of rage. 'My husband is at rest,' she growled, 'he was a good man.'

Sybil, her knees shaking, got up slowly and walked across the room to stand beside Duncan. She stared coldly at the woman. 'You're wrong, Absalon still walks this village. We have seen him,' she carried on, despite Daisy's angry gesture, 'he showed us his corpse buried up in the woods.'

The sudden shout of laughter made her jump.

'God, you don't know anything, you stupid woman,' shouted Daisy, hobbling around the table towards them, scattering bits of broken china with her cane. 'That's Kurt buried in the woods. My husband died at sea; an honourable death.'

'It was guilt,' Duncan said, shaking his head, 'guilt that killed them all.'

Daisy's face crumpled and she suddenly sobbed, a huge wracking sob that made her collapse against the table, her hands clutching at the tablecloth. 'He left me!' she cried out.

'Grandma?' whispered Serena, from her position near the wall. 'Don't cry.'

But she gave no sign of hearing her granddaughter, her thoughts entirely centred on her lost husband. 'He didn't understand, I did it for him.'

A chill ran up Sybil's spine as she listened to Daisy's heartbroken sobs, the old woman's memory still raw after all these years.

'What happened to him?' she whispered in Duncan's ear.

He tentatively put a comforting hand on Daisy's shoulder and muttered to Sybil, 'They all answered the call for the Dunkirk evacuation. I think they were so racked with remorse that they were desperate to make amends. They sailed off in their boats to help and didn't come back except for Bruce's grandfather,' he added bitterly, 'he made it back.'

He gently helped Daisy to the armchair and straightened wearily, passing a hand over his eyes he sighed 'And there you have it, the tragedy of this village that has never been forgotten.' Duncan glared defiantly at Daisy. 'Now I am going to take Sybil to her car,' and he raised a threatening finger to the Coppinger women, 'and don't even think about trying to stop us. The Coppingers,' he said suddenly, as though unable to contain himself any longer, 'have been the worst blight on this village and my family. Damn you all!' he cursed, and roughly grabbing Sybil's arm pulled her to the door.

Slowing as she passed Serena huddled against the wall Sybil stared coldly at the young woman. 'If my sister dies...' she began menacingly.

'She's not going to die,' Duncan said sharply. 'Now come on!'

They scurried out of the cottage and down the front path to the gate, Duncan only letting go of Sybil's arm when they reached the street but even then he was still visibly nervous and kept casting fearful glances behind him.

'What's wrong?'

'You have forgotten Bruce,' he said sharply. 'He still thinks you have his property. That little bag is worth quite a lot of money.'

Their footsteps clattered on the cobbles as they hurried up the deserted street; the evening was drawing in and the street lights were just coming on casting small puddles of warm light onto the ground. Sybil, struggling to keep up with Duncan who was surprisingly spry for a man of his age, managed to gasp out, 'My sister was right to be suspicious about this chocolate box village, it is a den of iniquity!'

Duncan snorted and slowed down, looking at Sybil with a hint of amusement on his face.

'Is she ever wrong?'

'No.'

'Then I am sure she will take great pleasure in saying "I told you so".'

Sybil's spirits were just beginning to lift as they left the cottage behind them and her thoughts were turning to her sister when behind them the squeal of the cottage gate echoed up the street. As one they stopped and looked back. Bruce had just emerged from the front garden and was walking purposefully towards them.

Panic gripped Sybil and she gasped, 'We won't make it to the car, he will catch us.'

Without a word Duncan snatched at her hand and hurried her towards Albert's cottage that was just ahead. The front door was closed but not locked; Duncan threw it open and pulled Sybil in after him into the dark hallway then slammed and locked it as Bruce, seeing where they were going broke into a run.

'Who's that?' came a querulous voice from the front room.

'It's us,' shouted Duncan.

'And who is us?'

Sybil pushed the door open and peered in at Albert who was sitting in front of the fire busy filling his pipe with tobacco.

'Evening,' he said calmly, looking up. 'What have you been up to now?'

'Bruce,' she said, sinking down into the chair opposite.

'Ahh,' he said, around the chewed stem of his pipe. 'Wants his property back, does he?'

'How did you know that?' she gasped.

His eyes twinkled at her over the bowl of his pipe. 'I know everything that goes on this village,' he said, and raised his eyebrows, 'I hope your sister is okay?'

'I don't know,' Sybil said miserably, looking towards the window where Bruce's shadow could be clearly seen against the heavy net curtains. 'I was trying to get to the car.'

'Ahh,' he said again, striking a match. 'And he is in the way.'

'I don't have the bag,' she said indignantly. 'Can't you tell him that?' she appealed to Duncan who had moved over to the window.

'He wouldn't believe you.'

'I don't know where it is!'

'I do,' said Albert, reaching down by the side of his chair. 'I've got it,' and showed Sybil the bag of amphetamines.

'How long have you had that?' Sybil asked angrily.

He grinned. 'A while; Joey brought it here, thought it would be safer with me.' He pushed it back into its hiding place and stretched out contentedly. 'And I'm not giving it to Bruce either,' he chuckled. He paused as a rapping sounded on the window pane.

'Albert. Open the door, I just want to talk.'

'No,' he replied loudly, and winked at Sybil who was cowering in her chair.

'Don't let him in,' she implored.

He blew a fragrant puff of smoke and peered at her through the smoke. 'The fun never ends with you around,' he said, and looked across at Duncan who was hovering nervously near the door. 'Come and sit down. He can't get in and if he does...' he smiled and reached down by the side of his chair and pulled up a double barrelled shotgun. Ignoring Sybil's squeak he laid it across his knees and lovingly patted it. 'I didn't like his grandfather, old Mathew Parish, and I really didn't like his father Frank and I absolutely loath Bruce. So any excuse to shoot him would be fine.'

'You can't do that!' exclaimed Sybil, 'That's murder.'

Albert removed the pipe from his mouth and stared at her. 'I'm not going to kill him,' he said earnestly, 'I'm just going to damage him a bit!' He jammed the stem back in his mouth and nodded happily. 'Been waiting for years for this opportunity.'

'Well I won't allow it,' she said firmly, 'there's been enough blood spilled in this village already.'

A shadow passed close to the window and they could see Bruce pressing against the glass and trying to peer through the net curtains into the dark room.

'Just open the door you old fools,' he shouted. 'She's nothing to you. All I want is my property back. Hand her over and the bag and I will give you a cut of the profits.' Receiving no answer he beat his fist against the window. 'Open the damn door!'

'Bugger off Parish,' shouted Albert, grinning with glee, 'You ain't coming in.'

The dark shadow moved from the window and Sybil whispered hopefully, 'Has he gone?'

'No, he hasn't,' replied Duncan, looking at her in exasperation. 'He's not going to give up that easily and he knows you will want to get to the hospital. So all Bruce has to do is wait.'

She sank her head in her hands. 'Poor Queenie, I must get out of here,' she groaned.

'He knows that,' said Albert, puffing away. 'As soon as you put your nose outside the door he'll pounce on you. And he doesn't play nice,' he added warningly.

'Then I will call the police,' she said, standing up. 'Where's your phone?'

'You can't!' Duncan left his position near the window and hurried over to her. 'Think of Daisy,' he implored. 'She would be arrested for murder and she's an old woman.' He stepped back quickly at the expression on Sybil's face.

'So is my sister and she is in hospital because of that family!' Sybil pointed her finger at the old man and said sharply, 'If you think that I am going to keep quiet about all of this then you must be mad!'

Hearing a low chuckle behind her Sybil swung round to face Albert.

'You're as feisty as your sister.' He removed the pipe from his mouth and waved it towards the hall. 'The phone is out there, go and ring the hospital and ask about Queenie, I'd be interested to hear how she is doing myself,' he admitted.

'I will,' Sybil said resolutely, 'and I'm going to call the Police as well.'

'No, don't do that,' he said, 'I have already called them.'

'What?' said Duncan, a look of dismay on his face. 'Why?'

Albert didn't meet his friend's eye, just concentrated on tamping down the tobacco in his pipe. 'I thought it was time,' he said simply, and then grinned slyly 'and if we are clever in what we say they might haul just Bruce off to the clink.'

Duncan nodded and walked slowly to a chair and sat down. 'We might be able to keep Daisy out of it,' he suggested hopefully.

'I don't believe you two!' Sybil said indignantly, and would have said a lot more but a shadow flickered across the window followed by a gentle knock on the door.

'Duncan. Are you there?' It was Daisy Coppinger.

'Huh!' grunted Sybil. 'Speak of the devil.'

'Duncan,' she repeated, 'open the door.'

He half rose on hearing her pleading voice, glancing nervously at Albert and Sybil.

'Sit down!' Albert said sharply. 'Nobody is setting foot in my cottage. We'll just sit tight and wait for the Police to get here.' He waved his pipe at Sybil again. 'I thought you were going to ring the hospital?'

She stood up and hurried past Duncan giving him a concerned look as she passed. 'Everything will work out for the best,' she said, trying to reassure him.

He looked up and just gave her a slight smile; the worried look remained on his face as she headed for the hall. Another rap on the door made her jump as she was reaching for the phone. Daisy's low voice came through the door.

'Duncan. Can you hear me? I need your help,' she appealed. Behind Daisy's soft tones Sybil could hear the low muttered promptings from Bruce then her voice came again, this time more insistant.

'Duncan,' she said sharply, 'you need to open the door. Think of your family.'

The phone still held in her hand Sybil peered back into the dimly lit room to gauge Duncan's reaction to this latest appeal wondering what Daisy meant by 'your family'. Was she threatening Duncan's granddaughter? she wondered.

'Don't you do it,' Albert mumbled, puffing out billowing clouds of smoke. 'She has no loyalty to you or this village, all she cares about is Serena and the memory of her husband.'

For a while there was silence outside the door as though Daisy was waiting for Duncan to respond. Sybil waited and listened then began to dial the number for the local hospital. There was a loud click just as it began to ring and the phone went dead. She looked at the phone in dismay.

'I've been cut off!' she cried out.

'Huh!' Albert snorted, 'that would be Bruce, clever devil, isn't he?'

'But I need to call the hospital,' Sybil gazed in frustration at the phone and jiggled the receiver. 'Damn and blast!' she muttered.

'Now, now, Sybil don't despair,' Albert replied, reaching into his pocket. 'In this age of technology there is such a thing as mobile phones, even for old duffers like me.' He held up an Apple iPhone and grinned. 'Bruce didn't take into account that I might have one of these; really useful,' he grunted, looking with pleasure at the latest model. 'I can ring anybody from the comfort of my chair.' He tossed it onto her recently vacated chair. 'Try that.'

But her attention had been caught by noises coming from the back of the house and she froze as a thud came from the kitchen. Bruce was trying to break in the back door and by the sound of the splintering wood it wouldn't be long before he was in. Albert swung round to face the door, his pipe dropping from his mouth.

'Damn him!' he spluttered, struggling to get out of his chair. He reached down and dragged up the gun and stood cradling it in his arms. 'Just let him come in here,' he declared wrathfully, 'I'll show him.'

'You're not going to show anybody anything, you idiot' said Duncan, picking up Albert's walking stick. 'It's time to go.'

'Where?' said Sybil.

'We'll go out the front while he's busy at the back, now come on.' He took Albert's arm and hurried him to the front door. They were just stumbling out onto the front step when an enormous splintering crash echoed through the house followed by the sound of Bruce's voice in the kitchen.

'He's paying for that!' growled Albert, trying to look back over Duncan shoulder. 'I have just had that painted!'

Chapter Fifteen

Outside in the street a number of people had gathered around Daisy who was tearfully talking in low tones; she stopped when she saw them emerge from the cottage.

'There she is!' Daisy cried, pointing a shaking finger at Sybil. 'She's the thief! She took my purse.'

A growing murmur greeted Sybil as she stepped forward defiantly. 'Shame on you!'

'A thief? So I am accused of stealing now, as well as assault!' She looked around at the onlookers. 'Are you all asleep?' she said bitingly. 'You're being led around by the nose by these Coppingers. Wake up and smell the coffee! They have been smuggling drugs for God's sake. And that is the real truth! They are nothing but common criminals.' Sybil looked into their hostile faces and a chill ran down her spine, she looked round desperately for Albert and Duncan. 'Tell them!' she pleaded. They shuffled up to stand on either side of her as Bruce and Serena emerged from the front door of the cottage. Bruce was clutching a crowbar in his hand which he raised and pointed at Sybil. 'Where's the bag?' he growled.

'See?' she exclaimed, staring at them. 'All he cares about is his smuggled drugs.'

'That's not true,' said Daisy, appealing to her neighbours. 'Bruce and I are very worried about my brother and the nonsense she has been telling him.'

Sybil's mouth fell open in shock and she looked at Duncan in dismay. 'You're her brother?'

He nodded miserably and she turned from him to stare at Daisy and caught the quick look of triumph on her face before it disappeared to be replaced by a worried and concerned expression.

'My poor brother,' she said slowly, 'what has she been telling you?' She held out a hand and beckoned him forward. 'Come over here Duncan, come away from that woman.'

'No, Daisy,' he said firmly, straightening his shoulders. 'Sybil has been telling the truth.' He looked at his friends and neighbours. 'She's right, Bruce has been smuggling and all the lies he has told about Sybil and Queenie are just an attempt to cover it up.' Duncan gestured at his sister in disgust. 'And all she cares about is Serena and keeping Absalon's precious reputation intact. Well,' he paused and glared at everybody, 'it has to stop.'

There was low murmuring as they listened to his words and Bruce, smiling slightly, shifted the crowbar in his hand. 'This is a smugglers village, that is who we are,' he declared, looking around the crowd. 'Aren't we?'

'Not anymore,' one voice called out from the back. 'Those days have gone and good job too!'

'Aye,' they all murmured, 'too right.'

'Those Parishes always were a bit flaky,' somebody muttered.

Bruce stared at the hostile faces. 'Well, damn you all,' he said angrily, before turning his attention back to Sybil. 'Now hand it over.'

'I haven't got it. It fell into the sea when we were struggling with Serena. If you want it you will have to go fishing out in the bay,' she said bravely.

'I think you're lying,' he said menacingly, and moved towards her then paused as Albert laughed.

'You're right, she is lying,' he said, and brought up the shotgun level with Bruce's chest. 'I have your bag of drugs and I'm confiscating them for the good of the community. And we as a village will decide what to do with them, and you!' he said pointedly. He looked at his neighbours. 'Is everybody in agreement?'

'You think you're going to stop me?' growled Bruce quickly.

'He's called the Police,' put in Sybil, 'and you'll be arrested.' Sybil looked at Daisy as she spoke and saw the shock appear on her face. 'And you too,' she said, 'for murder.'

There was a gasp from the assembled crowd and they all swung around to look at the old woman standing defiantly amongst them.

'I did what I had to,' she said proudly, holding her head high and glaring at Sybil. 'You wouldn't understand; somebody like you.' Her voice suddenly faltered and she seemed to suddenly sag in front of their eyes. 'Now I would like to go home,' she said weakly and looked appealingly around. 'Would somebody walk me back to my cottage? All this has been too much for me; I'm just an old woman.'

She had begun to shiver violently in the cold night air and her breath plumed out in the dim light from the street lamps. The temperature had dropped dramatically in the street and a freezing wind was blowing straight off the sea and whistling down the narrow space between the cottages.

Sybil's fingers began to tingle.

Far out in the bay and echoing across the water came the mournful clanging of a ships bell. Albert faltered and the gun lowered in his suddenly slack hand as he turned to peer through the passageway and out to sea. A dense black cloud, darker than the evening sky, was rolling swiftly towards the shore and from inside the swirling mist came the sounds of creaking rigging and waves crashing against the prow. The boat hidden within swiftly outpaced the mist and began to emerge. A fully rigged ketch appeared to their startled eyes as it sped towards the beach. In front as though pushed forward by the prow, a thin layer of ice crystallized over the tops of the waves and as it drew closer to the shore quickly spread up the beach crusting the shingle with a delicate layer of frost. It crept closer and closer to the cottages freezing everything in its path. The cobbles in the street turned white with ice and the white film crept up and over the spectator's feet as they watched in terror. Swiftly following the ice came a freezing, swirling fog which flooded up the beach and poured into the street. There was a thunderous noise as the boat ran aground on the shingle, its bell continued to toll, the sound resounding around the bay and ringing off the walls of the buildings. With each mournful clang the energy was sucked from the onlooker's bodies and they watched dumbly as a line of misty shapes disembarked from the ship and began to walk slowly up the beach. Striding in front was Cruel Coppinger leading his men to the steps between the cottages and ultimately to Sybil and the terrified villagers.

So many gaunt hard faced men poured out of the passageway and crowded around the living. More wraiths swarmed over the sea wall and drifted along the street to gaze on in cold faced disdain as they huddled together in the street unable to escape from the gathering dead. 'Do something!' Albert whispered in Sybil's ear, giving her a nudge and gestured to the ghostly figures waiting in the swirling mist.

'What do you want me to do?' she hissed indignantly.

'I don't know; you're the expert. You and your sister brought all this to a head,' he reminded her.

Sybil bit her lip and scanned the throng of pale faces gathered in front of her. They stood ranged behind the wraith known as Cruel Coppinger silently waiting. Waiting for what? she suddenly wondered, then as if in answer Sybil heard footsteps approaching along the cobbled street, coming from the church. 'It can't be,' she whispered. 'Queenie got rid of him.'

A dark figure began to emerge from the mist, the waiting figures parting as he moved slowly forward. It was Absalon.

'But Queenie sent him back,' uttered Sybil, aghast at his appearance.

'It will take more than your sister to get rid of that old devil,' Albert muttered, holding onto his shotgun tightly.

'What are you going to do with that?' she asked acidly, 'Shoot him? He's a ghost!'

'I know, I know!' he snapped.

A gasp came from the crowd as Daisy recognised the approaching figure. 'It's my husband!' She stumbled out into the middle of the street and peered through the dim light. 'He's come back,' she whispered. As he paced slowly through the rising mist six shadowy figures appeared at his side. With them came the darkness and as they passed each street lamp it dimmed, flickered and went out leaving only one light still burning over the gathered crowd. The men slowed to a halt just outside the circle of light, their faces pale and gaunt in the gloom yet their eyes burning with a dark purpose. The crowd, now silent, drew closer and watched in horror as Absalon slowly stepped forward. Staggering towards him Daisy reached out and asked pitifully, 'Why did you leave me?'

His cold eyes stared at her unblinking; sweeping the elderly woman from head to toe then turned away and searched the crowd looking for one particular person. An expression of frustration crossed his face when he saw that she was missing.

'She's not here,' Sybil said boldly, stepping forward. 'Haven't you done enough? You've ruined so many lives with your actions and you're still trying to control things from beyond the grave.' She gestured to Serena who was staring at him in a bemused way. 'Look at your granddaughter. She has lost her mind because of you.'

Absalon stepped closer and his expression grew colder, close behind the men followed, all staring fixedly at Sybil

'It's no good,' Sybil said, trying to stay calm. 'I can't hear you. I haven't my sisters' talent for communicating with the dead.'

'I can hear you grandfather,' cried out Serena, pushing her way past Sybil. 'I have always heard you.' She turned and faced everybody. 'This is the way it should be; we will control the village as always. Our village,' she crowed.

A horrified murmur spread throughout the crowd as they turned to face the dead that were closing in on them from all sides.

'Serena is right, what you are all afraid of?' Bruce said, thrusting Sybil out of the way. He spread his arms wide and appealed to his friends and neighbour, 'They belong here.' He pointed suddenly at Sybil, 'But she doesn't, she is the reason they have had to return. This woman is trying to destroy our way of life. We are smugglers,' he said triumphantly, then raised the crowbar and pointed it at Sybil. 'All we have to do is take care of her.'

'No!' said Duncan, stepping in front of Sybil to shield her from Bruce. 'Then you are not one of us either,' he said menacingly, and started to move towards the old man raising the crowbar to strike him down.

Bruce's step faltered and the weapon dropped from his grasp as Cruel Coppinger detached himself from the crowd of waiting dead and slowly paced towards him, a look of murderous rage contorting his face. He stopped just inches from Bruce, his white gaunt face twisted in disgust and he reached out an icy hand and grasped the man's throat. Bruce's skin instantly turned white beneath his fingers and as the ghost's touch began to burn and bite into his flesh he jerked back, gasping out, 'But I am one of you!'

Coppinger reached for him again and dug his thin icy fingers into the man's throat and watched in satisfaction as the skin froze under his touch. Bruce began to scream as the ice spread from his neck and travelled swiftly through his body. Ice crystals formed around his mouth muffling his wail and slowly crept up his face. His last pleading look was quickly smothered by a layer of frost turning his eyes milky white.

Bruce dropped like a stone to the cobbles.

As he toppled there was a hissing sound that mounted and swelled with triumph coming from the watching dead. Screams came from the crowd and some turned as though to run, but hesitated when they realised to escape they would have to push their way through the throngs of the dead.

'No,' shrieked Serena, and rushed to his side, she knelt and peered into his face. 'Bruce?' she whispered.

But from where she stood Sybil could see that Bruce was dead.

'Why?' Serena called out to the watchers, leaping to her feet. 'I brought you back. I opened the doorway between our worlds so that you could return!'

An eerie wailing rose at her words and long icy tendrils swiftly rose from the fog and blew around the young woman's body, clutching and grasping at her limbs. Serena shuddered at the cold touch.

'What's wrong?' she whispered to the watching Absalon.

'They didn't want to come back,' said Sybil. 'You summoned them against their will,' she shook her head and said slowly, 'My sister always says that for every summoning there is a price to pay, and they are expecting you to pay it.'

'But I gave them blood,' she cried out, jerking away from a ghostly hand clutching at her. 'Isn't that enough?'

Grey shapes slowly grew from the mist at her feet and moved to surround her. She shrieked. Faces appeared rising out of the swirling fog, hideous and gaunt, staring hungrily at the woman, so young and full of life. Vacant eye sockets stared at her and Serena shrieked again as they drew closer. 'Grandfather, help.'

He gave little sign that he had heard, his face remaining impassive as the grey spectres reached for her. Her flesh turned white from their deathly grip and she slumped to the floor as the life force froze within her. Serena's face began to freeze and through stiffening lips she managed to gasp out an appeal to her grandmother. 'Grandma,' she pleaded. 'Help me.' Her desperate gaze travelled from Daisy to Sybil as she slowly collapsed.

Daisy watched in horror as Serena lay on the floor surrounded by the grey spectres. Shrugging off a restraining hand Daisy stumbled through the swirling figures to reach her, but a wraith quickly rose up in front of her and blocked her path. A skull like face emerged from the mist in front of her, muscle and skin quickly fleshed out the grey bones. Recognising the long dead face she fell back.

'Not you,' she wailed, covering her eyes.

A dark hole began to appear in the middle of its forehead and blood began to ooze out and trickle down the still face. Daisy's legs buckled beneath her and she would have fallen but for Duncan who had hurried to her side.

'I had to do it. I'm sorry.' she whimpered and looked imploringly at Sybil. 'Help her please,' she whispered.

Forcing her quivery legs forward Sybil hurried to her side. 'Serena,' Sybil cried out, batting away the icy figures that tried to stop her. 'Enough,' she said sternly, kneeling she quickly wrapped her arms around the limp body and glared up at Absalon. 'No matter what she has done, she is still your granddaughter or doesn't that mean anything to you?'

The mist flowed around them both as Serena lay unconscious in her arms and Absalon continued to watch, unwilling or unable to save his kin.

'Do something Sybil!' Janet hissed, from the middle of the huddle of villagers.

'I don't know what to do,' Sybil said, she looked wildly at them, the mute appeal obvious on their faces.

Behind her there was a sudden clatter of footsteps as Jenny darted through the surrounding ring of ghosts and sped off down the street towards the cafe. Sybil watched Jenny disappear and a feeling of desolation entered her soul as her only friend in the village deserted her. Serena stirred and whimpered in her arms and Sybil looked down into her eyes, which once blue were now white and opaque. Mentally shaking herself she gently lowered Serena to the ground and stood up. Gathering her thoughts Sybil desperately racked her brains for a banishment spell.

'Banish now with spell and...,' she began haltingly, 'um...will? No, that's not right,' she muttered. 'Great Goddess of....protect us...Oh damn,' she suddenly cried out. 'I can't remember the spell. If Queenie was here...' she glared fiercely at the spectres crowding in around her. Icy hands reached out to her and grasped her throat as the dead tried to stop her uttering the banishment spell. Sybil's skin began to burn under their touch and she staggered back trying to escape the grasping tendrils. 'Thrice around the circles bound sink all evil...' she began desperately, swiping away the many hands that were clutching at her and trying to pull her down. 'Sink all evil to the ground.' Sybil began to choke as a hand gripped her throat forcing her to stop; she looked around desperate for help and heard in the distance running footsteps. It was Jenny dragging Queenie's case behind her.

A spark of hope flared in Sybil's heart and she managed to summon enough energy to stagger towards her approaching friend.

Jenny threw the case down at Sybil's feet and gasped out, 'I brought everything.'

'You're a genius, Jenny,' she said, and began pulling out Queenie's collection of 'special toys' as her sister called them.

'What about this?' suggested Jenny desperately, pulling out the scrying mirror and watching in fear as the shadowy figures began to reform and gather around Sybil.

'Not that,' said Sybil, throwing things out onto the road as she desperately searched for something that would help. Then her hands grew still as they closed on the one thing she could use. The herb long used to repel evil spirits. Sybil drew it out and clasped it to her chest sending up a silent prayer of thanks. She stood upright and faced Absalon and held out the bunch of dried lavender bound with a piece of old grey cloth. Drawing a deep breath she cried out, 'I call upon you Hannah, my blood kin, come to my aid and protect me from these unwholesome spirits. I summon you from the spirit world, aid me in my hour of need.' Sybil clasped the lavender tightly and stared at the ghosts hovering in front of her. 'Blood calls to blood.'

In the dead silence that followed the whole village held its breath and watched as little motes of light appeared hovering over Sybil's head, with them came a warm gust of lavender scented air that floated along the street and swirled gently around the frozen people.

Sybil smiled in relief and looked down at the grey cat that had appeared at her feet. 'Thank you,' she murmured quietly, reaching down and laying her hand on its head.

'A cat?' whispered Jenny.

'Hannah is more than a cat,' she replied quickly, wanting to reassure her. 'She is family and it is from her that we inherited our skills in the occult.'

The elderly grey cat padded forward, delicately picking her way through the puddles left by the melting ice. Around her the air grew warmer and was filled with the scent of new mown hay and blossom. She stopped in front of the watching dead. Small blue motes appeared swirling around the cat's feet, looking like little fireflies they swirled faster and faster blurring into one solid glow of dazzling light. Within this ring the body of the cat grew and stretched, expanding and flowing upwards into the form of a woman. As the light faded and fell away Hannah stepped forward and stared around the group of people, living and dead.

'Good evening,' she turned and looked fondly at Sybil, 'and to you, m'dear. I have come to aid you as asked.'

'I had no doubt that you would,' Sybil said huskily. 'I just didn't know what to do.'

Hannah nodded, pushing a stray lock of greying hair back under her lace cap. 'Don't you fret, m'dear. I will do what I can. Now,' said Hannah, surveying the ranks of the dead gathered around her. 'Gentlemen, it's time you were gone.'

An anguished whisper issued from the long dead throats which threatened to turn into a roar of protest. An icy wind soughed up through the passageway ruffling Hannah's greying hair and long grey dress.

'That'll be enough of that,' she said firmly. 'You don't belong here no more,' her voice softened as she attempted to comfort the tormented dead, 'but have no fear I will not banish you to walk in everlasting darkness. All will be set right and you will join your families in the spirit world and rest for ever in peace and joy.' Hannah beckoned Sybil forward. 'Come here m'dear.' She looked around at the cowering villagers who were watching open mouthed. 'All of 'ee gather close,' she instructed. 'This is much your burden as theirs, so with these words you will wish them well and help me send them on their way to everlasting peace.' Hannah took Sybil's hand and held it tightly. 'Now, clear your mind and focus your will. And we'll end this unhappy curse.' Hannah looked at Absalon and his men who had drawn closer to her and Sybil. 'All but seven will depart,' she instructed, gesturing Sybil to keep quiet and stilling her sudden protest.

Pointing to the ranks of the dead she spoke gently, 'It is time to leave. What was done was done and be it now undone. Return to thy rest and leave behind the hurt and memories of the past. By the light of this moon I cleanse you of taint and stain and return your spirits to their state of grace. Go now and complete your passage. Go and with our blessing be at peace.' Releasing Sybil's hand she held her hands out in a blessing. 'So mote it be,' she said firmly.

An expression of utter relief spread over each of their faces and their grim expressions slowly faded into joy as the shackles binding them to the village were released. As the ghosts retraced their steps back to the beach they began to fade, and as the silent crowd watched they dwindled away and diminished into little sparks of light hovering over the shingle. A gentle lavender scented breeze wafted them up over the beach and they floated skywards like a cloud of thistledown, higher and higher until they eventually disappeared into the night sky. The great ship that carried their spirits ashore slid slowly back into the water and sailed out into the bay disappearing slowly into the distance.

Leaving just the seven men behind. They gathered in front of the woman and gazed fearfully at her.

'Your burden is the heaviest,' said Hannah, addressing them. 'By your actions the death of an innocent was caused, but your sorrow is deep, this I can tell, and it is time you were released.'

Absalon bowed his head.

'You are all bound to this village and it is time for those ties to be cut,' Hannah said sternly, 'for everybody's sake.'

Thomas's father stepped forward, the pain evident in his eyes.

'My heart grieves for you,' Hannah said softly, 'but you will be reunited with your boy.' She then looked at Daisy who was still sheltering in her brothers arms. 'Poor foolish woman, she loved too deeply; loved somebody who perhaps didn't deserve such devotion. Still, her guilt is also heavy.' Hannah looked at Serena who was still laying on the cobbles, curled up in a foetal position, her blank eyes just staring into space. 'This poor child's mind has gone,' she said, laying a cold hand on Serena's forehead, 'and I can do nothing for her.'

Hannah's long skirt rustled as she straightened. 'Now let us cut the cords that bind you to this place,' she said to the seven men, and gesturing to Sybil and the rest of the villagers to follow, glided down the street heading towards the Coppingers cottage.

Following close behind Hannah and Sybil was Absalon and his crew; hesitating for just the briefest second Duncan gently took his sisters arm and guided her towards the cottage. Albert frowned and glanced across at Serena who was still lying on the cobbles, Janet and two of her friends kneeling by her side. Jenny, who was standing to one side, caught his look and moved quickly to his side.

She proffered her arm to the old man, 'Shall we?' she asked.

He nodded, 'I guess we had better,' he glared at the rest of his neighbours who were hurriedly disappearing into their cottages, 'as they are running off to hide, it behoves us to witness the final act, don't you think?'

'Absolutely. We have seen it this far. How worse can it get?' she said, smiling nervously.

Chapter Sixteen

Inside the cottage Hannah walked purposefully down the hall to the living room. Sybil, close behind her, paused in the doorway uncertain as to why she had led them back to the cottage.

'Hannah?' she asked.

Hannah was gazing up at the old photograph of Absalon hanging over the fireplace.

'Get it down Sybil.'

She hurried forward and reached up for heavy framed picture. 'Why?' she asked, as she carefully lifted it down.

'You will see.'

Laying the picture on the fireside chair she looked at Hannah who gestured for her to turn it over.

Tucked in the frame was an old brown envelope. Carefully opening the envelope that was brittle from age she pulled out a thin piece of paper and glancing up at the eager figures crowding forward she began to read the shaky copperplate handwriting.

To whom it may concern,

We, the undersigned confess that we knowingly took part in the unlawful trade of smuggling during a time of war and by our actions caused the bloody murder of the boy Thomas Puckett by an enemy of our country.

We vow that no mention of this dreadful time will pass our lips but we are determined that no innocent blood will ever be spilt in this village again and so give our most solemn blood oath that smuggling will never be tolerated in the village of Bindon and that all such trade will cease now and for evermore.

May our spirits for ever walk in torment if this oath is broken.

So say all of us.

Absalon Coppinger
James Puckett
George Riggs
John Bishop
Joseph Peach

Mark Bartlett
Mathew Parish

Beside each name was a thumbprint in blood.

Sybil stopped reading and looked up into Absalon's eyes. 'So you were bound here by your own oath,' she said quietly. 'And even worse it was your own grand-daughter who was doing the smuggling'.

He nodded slowly and a look of pain momentarily crossed his face as he looked at his wife slumped on the sofa.

Hannah stepped forward and gently took the letter from Sybil's hand. 'I think you have suffered enough, all of you. It is time to go.'

There was an anguished wail as Daisy cried out in protest, 'He can't leave me again.'

'Hush now. You will be together again in due course.' Hannah turned back to face the men clustered around Absalon, her gaze picking out Thomas's father. 'You should be at peace; it is time to join your loved ones.' She looked sternly at the villagers, 'Although a blood oath is a serious thing and not put aside so easily I have been given permission to break it, and as I doubt that anyone in this village will tolerate smuggling again it is safe to do so. So now,' she said calmly, gazing at the remaining seven men, 'be at peace.'

With this Hannah dropped the letter into the fireplace and as the thin piece of paper fluttered down onto the dead coals it burst into flames. The confession and blood oath was burnt to ashes.

'With the burning of this oath I set you free,' Hannah said softly. 'Take your leave and may the angels guide you to God's healing light. So Mote it be.'

A sigh like a gentle wave breaking on the sea shore filled the room, the front door swung slowly open and the men moved swiftly towards the sunlight that flooded the gloomy hall of the cottage. Outside the village was as it had been during their lifetime; the sound of laughter filled the air from the children playing in the street and women pausing in their chores gathered at their front doors to gossip. The men stepped eagerly forward recognising the long dead faces of their families gathering to welcome them home. Except for Absalon who paused on the threshold, he gazed back into the dim room and bowed his head to Sybil.

'Thank you,' he said simply, then stared across the room at Daisy who watched him in weeping silence. 'I will be waiting.'

Absalon then walked swiftly to the door and followed his crew out into the sunshine.

The sunlight slowly began to fade as they disappeared from view, but behind her Sybil heard Duncan cry out as he recognised the young boy in the street and moved as though to follow Absalon through the doorway. Hannah put a gentle hand on his shoulder.

'No Duncan, it isn't your time yet.' She smiled regretfully at Sybil, 'But it is time that I went home,' she said, moving towards the door. She paused before stepping through, 'Don't be sad Sybil; I have no doubt that I'll be seeing you and Queenie soon.'

Hannah smiled around the room in farewell and then walked out into the darkening street. Behind her the door swung shut.

There was silence in the room until Duncan pushed past Sybil and jerked the door open. Outside the street was quiet and empty, the darkness lit only by a few twinkling stars in the night sky.

The night air was cool and fresh after the stuffy atmosphere of the cottage. Sybil leant against the gate for a minute and rubbed a tired hand over her forehead.

'Are you off then?' enquired Albert, who was hobbling along the path towards her.

'Yes,' she said, 'I must get to the hospital.'

'Well, it's going to be very dull without you two here.'

'I am leaving you with quite a mess to clear up,' she apologized.

Albert looked up to the end of the street where he could just see the flashing blue lights of a police car. He grunted. 'Don't worry Sybil, we'll weather this storm. You had better go,' he urged, 'before you get caught up in any questions.'

She stared at the flickering lights and could just make out the silhouette of an officer walking down the street.

'Yes,' said Sybil, then looked sadly towards the church. 'What about Thomas?' she asked suddenly. 'Is he at rest?'

'I think so,' Albert said gruffly. 'Seems to me he was the sprat to catch the mackerel.' He grinned at Sybil's baffled expression. 'I guess Absalon would have been waiting for somebody like you and Queenie to come here, and all he had to do was dangle Thomas in front of your nose and you were off, hot on the trail.' He grinned again. 'I told you he was a clever bugger.'

'A Cunning Man indeed!' she said.

Chapter Seventeen

Queenie lay still and quiet in the hospital bed, surrounded by flowers sent by anxious friends she slept on unaware of her sisters' presence at her side. Her cold hand was held tightly in Sybil's as she gazed at the pale and bruised face.

'Poor old thing,' she murmured, stroking a lock of hair back from her forehead.

'Good job she's asleep,' said Gordon, entering the room with a cup of coffee in his hand, 'calling her that,' and placed the cup on the bedside cabinet. 'Don't worry Sybil, she will be fine,' he said gently, patting her on the shoulder. 'Queenie will be up in no time at all.' He looked round as the door opened again and Kitty pushed her way in with her arms full of flowers.

'They have just been delivered,' she said, laying the flowers down on the foot of the bed. Kitty peered at one of the notes pinned to a beautiful bunch of pink roses. 'Who is Albert?'

Sybil grinned weakly. 'A resident of Bindon. He took a fancy to Queenie; thought she was a tough old bird, which I think coming from him was a compliment,' she said wryly. Sybil gently patted her sister's hand. 'Look dear, more flowers for you.'

There was no response and Sybil blinked back a tear. 'I wish she would wake up,' she said mournfully.

'She will, when she is good and ready,' consoled Gordon. He pulled up a chair for Kitty and then perched on the end of the bed. 'I have been talking to a friend who works for the Customs and Excise.'

Sybil pricked up her ears. 'And?'

'He was being a bit cagey about giving too much away but reading between the lines I think they have had their eye on the Bella Venture for some time; they had a tip off from the Dutch authorities so I think it was only a matter of time before Joey was caught.'

'That makes sense, I suppose Serena still had contacts in Amsterdam. What about the rest of them?'

'Well... he wouldn't tell me too much, ongoing investigation as he called it. Oh,' he said suddenly, 'I mentioned the salt, you remember? In the bags? Apparently that is an old trick; the cargo is dropped over the side weighed down with bags of salt. And all Joey had to do was wait for the salt to dissolve over the course of a day or two and just hang around until it popped up to the surface. Very neat,' he said, grinning.

'Clever devils, aren't they?' a weak voice said from the bed.

'Queenie! You're awake.'

'You were making so much noise,' she grumbled.

'How are you feeling after your adventure?' asked Gordon.

'I'm feeling a bit worse for wear.'

'Time for a new hobby, I think,' Gordon said firmly.

She stirred slightly and said slowly, 'I think you're right, I have decided that I am going to learn to knit.'

'Good idea.'

The little cottage in Medbury was overflowing with flowers and little gifts for Queenie, waiting for the day she was released from hospital. Sybil, knowing her sister, ignored the Doctors suggestion of a few weeks convalescence in a care home and packed her sister into the little yellow car and whisked Queenie back to the peace and quiet of the village.

Tired from the journey and still weak, Queenie had collapsed into the fireside chair and closed her eyes. Still deathly pale, she had lost so much weight from her illness that her clothes were hanging from her frame and dark hollows had appeared in her cheeks.

She remained quiet and listless all the following week; with her appetite gone she took little interest in anything. In exasperation Sybil placed a ball of wool and a pair of knitting needles on her rug covered legs.

'Here,' she said. 'You wanted to learn to knit.'

'Thank you,' Queenie said meekly, and picked up the ball of wool. 'How do I cast on?'

For the next few days Queenie quietly struggled with the wool, eventually producing an irregular shaped square of knitting full of holes.

She held it up and showed her sister.

'How is that?'

Sybil put down the sleeve she was finishing and gazed at the sorry piece of knitting.

'That's very good dear,' she said encouragingly.

Queenie's brow puckered as she scrutinised her effort. 'I think I need more practice,' she sighed, rubbing her forehead.

'Headache?' enquired Sybil solicitously.

'Just tired.'

Queenie laid down the needles and wool and stared into the fire.

'How about a nice cup of tea?'

'Okay,' she replied listlessly.

Queenie closed her eyes and leant back against the chair, half listening to Sybil in the kitchen while her thoughts were still full of Thomas and the village. Although Sybil had reassured her that the situation had been dealt with Queenie still couldn't rest easy, feeling that she had failed Thomas in some way.

Underneath her fingers the wool twitched.

'Stop it Nigel,' she said wearily.

It moved again and she opened her eyes, expecting to see Sybil's little dog playing with the ball of wool. But Nigel was lying asleep on the hearth. Queenie looked down at the knitting lying on her knee; stitch by stitch it was being slowly unravelled.

'Do you know how long that took me?' she asked the empty room.

A low chuckle came from the hearth as the last stitch was pulled from the needles and they clattered to the floor.

'Who's there?'

A slight scuffling noise came from the hearth and Nigel raised his sleepy head to look at the figure slowly appearing next to him. Thomas, sitting cross legged on the rug, grinned at her. Seeing his gap toothed smile a sudden weight was lifted from Queenie's shoulders and she smiled back at the little boy.

'Thomas,' she said, 'what a nice surprise!' Queenie leant forward and looked searchingly at him, 'And you are okay?'

Thomas nodded and reaching over pressed a sprig of lavender into the palm of her hand. Queenie stared down at the fragrant bloom and then smiled to herself.

Seeing the look of understanding appearing on Queenie's face Thomas stood and ran towards the door which, as he drew near slowly opened. Outside it was a beautiful day and his father James stood waiting in the sunlit street for his son. Thomas paused for an instant in the doorway and looked back at the old woman.

'Thank you,' he said simply.

And the door closed gently behind him.

'Who was that?' asked Sybil.

The unexpected voice made Queenie jump and she turned back to the sprig of lavender in her hand before answering.

'I think it has just been pointed out that I was not put on this earth to knit and that I am here for another purpose.'

'I could have told you that!' replied Sybil testily. 'I was beginning to think you would never snap out of your black mood.'

Queenie grinned and kicked off the rug covering her knees.

'Mood? Me?' She rubbed her hands together and stared at the tea tray Sybil had just carried in. 'Where's the cake?

'You are feeling better,' said Sybil, smiling with relief.

'Well go on Sybil, find some cake. Preferably something chocolaty, and then...' she grinned, the old spark back in her eyes, 'we can plan our next adventure!'

Historical Note:

Smuggling was rife around the south west coast during previous centuries as this illicit trade became more profitable than fishing and farming. Many of the impoverished families living on or near the coast, and struggling under heavy taxes from the Government, became involved directly in the trade (or indirectly by turning a blind eye to nocturnal movement of cargo).

Worbarrow Bay (Widbarrow) has a long history of smuggling during the 17th, 18th and 19th century as it is an ideal landing site due to the deep waters of the bay. Although the village is now deserted since the military requisitioned it in 1943, it is still possible to walk along the shingle beach from the village and visit the genuine smugglers cave at Mupe Bay. Smuggling gangs working out of Lulworth would load the cargo here onto the backs of ponies and travel through the gap in the cliffs transporting it throughout the country.

In October 1719 a smuggling run of unprecedented size was landed on the beach, it involved no less than five ships simultaneously unloading, and an observer described "a perfect fair at the waterside, some buying of goods and others loading of horses; that there was an army of people, armed and in disguise, as many in number as he thought might be usually at Dorchester fair, and that all the officers in the county were not sufficient to oppose them"

There were many smuggling gangs working along the south west coast at this time, Isaac Gulliver, Roger Ridout, Jack Rattenbury, the Hawkhurst gang but none had such a bloody thirsty reputation as Cruel Coppinger.

If you wake at midnight, and hear a horses feet,
Don't go drawing back the blind, or looking in the street,
Them that asks no questions isn't told a lie,
Watch the wall my darling, while the Gentleman go by.
Five and twenty ponies,
Trotting through the dark,
Brandy for the Parson,
'Baccy for the clerk;
Laces for a lady, letters for a spy,
And watch the wall my darling, while the Gentlemen go by.

Rudyard Kipling

Elizabeth Andrews lives in the West Country and is known for her love and knowledge of Britain's folklore and is a regular contributor to magazines and periodicals.

Her best-selling book 'Faeries and Folklore of the British Isles' is an illustrated guide to all the magical creatures that populate Britain. Her next book 'Faerie Flora' explores the myths and legends surrounding our most common flowers and plants.

It was during the research for this book that she stumbled across the strange and intriguing tale of Hannah, the most famous witch in Devon. This became the basis for her novel 'The Lavender Witch' the first in this series featuring the psychic sisters.

Illustrated
Faeries and Folklore of the British Isles
Faerie Flora

Fiction
The Lavender Witch

Children's Illustrated
The Faeries Tea Party
The Mice of Horsehill Farm
Teasel's Present
The Great Storm
The Whale's Tooth

Printed in Great Britain
by Amazon

86645279R00113